FERAL BREED FIGHT CLUB

THE COLLECTION

ELLIS LEIGH

CLAIMING HIS CHANCE

FERAL BREED FIGHT CLUB, BOOK ONE

After a long year of tragedy and battles, Cahill of the Southern Appalachia pack is hoping to spend a little time alone on his mountain. But with no mate to worry about, the safety of the pack falls on his shoulders, as does paying off the guards he'd hired to keep the mountain safe while he was away. Protecting the pack means heading off to participate in an underground fight club where shifters take to the ring for fame, fortune, and debt repayment. A ring some don't make it out of alive.

To the owners and fighters at The Pack House, Trinity and Piers seem like any other mated couple. And that's exactly what she needs them to think. Years of running from the truth has set Piers on a path headed right into the fight cage, and Trinity has followed, even though the violence and the noise are something out of her nightmares. But the two have plans, and a handful of fights is all that stands between them reaching their dreams and banishment...or death.

. . .

When Cahill sets his sights on Trinity, nothing can stand in the way of the fighter getting his fated mate. Not the heavy debt his pack must repay, not the other fighters out to show him who's stronger and more skilled in the ring, not even the possibility that she may be mated to another. Once a fighter, always a fighter—and Cahill's more determined than ever to throw a knockout punch for the chance of a real win with the woman of his dreams.

———

ONE

Cahill

"It's them. They're finally home."

The call carried down the hill, the heavy drawl a balm to my ears. Perhaps to my Alpha as well.

"You hear that, Cahill?" Alpha Killian asked, his eyes locked on the forest hiding our packlands from view. "We're home."

I blew out a heavy breath, unable to speak. We were *home*. Back with our pack, our family, and our friends. Back where we belonged. And even though I'd be going home to an empty cabin, at least I was back on our mountain. At least I'd survived.

"I don't think I can handle a big crowd." The only female in our small party clung to the side of her mate. Beta Gideon kissed the top of her head and tightened his hold on her, ready to protect her even if it was from those who only wanted to welcome her home.

"We'll go straight to our cabin," Gideon whispered. His eyes met mine over Kalie's head, and I nodded. It was time for me to get back to work, to pick up the reins of being head of security for our pack and protect those who needed it. And Kalie definitely needed it.

As we came around a bend in the drive, the air practically shimmered with anticipation. Southern Appalachia pack shifters lined the road leading to our mountain, but they didn't approach. They stayed back, watching us with wary eyes, anxiety high as the four of us passed a row of armed guards stretching across the drive. They were the protection we'd left behind, the shifters I'd hired to guard those who stayed on the mountain while Alpha Killian, Beta Gideon, and I raced off to bring back a packsister who'd been taken from us. From their guns to their camouflaged uniforms, their icy stares to their heavy, black boots, the men I'd left in my place were the baddest, most intimidating I could find. I couldn't blame my packmates for being on edge.

"I want the guards off this land as soon as possible," Killian said, hiking up his bag on his shoulder. "This pack needs to heal, and they're not going to do that with soldiers surrounding them."

"Understood," I replied, eyeing the guards over my shoulder. I hadn't expected to be gone as long as we had been, and I wasn't sure what the cost of their protection would be. Shifters like them weren't exactly known for accepting an IOU. What should have been a week-long trip had morphed into months away, and our pack had taken the brunt of the stress of being left behind. Like us, they were tired—on edge, physically and emotionally. The past year had been a fucking whirlwind of both the highest highs and the lowest lows. And now I needed to pay the piper for doing my job while I'd been gone. *Fuck.*

Our pack stood on the edge of a precipice, watching, waiting. With each step, they seemed to creep closer, anticipation rolling off them. Until finally, the restraint of the group reached its limit.

A breathy, relieved call of "Killian" set things in motion. The Alpha's curvy mate was the first to break from the crowd. She raced forward as soon as we trudged around the final curve, practically leaping across the boulders lining the driveway to get to him. He dropped his bag and snatched her out of the air as soon as she was close enough, the two becoming one in a heartbeat. Their connection was like that—bright and bold, something no one could deny. The pack practically sighed in relief at seeing their Alpha male and female back together.

Pack Beta Gideon continued up the hill with his arm securely around his mate Kalie, both looking haggard but smiling politely at the other shifters who were practically itching to place hands on the couple. The second-in-command and his mate were quieter than Killian and Lyra, less show biz. Their love for each other was something you simply understood. It was in the little gestures, the help they offered one another, the subtlety of their smiles. Quiet but mighty, their bond was just as intense and unbreakable as the other mated pairs in our pack, but it had been stretched hard. Hell, raked over the coals might have been a better term for what those two had been through.

"Omega Kalie is home, my friends," Killian hollered, his voice loud and deep as it practically shook the rocks underneath us. "Come, welcome her and Gideon back to the mountain."

Members of the pack rushed forward, grabbing the couple's bags, following them along the long and winding incline leading to their cabin. The pack whispered almost continuously, sending prayers and thanks to the fates and quietly hissing threats to those faceless enemies who might dare another attack. The hardiest of our group walked beside them, already on guard. Prepared to defend the beloved couple with their lives if needed. Kalie had been missing for months, having been kidnapped during an attack on our pack that'd left numerous members dead. Just the fact we'd found her at all had been a blessing. There was no way we would let anyone come near her again.

Making sure of that was my job, especially since no one would be waiting in the crowd to welcome me home. Not specifically, anyway.

I grabbed one of my packmates—a hulking brute named Eachann, who had nearly lost an arm in the battle that took Kalie from us. He looked better, though. Well healed. And brutally, savagely ready to protect his own.

"I want a perimeter surrounding their cabin. Leave enough room so they can't sense you, but make the line deep. They need privacy *and* protection."

"Yes, sir." He grabbed my forearm in welcome and gave me a half smile. "It's good to have you back, Cahill."

"It's good to be back." I nodded and released the man to do his job, knowing he would treat his responsibility with the attention it deserved. Eachann had fought by my side a thousand times, had grown up with Killian and me on this mountain. He and Gideon were practically brothers. Gideon would appreciate my choice of leader for his security detail, as well as the privacy we'd give him. Kalie and Gideon needed time alone if they were going to recover from the shitstorm they'd been through. As did Killian and Lyra, though for different reasons. Lyra had looked exhausted when she ran for her mate, though I'd bet she'd handled herself and the pack with a skill few could muster. Still, I had a feeling she wasn't going to let Killian out of her sights for days. That left my non-mated, no-family-left self to deal with...everything.

"You're back, Cahill of the Southern Appalachia pack." A huge shifter with a menacing air approached from the line of guards, glancing over my shoulder as Killian walked past with his mate still in his arms.

"We are. Thank you for your protection while I was away." I offered my hand, a decidedly human custom but one that felt right for the moment. He stared at it—the traditional arm-grab of our kind being something he was probably more familiar with—then shook it with enough force to make my bones pop. I clenched my teeth as I endured the pain, but I didn't drop eye contact. This guy was a total thug, a mercenary. He wouldn't respect anything I had to say if I showed weakness.

"Time for your pack to honor our deal." The security guard pulled a phone from his pocket and tapped the screen. "Due to the change in plans and the new amount owed, I'm no longer able to negotiate the fee. You need to talk to my boss."

I pressed the device to my ear and waited through two rings as my stomach sank toward my feet. A year ago, I would have said something cocky just to get a rise out of the guard. But after the hell we'd been living for the past few months, I had no interest in mouthing off. I wanted to pay my debt and be done with...everything.

The voice that eventually came across the line sounded almost gleeful, so much the opposite of me. "Alpha Killian, my boy. So glad you made it back from the battle at Merriweather Fields."

"I'm sorry, sir, but Alpha Killian is unavailable right now. My name is Cahill, and I'm his head of security."

Silence. I glanced at the guard, who simply looked back with a glare that might have made lesser men nervous. But after the battle at Merriweather, fighting beside shifters with strength I couldn't imagine and witches who could do things I once thought impossible, his brand of brute force couldn't scare me. I knew he was a weak opponent compared to what I'd faced.

The man on the other end of the phone sighed. "Well, this is a bit of a disappointment. I had hoped to speak to Alpha Killian in regards to payment."

"You can speak to me, sir. I have authority to handle payment." I turned my back to the rest of my pack, knowing Killian would want to be involved if he knew what I was doing. But he and Lyra needed to reconnect, and the pack needed their Alpha to help them feel safe. Kalie needed her mate to help her heal from whatever horrors she'd lived during the months she'd been held against her will, which meant Gideon was out as well. I was officially the third-in-command, and I would handle whatever came up.

"Very well, Cahill of the Southern Appalachia pack. We have an underground boxing club of sorts in West Virginia that we'd like Killian to participate in. He would have to win just one fight, or lose five, and the debt of the pack would be cleared."

My throat clamped down on an instinctual growl my human mind knew couldn't be released. Underground boxing club? His language didn't fool me. Those words were a polite way of saying they ran illegal cage matches between shifters for human spectators to watch and bet on. While the practice wasn't sanctioned by our leadership—and was certainly illegal by human laws in the states where the fights occurred—they were still well-known enough even to a pack as closed off as ours. Some fight rings hosted matches that were to the death, some lasted until one opponent couldn't stand anymore, but all of them had the same base rule—no shifting. Each contestant had to fight in their human form, which was hard for us. We fought better when we let our animal instincts rule. Even the strongest Alpha could fall during a human-form match. And if there was one thing we couldn't afford to lose, it was our Alpha.

"Alpha Killian is needed on packgrounds for the foreseeable future," I replied, keeping my voice steady even though exhaustion was quickly creeping over me. "Perhaps there's another payment method you'd accept."

"No," he said, voice curt. "I want a strong fighter in West Virginia, and your pack is rumored to have some of the largest and toughest shifters around. Word of the battle at Merriweather has spread far, my friend. I want a Southern Appalachia fighter. That's the only payment accepted."

Ah, there it was. The opening I needed, the opportunity to take care of things myself and relieve Killian of the duty. He didn't *specifically* want Killian as the fighter, just a strong fighter from our pack. Having been raised with and taught by Killian himself, I knew I was one hell of a tough fighter. The guy on the phone didn't know it yet, but he'd see. As much as I wanted to stay with my pack and enjoy the quiet peacefulness of our mountain home, we had a debt to pay. And I fully intended on paying it myself.

Steeling myself, I pulled on every vestige of confidence inside of me as I said, "I'll take Killian's place in the boxing club to resolve the debt."

Silence again from the mystery man, and then an almost excited... "Are you pack Beta?"

Gotcha. I smirked, knowing exactly how to impress someone like him, though I'd need to fib a little. There was no way I was letting him know about Gideon. "No, sir. Killian's sister, Moira, was our pack Beta, but she's found her mate as the third in the triad of the President of the National Association of the Lycan Brotherhood. I'm the head of security for the Southern Appalachia pack, though. I've grown up with Killian and his sister, have fought with them and against them since I was a pup. You would not be wrong to put me in your ring, sir."

I waited. The only sound a subtle whooshing noise through the receiver as the man processed my offer. I wasn't worried, though. He wanted our pack because of our reputation, and I had the experience to prove those rumors true. We were big, tough, and hard to win against in a head-to-head battle. The only reason the attackers had gotten a single foothold in our pack a few months ago was because they'd come in like snakes. Instead of challenging us forthright, they'd gone after our weakest links: our elderly and our youth. I'd lost both of my younger sisters that night because the bastards had been too cowardly to face our grown shifters directly. A fact that had fueled my rage through the battle at Merriweather. Once the fight was over, though, that rage had dissipated. In its place, filling a giant hole inside me, was a sea of guilt over how many mistakes I'd made and the numbing realization of how much I'd lost.

"Three fights, not one." The man's voice over the speaker pulled me from my spiraling thoughts. "And you'd better be good enough to make us some money right from the start. You screw up in your first fight, and I'm calling Killian down here to finish off your contract."

I nearly sagged in relief. This I could do. I could fight. I didn't want to—I'd had enough fighting for multiple lifetimes already—but I wouldn't put my pack in danger. Three fights, good ones, and I could come home to my mountain and bask in the silence as I mourned my sisters. That was all I wanted. Plus, Killian would be safe, and Gideon would be able to take care of Kalie as he needed to. Those two facts alone were well worth the cost.

I took a deep breath and gave myself over to the need to pay for as many mistakes as I could. "Understood, sir."

He disconnected the call with a grunt. For a split second, I wished I had let one of the others handle the debt we owed. I needed peace, calm, and quiet after what we'd been through, but there was no one else who deserved the burden as much as I did. I scratched at the burn marks on my arm, handprints left behind by a witch I'd attacked. I'd been so sure I was right, so solid in my convictions, but she and her sisters had proved me utterly wrong. They'd opened my eyes to things I'd misunderstood my entire life. And I'd failed them, exactly as I'd failed my own sisters. Perhaps quiet and peace just weren't in the cards for me.

With little more than a glance his way, I handed the phone back to the guard.

"You're smaller than many of your pack. Our fighters are big, mean, and well-trained. You should have let your Alpha come."

I shrugged. "I don't need to be taller than my opponent to win a fight."

He huffed a laugh. "You won't survive three fights in our ring, boy. Though hopefully you can hold on long enough to make the bosses happy before your opponent tosses your ass out of the cage."

I used my thumb to wipe the corner of my mouth, letting my lips turn up in a cocky grin, confidence making me arrogant. "I'll fight and I'll win because I'm good, not because I'm the biggest. But go ahead and bet against me. Your lost money can line your boss' pockets."

He glowered, a small rumble coming from his throat. "Say goodbye to your pack, Appalachia. We leave in the morning."

TWO

Trinity

"Your mate's a good fighter. Always such a nice, slow build to an explosive finish. He's earned his nickname of Tidal."

Fighting back an irritated frown, I hurried after the handler toward the medical rooms. Did he have to talk? Couldn't he be silent as he took me to see if Piers was still...*shit*. I couldn't bear to think it. The cheers of the crowd from the arena bounced along the concrete walls. The noise made my wolf anxious, made her pace inside my head. Made me long to shift. But that was the last thing I should do in this...hell. This training center and arena for studying the art of violence.

Piers, just get to Piers and worry about the rest later. I let my thoughts keep me focused on the task, but it was getting harder and harder to pretend with every day. I hated this place. Hated everything around me. But I had to stay in character, had to keep living a lie. It was what needed to be done. For Piers...for the future we'd planned. We were so close to achieving what we'd been working for.

"Yes, yes, he has. I'm quite proud of him." My heels clicked on the concrete floor and my heavy dress restricted the length of my stride as I struggled to keep up with the man's giant steps. I wished I could hike up the skirt, kick off my shoes, and run, but I had to stay in character. The heels, the sexy dress, the heavy makeup—all of it helped me play the part. All were expected and not to be overlooked. I needed to be seen as the beautiful, sexy mate of a prizefighter. Arm candy. Untouchable. The alternative... Well, it wouldn't be good for me.

This building, this disgusting concrete box in the middle of the mountains that reeked of blood and sweat, was also chock-full of testosterone. A toxic cocktail to my kind for sure. Shifters loved to fight, loved to let their animal side loose and work off their aggression, but what happened here wasn't natural. It was filthy, muddied with hormone shots and scented air pumped through the vents to keep the shifters on edge and ready to battle at all times. Hell, the smell worked *my* animal side hard, and it was filled with *female* pheromones. I couldn't imagine being one of the men in the rings—the scent of mating and rut in the air, another male shifter in your face, threatening and probably dangerous. I'd lose control of my wolf in a heartbeat, and she was a gentle beast.

After what seemed like a mile-long jog down the endless hallways, the handler reached a dented and scarred door and pushed it open. He didn't move through, though. Instead, he stood taking up most of the entryway. Blocking my path. With a much more interested expression on his face than I'd noticed before, he looked me over, his gaze almost a physical sensation. Eye-fucking me...the bastard. I bet he thought he could get a reaction out of me with this stunt. Perhaps a gasp or a little shiver of my exposed shoulders. A tiny little taste of my fear.

As if.

Let him look, let him play his games and think he was somehow dominating me. I'd been raised in a rough pack of men who tried to push that traditional subservient-women values crap some packs seemed to thrive on, but not the females in our group. My packsisters had been involved in physical fights, refused matings, and psychological warfare the likes of which this guy had probably never even heard about. The women of my former pack had taught me well, and when we left, I was thrust into worlds of seedy characters and men who saw no issue taking what they wanted from those they saw as weaker. But Piers and I had survived...together. This handler wanted to play games with me? Great. I was a goddamned professional athlete in the battle of the sexes. And I wasn't afraid.

"In you go, little lady."

I tucked my head toward my shoulder, keeping my eyes down. Playing the sweet, innocent, helpless woman desperate to get to her injured mate. If he only knew.

"Thank you," I nearly whispered.

His growl was low and barely discernable, more something I felt than heard. "It's not a problem."

I fought back a snarl as my arm brushed his chest, my wolf ready to show herself. Particularly her teeth. Gentle or not, she'd defend us to the death, a fact that might end up working in my favor in this place. *Last one*, Piers had said when we moved here. *Last time we have to run this con, then we'll be set.* He'd better have been right.

Once I spotted Piers, though, all acts fell away. I didn't even give the handler a second glance as I rushed across the room to the gurney. Lying there, covered in blood and sweat and dirt, was Piers, the man who'd been at my side practically since birth. The one I needed to be okay to feel safe. And he was a mess.

"Hey, Trin." Piers tried to reach for me but dropped his arm, groaning with the effort. Heavy slash marks cut through the flesh of his shoulder, knitting together slowly. He looked pale, probably from the pain. And there was very little I could do to help him.

"Good fight, Tidal," the handler called from the still-open doorway. "I'm pretty sure the other guy's going to need to have his jaw reset after you got that hit in at the start. How many times do you think you broke it? I swear I heard five crunches of those bones."

I glared over my shoulder at the handler. "Can we please have some privacy?"

His lip turned up in a show of aggression, but he still nodded and stepped out into the hall. I didn't move until he closed the door behind him, and then I let myself relax into who I really was.

"Damn it, Piers. What were you thinking?" I grabbed the gauze and saline, cleaning his shoulder wounds, keeping my hands busy to stop my mind from exploding. I thought the blows he'd taken had looked bad from the spectator seats during the fight. Here, so close that I could see every mark, I knew the fight had to have been ten times worse than I imagined. I had no idea how he'd walked out of the ring at all.

"It's not as bad as it looks." Piers hissed as I wiped the blood away from a split on his cheek. "Only the shoulder will take more than a few hours to heal. Besides, I stomped that fucker. Won that fight as if it were nothing."

"Nothing," I huffed. My eyes burned with unshed tears as I looked over his body. His skin was positively littered with *nothing*. Cuts, splits, tears, bruises... Even with the rapid healing of his shifter blood, it would take days to recover from this. "Doesn't look like it was nothing to me."

Piers grabbed my arm, halting my cleaning of his wounds. "Stop it. You're worrying too much." He dropped his voice, pulling me closer to whisper in my ear. "Five fights, remember? I win five fights and we're set to start that life I promised you.

You can buy some land, set up a pack of your own, and bring together all the orphans and shifters who've been kicked out of traditional packs or are alone for whatever reason. Others in our situation. Everything I promised you when you followed me after I was kicked out of the pack. Every dream you've ever told me, I'll make sure comes true. Five fights, Trin, and I've already won three. Just two more."

I nodded, tears finally falling. "I know. But it's not just for me. It's for both of us."

"I can be happy anywhere." He pulled back, eyes staying locked on mine. "I know you hate this place, but it'll be over before you know it."

I shook my head. "It's just so loud, and I hate not being able to shift."

He fell back against the gurney, his eyes going unfocused as a grimace of pain passed over his face. "Shit, Trin, you know the rules. Plus, I can beat just about any guy in this place in human form. If you shift, you risk getting us kicked out. And hell, if they shift, I can't even follow them and fight in my animal form." He stared into my eyes, his telling me all the things his words couldn't. All the secrets we had to keep. "If I shift, they'll kill me. And you'd be on your own."

I took a deep breath, trying to rein in my anxiety. "I know."

"Two more, and we're out of here. You can get everything you've wanted all these years."

I sighed, hearing the sadness in his voice. He liked it here, liked the fighting and the decidedly male atmosphere. He'd leave, though, for me. For the promises he made me so many years before. For all I gave up to stay with him.

I ran the gauze over his eyebrow with shaky hands, guilt heavy on my heart. "This one might scar."

His lips lifted up into a close approximation of a grin, a

shadow of that same goofy smile that'd been my downfall since we were toddlers. "Bonus, then. Chicks dig scars."

I rolled my eyes. "Not this chick."

Before he could answer, there was a knock and the door swung open. One of the owners of the underground fighting ring strolled into the room, his dark, pinstriped suit at total odds with the filthy surroundings. Not that my sequined evening gown fit in, either.

"Piers, my boy. Good fight, good fight." He approached the gurney with a smile, completely focused on Piers. I moved to the head of the bed, knowing my job was to be invisible. I was nothing to him. If it weren't for the fact that Piers had put his foot down, I wouldn't have been allowed in the training areas of the arenas. No women were unless they had a specific job. Mine was being Piers' mate.

Speaking of which, the man in question boosted himself up with his elbow, shaking the owner's hand when offered. "Thank you, sir. I hope it was a success for you."

"Of course it was." The owner's gaze locked on Piers' shoulder, a sharklike expression in his eyes. "Next time, I want you to slow it down a little more. Make the show last. The longer the battle, the more bets the humans make."

"Take more?" The words tumbled from my lips unbidden. I stared, my wolf wanting to slash this creep across the face and force him away from Piers. "He's lying here with broken bones, covered in his own blood, and you want him to take more?"

The man's face hardened, though he still refused to look at me. "Piers, we allowed you to bring your mate because we respect the mating bonds. That respect needs to be reciprocated for our efforts."

Shit. Piers turned his head, eyes locking on mine. I knew I'd screwed up, he knew I'd screwed up, and he was imploring me to behave without words. *Two more fights, just two more and I'll be free.*

"I apologize, sir." I kept my voice soft and hung my head, unable to wipe the anger off my face, the words I knew I needed to say vile on my tongue. "I'm just upset. I've never seen him bleed so much."

"Men bleed for many things, little girl. Money, power, sex... that's our world. That's our life. Deal with it, or move the fuck on and get out of your mate's way. He's going to bring in a lot of cash with that fighting style of his. A lot. The five fights for a million dollars deal we struck may be just the start of his career."

Piers pinched me as the owner turned to leave, a signal to do what needed to be done. I jumped and followed the man to the door, once again playing the role of Piers' quiet, meek mate. Knowing this one, this particular lie, was going to sting.

"Of course, sir. Thank you for the opportunity. My mate and I are very" —I forced my lip not to curl in disgust— "*appreciative* of your generosity."

He grunted and strode into the hall, disappearing quickly through the maze of the back offices. When I could no longer hear his footsteps, I leaned out to check for anyone else nearby. I needed a few minutes of privacy with Piers, and shifter hearing was too good to risk this particular conversation if anyone was in the vicinity.

I was about to step back inside the room when the doors to the training room at the far end of the hall banged open and four men walked into the hallway. They stood with wide eyes, arrogant posture, bags over their shoulders, and no bruises...new fighters. My eyes darted to one as if on instinct. He was taller than the rest, tanned a deep golden brown with a jawline that seemed chiseled from stone. Even from far away, I could see the hard set to his eyes, the ferocity in his stance. He wasn't really bigger than the rest of the men in his group, but he definitely appeared meaner. Tougher. With what looked like burn scars along one arm and an intense expression that brooked no room for error, he looked like a storm brewing in human form. I'd seen men like him before. He'd be a tornado in the ring.

"Trin? Help me dress this wound, would ya? I want to go back to our room." Piers crept up behind me, leaning out into the hall to grab my elbow.

I ripped my eyes from the new recruits and followed Piers back into the room. "You shouldn't even be out of bed yet."

"Quit worrying and just help me, okay?" His tired, irritated voice was my undoing. He was injured, and I was too busy ogling the new recruits to have noticed him struggle off the gurney. I felt the urge to keep an eye on the new guy, but that would have to wait. Piers needed me, and I had a duty to uphold.

"Yes, dear."

THREE

The place where the fighters lived, trained, and eventually beat the shit out of each other was an unassuming concrete block structure. Other than the rock mountain wall it basically rested against, there was nothing remarkable about the squat building tucked deep in a thick forest of trees. It could have been mistaken for a garage or simple storage facility unless you saw it from the back. That's when you got an idea of the size of the place, the huge edifice stretching long past where any normal building should have ended.

One of the guys we'd picked up along the way, a young shifter named Beadan, whistled. "Damn, that's one big-ass building."

"Sure is." I glanced at the other two men we'd driven in with, all four of us new to the fight scene here but looking for some kind of payment. For me, it was duty and to pay off my pack's debt for the security detail we'd used while traveling. For the rest, it seemed like they were looking for money. Something all young, strong-willed wolves needed. We tended to be kicked out of our packs once we reached maturity, too many Alphas afraid of having potential usurpers nearby. I was lucky. Killian knew his strengths and had enough confidence to keep the adult males in his pack, to keep families together as had his father before him. These boys...well, they'd had it a little rougher.

"This is the largest fight facility in the Southeast," the handler who'd driven us down said as he stepped in front of our small group. "For the length of your contract or longer, you will live, eat, sleep, practice, and fight within these walls. You will not leave the building unless a trainer or handler has approved your trip. You will remain aware of your surroundings at all times. We put on fights for human spectators, and they must never learn of our secret. Is that understood?"

He glared at each of us in turn, waiting to move on to the next until we nodded our understanding.

"And one more rule," he said, face hard, looking like a man ready to fight a battle of his own. "You will not shift on our property. Not inside, not outside, and for the sake of wolf shifters everywhere, especially not in the ring. You shift, you're out. No money, no release of debt, no second chances. Am I understood?"

We each mumbled our agreement, every one of us looking a little wary. Not shift? My wolf would not be thrilled, but I had enough control to make it through a few weeks if necessary. Some of the guys with me were young; it would definitely be harder for them.

"As you've accepted the rules, I only have one more thing to say." The handler stepped back, bowing dramatically even as his lips turned up in a wicked sneer. "Welcome to The Pack House. Now get inside and get ready to have your heads busted."

The new shifters walked toward the building with hurried steps, all of them talking excitedly. Anxious to get started. I didn't feel the same excitement as the rest of the guys around me. I was just here temporarily. Three fights. The quickest way to get back home was to fight three fights, which meant I needed to win three fights. I wasn't exactly known for being a graceful loser. In fact, I was better known for a hot temper and an almost obsessively competitive nature. But I was ready for a change. After everything I'd seen over the past year... Yeah, change was good. Nice, quiet, easy change. Life could slow down any time now.

Just three fights.

We walked inside the gym together, all four of us pausing inside the doors. *Oh hell.* The air had a moist, almost physical feel to it. Sweat and testosterone buffeted my senses, the smell of female teasing my wolf, along with an overriding sense of blood in the water. This place was a veritable gold mine for any shifter who liked to let his animal side get aggressive. Hell, even I was having trouble controlling my snarl in the hormone cocktail. No wonder these fights made so much money—my kind would kill each other in the ring instead of shifting if they lost control in this environment. Something I really needed to remember.

Before I could move farther into the darkened space, something out of the corner of my eye made me turn. The rumble echoing through my mind was one I'd never made before, a noise my inner wolf had never sounded. It was deep but not threatening, more wanting than anything. A craving of sorts. And it was directed at a woman.

Short and round, curvy in a way that had long fallen out of favor in human culture, she stood just outside a doorway down a long hallway. Shadows darkened her face, keeping her eyes hidden from me, but I felt a pull to her. Something drawing me toward the female. Before I could act, a man, naked from the waist up, leaned out the door and took her elbow in hand, gently tugging her inside. My wolf side raged, a cacophony of snarls and growls that made no sense at the moment. I clenched my fists, hiding the claws that had erupted and breathing hard so as not to shift further. So as not to stalk down that hallway and barge through that door.

"Yo, Appalachia."

I jerked, dropping into a slight crouch. My wolf edged forward, snarling viciously in my mind. My eyesight sharpened as I focused on the man who'd called the ridiculous nickname they'd given me. Sweats, clipboard, thick arms and neck. A trainer, I assumed. No threat. Not to me. To her, perhaps...

Fighting off the urge to bare my teeth at the intruder, I nodded. "I'm here."

"Yeah, I can see that. In the ring, kid. Time to see what you're made of."

I took a deep breath, nearly shivering as the scented air deluged my senses. So not helping me stay in control. "Where do I change?"

The guy snorted a laugh. "Drop trou wherever. You're in ring three."

My feet felt leaden at first, unable to move. Unwilling, more like it. But I did, I moved. And it got easier with each step. I wove my way through sweaty shifters and blood-splattered boxing rings until I found the one with a large three painted on the side, forcing my mind to focus the whole way. This was it. Time to settle down and rein in my instincts. Fighting was an art, a craft I'd learned over decades of skirmishes and practice bouts. While my wolf's strength and speed were welcome, his instinctual responses to threats were not. In a fight was where the true balance between man and beast came into play.

I tossed my bag on the bench and took out a cup and a pair of sweat shorts. I yanked my shirt over my head and dropped it in the bag, doing the same for my jeans once I'd slid them down my legs. As soon as I'd re-dressed in my fighting gear, I climbed into the ring. The floor bounced a bit under my weight, so I took to the balls of my feet and hopped around. Seemed very much like a regular boxing ring, though I had little experience with them. I'd always fought on dirt and rock, outside in nature with my packmates. This was very, very different.

Beadan climbed in after me, looking cocky. "You ready to go down, Appalachia?"

I huffed a laugh, mimicking his moves as he began to circle, but pushing him to my pace. Almost herding him. "You think you can handle me, kid?"

"I've beaten bigger."

"Bigger doesn't mean better."

"Said no woman ever." He came at me with a snarl, swinging hard. I edged back, avoiding the hit, keeping myself in check. Patience in a fight was the difference between winning and losing. Let the kid wear himself out. I had all damn day.

We circled and jabbed for a few minutes, him attacking, me feinting away. I stayed on the balls of my feet, ready to move at any second. Never pushing the fight to a more aggressive level. Beadan was breathing hard, his eyes nearly glowing as his wolf took more and more control of his mind. I was close to winning. Just a few more minutes. A little bit—

I nearly froze in place when I noticed the smell. Daisies and fresh water. Natural and clean. I spun, looking for the source, feeling a need inside my heart that hadn't been there before.

The woman from the hallway stood at the edge of the ring, almost dwarfed by the half-naked man practically wrapped around her. Her deep blue gown sparkled under the low lights, making her shimmer in a way that seemed almost angelic. But the low-cut neckline and the way the fabric hugged her was pure sin. She was a rose in the middle of this pile of garbage, a flower growing through a crack in cement. And when she looked up at me, her brown eyes meeting mine for the first time, my entire world tilted.

Motherfucker.

My wolf snarled loud and harsh, wanting to move closer, to knock that fucker's arm off our mate. And she was our mate. I knew it the second our eyes met, felt the connection to her. And by the way her painted lips fell open and her eyes went wide, she knew it, too.

I had taken one step in her direction when I sensed Beadan come closer. Images flashed in my mind—my mate with that man's arm around her, the younger of my twin sisters laughing as she ran away from me that last night, a fierce witch standing up to the worst of our kind with a bravery I admired. And falling dead at her enemy's feet anyway.

My response was natural, automatic...completely inhuman. My wolf saw Beadan as a threat to our mate, and that just wouldn't do. I turned with a snarl, swinging my arm in an upward arc, the full weight of my body behind it. My fist connected with Beadan's chin, knocking him backward in a cloud of blood spray. He fell to the mat like a rag doll, unconscious. I loomed over him, pumped up, ready to defend my mate against the threat he had posed, my human side trying to edge through the curtain of animal rage in front of me.

Shit.

"Hey, Tidal," a trainer yelled from the other side of the ring. "How about you keep that mate of yours tied up in your bed, yeah? She's upsetting the hormones of the new guys."

My head swam, nothing making sense as I stared after the woman who'd just sent my whole world off the edge. Tidal was mated to my mate... But how could that be? I knew of triads, of course—hell, I'd seen Moira and her two mates interacting at Merriweather Fields—but I'd felt nothing but rage toward the muscle-bound shifter who held my mate. And she was mine, I knew it. Could feel it all the way down to my toes. But who the hell was he, and why did people think they were mated?

"Good job, Appalachia." Clipboard up and scribbling furiously, my trainer didn't seem to notice how close to shifting I really was. "Next time, try not to kill your opponent. It's going to take him a couple of days to get over that hit."

I glanced back at Beadan, his still body shoving off the protective haze that'd taken me over. The poor kid was laid out, two guys in white hovering over him. Medical folk, I guessed.

"What the fuck..." I whispered. I glanced down at my hands, the one bruised from hitting so much bone. One of the white coats glanced my way.

"It's the pheromones in the air. They make it easier to attack your own kind without provocation." He stood, holding one end of a stretcher they'd put Beadan on. "Don't worry. You'll get used to them."

But I knew he was wrong. I'd lost control, very possibly scaring the mate I had yet to meet and nearly killing a kid who'd really done nothing wrong. I wouldn't just get used to this place. I couldn't. Not if I was going to figure out what the hell was happening around here and why my mate seemed to be claimed by another.

FOUR

Trinity

Mate...mate...mine. I stood frozen in place, those words on repeat in my head. I hadn't expected this, hadn't been prepared, but there he was—my *mate*—in all his half-naked glory. His eyes were locked on mine, the huge man in the ring staring so hard I could almost feel his gaze on my body. And he was huge. From a distance, he'd seemed smaller, but he had to be well over six feet tall, and while not bulky, he was definitely made of solid muscle. Solid muscle barely contained behind a pair of loose gray athletic shorts and practically glistening under the lights. By the gods, the man was...so much more than I'd thought.

I'd also been wrong about him being a tornado in the ring. He was more like a river, weaving its way around the rock in front of it as if in surrender. When really, it was slowly cutting through everything in front of it. A true force of nature. I knew he'd win the fight, knew he'd conquer that rock at some point, but I wasn't ready for him to spin and strike the way he did. I gasped as my mate hit the smaller man in the ring. So brutal, so vicious. So oddly sexual and repulsive at the same time.

Blood sprayed into the air, the smell making me sick to my stomach. The sight making me want to run away and hide. But I wouldn't, not from him. He was meant to be mine. No matter his faults, no matter his flaws, the fates had linked us together in some haphazard way. And as much as I hated the idea of falling for a man who liked to fight, there was no stopping my attraction to him. No way to quell the inferno waiting to burn me alive.

"Hope I don't get the new guy next time," Piers said, chuckling. "That'll be a quick, boring fight."

I frowned, staring at the back of my mate, too sick to worry about matchups and skill levels. Too obsessed to tear my eyes away.

"Hey, Tidal," a trainer yelled. "How about you keep that mate of yours tied up in your bed, yeah? She's upsetting the hormones of the new guys."

I cringed, wishing I could disappear as shifters around the room laughed out loud. I hated being singled out, hated how they stared and undressed me with their eyes. Hated that there was nothing I could do about it without revealing our lies to the world. But this was what we'd agreed to do, and so I fought the urge to run away and hide. Piers promised me his reputation would keep me safe, so I deferred to his plans.

Two more fights.

"Can we go now?" I asked as Piers waved his hand at the trainer in a "Yeah, yeah...working on it" sort of way.

"That might be a good idea." Piers ushered me away from the ring, leading the way to our room. *Our* room...*shit*. This was going to get messy. "You'd better toughen up a bit, Trin. Can't have you fainting just because of a little blood and some good-natured ribbing."

"I didn't faint," I snarled. I stayed close to his side, almost afraid to look back. My mate would see us together, he would think...*double shit*. If he said a word about what just happened,

Piers and I would be in a heap of trouble. A thought that nearly made my blood run cold and my knees go weak. Something that couldn't happen out here, not yet. Not with witnesses.

"Close enough." Piers directed me around the middle set of rings. "Your whole body was stiff. I thought for sure you were going down."

Going down...yes, yes, I was. Going down a path that we'd never discussed. A dangerous one neither of us was ready for. But there was nothing I could do, nothing I could say yet. I needed to feel out this new guy, see if he could keep a secret. See if I could trust him with Piers' life.

Shaking off the fear crawling up my spine as best I could, I lifted my chin and rolled my eyes. "I wasn't anywhere close to fainting. Besides, that was a rough hit. Even you have to agree."

"True. A hit like that to the chest could kill a shifter. We may heal quickly, but a stopped heart means no blood flow, and no blood means lights-out for good."

Piers paused to watch another pair spar in a corner ring, his eyes tracking each move. Learning. Looking for weakness. He was good at this life, and he seemed to like the skills he learned here, something I couldn't grasp. I clung to his arm, willing him to keep moving, desperate for a place to hide. For quiet.

He didn't take my hint. "The bosses want me to make my fights last longer."

"I remember."

"It'd be easy with that kid who just got knocked out, you know? I could fake taking a few hits, dance around a bit, then knock him on his ass. Easy win." Piers leaned over, bringing his lips to my cheek, whispering softly for only me to hear. "But that other guy? He'd be harder to beat while putting on a show. That'd be a true fight, one I'd need to totally focus on. I think I could take him, but it'd be tough. He's a smart fighter; I might not win."

I nodded, understanding. If he didn't win, he might not walk out of the ring. Hell, he'd won his earlier match and had still ended up in the medical wing. Shifters were rough, tough fighters. Even an easy win could cause physical damage. Plus, an easy win wouldn't make the bosses happy, and if the bosses weren't happy, the money could stop.

We needed that cash.

Piers pulled away, watching the fighters again, that analytical expression back in place. Unable to resist, I peeked over my shoulder to the ring where my mate still stood. He was looking back at me, his eyes hard, his entire body exuding a tension that spoke of pure rage. He scared me, there was no denying that, but he also intrigued me. He'd seemed so calm in the ring, so comfortable. He hadn't just attacked the kid as some of the others would have. He'd hung back, let the kid take him on, had seemed smart and calm. But then he'd flipped some sort of switch, and the vicious blow had been the result. What had made him react like that? What had caused him to lose his cool?

"C'mon, Trin," Piers said, pulling me mentally and physically away from the ring. "Let's grab something to eat."

I kept my eyes on my mate for as long as I could, letting Piers lead me where he wanted me to go, unable to look away from the statue in the ring. Terrified and turned on all at once for a man I hadn't met yet.

———

At sunrise, I took off on my own for a stroll through the woods. I needed fresh air. I'd been cooped up with Piers all night, keeping an eye on his injuries, making sure he rested, hiding in the room we shared so as not to have to deal with the secrets eating away at me. I couldn't tell him, not yet, not until I figured out a plan. Until I knew what was best for all of us.

I took the path leading deep into the woods, along the backside of the rock face the building nestled against. There was a small river back there, one no one else was able to frequent. Really, the entire area outside the gym was off-limits to the fighters. Something that worked in my favor as it was the only place I could get away from the noise and the stress, the only place I could truly be alone. The only place I felt safe.

I loved to explore the hills out here, to traipse between the trees on two legs. My wolf longed for release, but that wasn't possible. Not until we left this place. I couldn't imagine staying human for as long as some of the fighters did, though from what Piers told me, the owners demanded the men not shift to keep their animal sides on edge. Caged. Ready to blow.

Dangerous.

When I reached my favorite tree, I sat against it and settled in to watch the world go by. I itched to shift to my wolf, but I knew better. It wasn't just because of the rules of the club owners, either. In a world run by men, it was better to be safe than sorry. There was only one other female I knew of within the training facility—a doctor. Women spectators came into the building, but none was allowed in the back. Our shifters were too animalistic, too hyped-up on hormones. A human woman in close proximity would be an easy target, a female in wolf form would drive them positively over the edge. It was why Piers and I stayed so close, why I rarely left his side. Why I loved taking to the woods to escape the toxic testosterone of the world I was currently stuck in while the men worked with their trainers. While they were too distracted to notice me missing.

The deliberate crack of a twig broke the silence and caused me to flush with irritation. Only Piers would be dumb enough to leave the gym during training time. *He's going to get himself kicked out.* "I can be alone out here you know, Piers. It's safe."

"My name's not Piers."

I spun, totally alert, my body responding immediately to the unfamiliar voice. Hot, thick, deep...definitely not Piers. The man from the ring, my mate, stood before me in jeans and a dark shirt that only highlighted the muscles beneath it. I didn't stand, couldn't, seeing as how my legs refused to cooperate with my brain. Holy shit, he was handsome. Large and obviously powerful, he towered over me, yet I wasn't afraid. He had an air about him, an inherent gentleness that his physical appearance belied. Plus, he was my mate. I knew he wouldn't hurt me.

"You're not supposed to leave the building."

He shrugged, the picture of casual confidence. "Some rules are meant to be broken. It's too pretty out here not to take advantage of the view."

His eyes danced along my body in a way that made my heart race faster. My wolf practically preened under his gaze, wanting me to move closer.

"Appalachia, yes?"

He smiled, charming and sweet. "Only in the ring. My name's Cahill. May I join you?"

"Yes, of course."

He sat on a patch of grass, keeping a few feet between us. Giving me space, something I much appreciated. I sat with my back against the tree and waited for...something. The silence stretched, turning awkward. A weight against me. I searched my mind for anything to say, some witty remark to make. When nothing came, I resorted to commenting on the obvious.

"You're a fighter here."

He cocked his head. "Yes, or I soon will be."

I nodded, unable to hold his gaze for long. He made me feel bared to him, stripped down in some way, and I kind of liked it. The heavy silence returned. I tapped my fingers against the ground, looking around desperately for something to inspire more conversation. Cahill appeared calm as he watched me. His face turned slightly into the rising sun, his dirty-blond hair almost glowing in the light, his lips quirked up into a subtle smile.

Finally, I let my mind and my eyes wander, hoping for inspiration. Strong chin, long neck, thick shoulders, arms that—

"How'd you get those?" I asked, pointing to the scars on his forearm. The same scars I'd noticed the day before from far away. The ones that looked like a messy handprint had been branded onto his skin.

Cahill glanced at the marks. "Got in a bit of a scuffle with a fire witch."

"Really? That's sort of...not wise."

He shrugged, his brow furrowing, a sense of sadness rolling off him. "It was my fault. I was being a judgmental ass when I shouldn't have been. She did the right thing by reminding me of her power."

A sharp snarl escaped me. Cahill's eyebrows rose in response, and I coughed to cover up the flaring of my sudden protective instinct. My mate had been close enough to a witch to have handprints scarred into his flesh. That thought both terrified and infuriated me. While human me oscillated from fear to rage, my wolf was solid in her opinion of his statement. How dare they touch what was hers?

"So she burned you to teach you a lesson?" My lips pursed as all the rotten things I'd learned about witches flitted through my mind. Things I'd never been able to confirm myself. "From what I know about witches, that sounds like something they would do."

"She burned me to defend herself and a human kid." His eyes met mine, fierce and bright. Honest. "She was right to fight me, and I was lucky this was the only mark she left behind. I can't blame her being a witch for *my* ignorance."

I sat back, not having realized I'd been leaning toward him.

Ready to jump, to defend. But he didn't look like a man who needed protecting. He looked like a man who'd lost a friend somehow. "You have an interesting take on witches."

"The fire witch's sister saved my life in a fight they didn't need to be at." He cocked his head, looking me over in a way that made me shiver. "They defended the leader of the North American Lycan Brotherhood alongside us, and they lost one of their sisters protecting a fellow shifter."

"I've never heard of shifters and witches fighting together."

He chuckled harshly. "Neither had I, but then we did, and it was great. They changed my entire view on other supernatural beings that day. I've learned to be much more accepting—" he paused, frowning "—or at least, I'm trying to. I don't want to be that hothead kid who was too arrogant to do anything but strike out at those who are different. I want more calm around me, more quiet. I've seen enough violence for three lifetimes."

My heart leaped in my chest. I struggled to keep words from tumbling from my mouth, to keep my smile from breaking free. I wanted to hug him, to pull him close and say *me too*. Maybe, just maybe, the fates knew what they were doing after all.

"That's good," I whispered, my smile unstoppable. "Quiet and calm is...really, really good."

"So," he said, all long and leading, his eyes locked on mine once more. "Piers?"

I raised an eyebrow. "Yes?"

"That the guy who was hanging all over you last night?"

I looked toward the river, unable to hold his gaze a moment longer. I'd known this would come up, but I wasn't ready. I didn't know what to say yet. So I dodged the question. "Was he hanging? I hadn't noticed."

He made an irritated sound like a wolf chuff but in human form. I bit my lip, watching the water float by as a lead ball took up residence in my stomach. I hated not being truthful, but I couldn't tell him anything about Piers. Not yet. He may have been *my* mate, but that didn't mean I could trust him with Piers' life. We'd be done with this place soon enough, and then we could move on to other things. Safer things. Things that involved this new mate I'd come across.

"If not hanging, then what would you call it?" Cahill asked, his tone softer, the words spoken in a way that made them mean so much more than a simple question. I allowed myself a moment to look him over. There was a vulnerability underneath all that muscle, a soft spot. Having been a pack wolf my whole life, I knew how much power I wielded over him. As his mate, I could choose to refuse him. I could deny the fates. He knew that law, and from the look of him, he feared it.

I cocked my head, desperate to tell him the truth but knowing it was a bad idea. So I gave him what I could. "I'd call it protecting."

That made his head whip up. "Protecting you from what?"

I raised an eyebrow. "Who said he was the one doing the protecting?"

He stared. Seemingly unable to form words. I held his gaze, keeping mine firm.

"Okay then, no hanging." He crept closer, barely even blinking. "The trainer called you his mate."

I bit my lip. "He did."

An inquisitive look that made my heart race crossed his handsome face. "You're not going to elaborate on that?"

"I can't," I whispered, my hands shaking.

He gave me a nod and crept forward a few more inches. "You protect each other."

"Very much so."

"And yet you're out here alone."

I leaned forward, lifting onto my knees, wanting him closer.

Needing it. "The fighters aren't allowed to leave the building, and the early-morning training sessions keep everyone busy. You should be inside, not out here pretending to want to know about my friend."

"Is that what you are to each other?" Cahill drawled, the words all soft and sensual as they rolled off his tongue. As his knees came to rest against mine. "Just friends?"

I licked my lips, his proximity making me anxious in the best way. Making my defenses weaken.

"No. He's very important to me."

Cahill bristled, looking ready to fight. Looking ready to kill the one person in my life I could rely on. *Shit.*

FIVE

Cahill

A growl slipped through my lips at her casual mention of this Piers guy being important. Fuck. I didn't need trouble right off the bat at this place, but she was my mate. *Mine.* I wanted to be the one protecting her. Wanted to claim her, mark her, keep her to myself. I wanted her with a passion I'd never experienced.

She was my one and only chance at having a life enhanced by my soul mate, and I was willing to do whatever it took to keep her by my side. I would fight, kill, die...just to make her happy. But I couldn't be impulsive, couldn't risk my chance at getting what I wanted. What I needed.

I coughed back my wolf's warning, having no idea what to say. She acted as if she didn't realize we were mates, as if she didn't feel the pull. Or maybe she did but was fighting it for some reason. Maybe she—

She leaned closer, snatching my attention back from my spiraling thoughts. I watched her closely, noting every breath, every shiver. Every inch of pale skin exposed to my eyes. Her breath washed over me, her flowery, fresh-water scent a total tease to my senses. So clean…so purifying…like a rain. My own personal raindrop. A raindrop I'd already scared once when I lost control.

"Your wolf sounds strong," she said, her voice low, a murmur on the wind. "Mine is very intrigued by him. She's practically panting to get her chance to meet you, but we can't shift here. It's against the rules."

My wolf rushed forward, making my eyesight sharper as he tried to push my human side out of the way. I sank my claws into the earth, fighting back the urge to grab her and pull her closer. Pull her against me. Instead, I growled, pushing words past the rumbling sound as best I could.

"I've never really been one to follow the rules."

Her lips turned up in a sarcastic sort of smile. "No? But you're a pack wolf…right?"

"Yes," I hissed, the smell of her making me crazy. "I'm the head of security for my pack."

She hummed a single note softly, almost as if she were thinking over something. "I'm not sure whether to be terrified or impressed."

I huffed an almost whiny sound, fighting to keep control. "Never terrified. Not of me. Not of my pack."

She inched closer, her lips almost on my skin. "Packs have rules. Lots of them. They kicked Piers out when he couldn't follow them."

I stared into her eyes, pieces of a puzzle falling into place but still leaving massive holes in the overall picture. So Piers had gotten kicked out of his pack, probably when he came of age, like most male shifters under weak Alphas. But that didn't tell me about her…about why she was with him. About what their relationship was like.

"The only thing that can get you kicked out of the Southern

Appalachia pack is to do harm to another member. We don't force our males to leave."

She blinked, almost looking surprised. "And your women? Do your rules say they must be subservient to their male mates?"

My shoulders shook with the force of the laugh I coughed out. "The only way a woman in our pack is subservient is if she wants to be. Our Alpha's sister helped run the pack, and she made sure the males in our pack knew from the start that any woman brought onto our mountain would be well aware of the power they held over us."

She grew quiet, thoughtful, staring at a spot over my shoulder. I watched her silently as I waited for her next question. For the next roadblock her mind seemed to be throwing up against us.

Finally, her wide eyes met mine once more. "It sounds too good to be true."

"It's not. You could be happy there with me. You'd be loved and respected as a woman of the pack, but also as my ma—"

"Don't." She placed her finger over my lips, silencing me. Her eyes were wide, almost fearful. Aw, fuck. I would *not* scare her again. But the scent of her swamped me, the warmth of her skin making my cock so hard it hurt. Had we been in the building with its pheromone-filled air, I'd probably have her on her back already with my teeth in her neck. Thank fuck we were outside. I could control myself here...mostly. Still, my chest vibrated with the strength of my growl, my eyesight sharpening as my wolf side tried to take control.

And this girl, this beautiful woman, sat before me and played with fire. She smiled up at me, all wide eyes and simple beauty, rubbing her finger along my lips like a treat. Like she had to touch me, to explore my features. Like she wanted me. I could smell her arousal on the air, hear the way her breathing had picked up. Something between us had turned hot and needful, a moment of desire hampered by fears I had yet to understand. But I would... and soon. I'd do anything to make her feel safe with me, to show her how much I was willing to do for her. To prove I was a good man to have as a mate. I'd made enough mistakes over the past year; I wouldn't make any more, especially not where she was concerned.

With shaking fingers and a ball of arousal burning hot and heavy in my gut, I grabbed her hand as she dragged her thumb across my bottom lip, breathing hard, fighting every animal instinct I had, desperate to remain a gentleman. Mindful of the precipice we stood upon when it came to our relationship.

"What's your name?" My words came out rushed, breathy. Probably not at all what she was expecting from me, but I had to know. I needed to learn everything about her. Starting with the basics.

She slid her hand out of my hold, her movements slow and almost hesitant. "Is that really all you want to know?"

"No, but it's a start."

She leaned closer, her arm brushing mine. "My name's Trinity."

I practically whimpered, fingers buried in the soil, holding tightly to the ground, still resisting the urge to grab her. To yank her to me. To kiss her until she couldn't see straight. Her tongue flashed against her lips, and I nearly howled. Every inch of me hurt, all my focus on locking my muscles down so I didn't do anything stupid. So I stayed in control.

"You're not as scary as I thought," she whispered. Such a simple phrase, barely a handful of words, and yet too powerful to pass over. My growl stopped, my body froze in place. Every flame of desire for her went cold, every need disappearing into nothing.

"You thought I was scary?"

"That...the way you hit that man in the ring." She shrugged as if it wasn't important, as if the idea of her being afraid of me wasn't one of my biggest fears. "It was a little more than I expected to see."

"I don't—" I shook my head, memories of that hit blending with pictures of our pack after the attack. Of my dead sisters lying in the dirt in front of their cabin. Of teeth and claws and screams and bodies falling. A shifter...a witch...a friend. So much violence and death in such a short time. So many moments I could have done things differently.

Moments I couldn't change, unlike the one I found myself in right then.

"I didn't want to hit him like that," I said, trying my hardest to make sure she understood. To show her I could be honest and open with her. "I didn't mean to scare you, and I didn't hit him like that to show off. My reaction was about protection. He crept up while I was focused on you, and I thought he was a threat."

She sat silent for many seconds, time slow and heavy as it passed. I wished with everything I had that she believed me, that she'd understand how a threat to her would send me into a rage. That my need to keep her safe outweighed everything else.

That she wouldn't think I was a lunatic.

After an eternity that probably only lasted ten seconds, she inched closer, bringing her face directly in front of mine. "Why did you want to protect me?"

"Because..." I licked my lips, the fire within flaring brightly once more by her proximity. The taste of her skin on my flesh had me shuddering, the memory of her touch on my lips something visceral and incendiary. My God, she was sweet. I wanted more of her. Lots more. I didn't want to fight the pull anymore. Not for another second.

"Tell me," she whispered, her breath washing over my lips. "Don't say the word, but tell me. I need to hear it."

With little more than a breath, I whispered the only truth I could. "Because you're mine."

She sagged against me. All I knew was her, all I felt was her body pressing to mine. My raindrop had become my world. And when she sighed, when she closed her eyes and smiled so soft and pretty, I knew I was done. That flame of desire exploded, burning everything in its path. Every obstacle, every barrier... gone. There was nothing but her and me and the beating of our hearts as one.

Until the explosion of sweetness on my lips.

SIX

Trinity

Oh God, his lips. Firm and demanding, but with a hidden softness to them. Just like the man himself. We came together in a rush, neither person making that first move. Was I kissing him or was he kissing me? As his tongue brushed against my lips, I opened for him and quit wondering. It didn't matter who made the first move, who leaned in first, who started the fire. We were blazing, nearly out of control, and that burn was the best feeling in the entire world. Kissing Cahill was a much different experience than kissing the random shifter men I'd grown up with in the pack. Those boys were like placeholders, teachers who never got close enough to take more than the physical. Cahill was mine, my mate, someone to whom I could give my entire heart. Someone I worried I would never find. Someone I couldn't technically have. Yet.

But for one moment, for one brief, glorious minute, I pretended none of those things mattered. I imagined we were truly alone, safe somewhere far away from this hell, with no obligations to the rest of the world. And when his hands grabbed my hips, I didn't resist him. I let him tug me closer because I wanted him to. I wanted to feel his body against mine. I wanted one more minute in the fantasy. I deserved that much, didn't I? And he deserved the same. Deserved more than me. More than a mate who kept secrets from him.

Piers.

I pulled away, gasping for air, my hands shaking as they clutched at his shoulders.

"We can't."

"Can't what?" His tongue peeked out, and he licked his lips in a most obscene way. I nearly attacked him. What I wouldn't give to be kissing him again. To feel those lips on mine. On me.

I shivered. "Cahill, we can't do this."

"Do what? Kiss? Because I'm pretty sure we were doing a bang-up job of it just a few seconds ago."

I untangled myself from his arms, hating myself for having to let go, ducking my head to hide the desire in my eyes. "No, we can't do this. Any of this."

One finger slid under my chin, gently lifting my face. I nearly whimpered when my eyes met his. He looked at me as if I held the key to his world, as if I was more than just a pack wolf with a secret or ten. He looked at me as if I mattered.

"Why not? What's going on?"

I swallowed hard, knowing how much this would hurt him. Readying myself for the rebound heartache. "I can't betray my... Piers like that."

"Piers." His back stiffened, eyes hardening. "Who is Piers to you?"

I wrung my hands as I stood up, refusing to lie. I couldn't, not to him. Not to my mate. But I couldn't tell the truth, either. "I...I don't want to say. But he only has a handful of fights left."

"What does that have to do with anything?"

"Please," I whispered as my heart cracked slowly, painfully

deep. "I know it's confusing. But I can't tell you. I can't risk it. Once he's done fighting, we can leave here. Everything will work out then."

"Trinity, really, I don't understand. What can't you risk?"

I bit my lip, facing him. Terrified. "Piers. I can't risk him."

His eyes went cold and dark before he turned away from me. "I see."

"No." I gasped at the pain in my chest, at the way my heart screamed for Cahill. I jumped toward him without thought, without plan, grabbing on to his arm, thumbing the edge of his scars and forcing him to look up at me. "You don't know, and that's my fault. But it's not what you think."

Cahill sighed, his hands coming to hold my elbows. To hold me in place. "Then tell me."

The pain was excruciating, my heart ripped in jagged pieces. But there was nothing I could do. "I can't."

He growled again, this one softer, higher. More pain than aggression. "But you're my—"

I pressed my finger against his lips again, silencing him before he dared to say the word. I wanted to hear it, wanted to yell it from the rooftop and let the whole world know he was mine, but we couldn't. And that might have been the moment my heart fell apart, flayed open by the secrets I was sworn to keep.

Dropping to my knees before him, I dragged my cheek along his, nearly purring at the scruff as it scraped my sensitive skin. Giving him a brief taste of what he wanted, scenting him as mine. Higher still, just a bit, so I could whisper in his ear. So I could close the one door I desperately wanted to keep open.

"We can't say it. Not here, not where the others can hear us. I know what we are, but we can't say the word."

Cahill grabbed my hips, his touch harsh and nearly painful. "Why? Please, tell me."

"I can't, but know this. Once Piers' last fight is done, I can be yours completely. We'll leave here; I'll go wherever you do. Just...give me time." I pressed my lips to his cheek and closed my eyes for one second, breathing him in, clinging to his warmth and his touch. And then I jumped up and ran.

The pain nearly brought me to my knees, but I still raced as fast as I could for the complex. I knew Cahill could catch me if he wanted to, if he chased me, but I hoped he'd stay put for a minute. Nothing good could come from him chasing me. I had to be ahead of him. If the other shifters knew, if they saw us together, it could destroy what we'd been working for. What Piers had been working for.

I slipped into the gym unnoticed, reeling from the pain and needing to hide in my room so I could finally release the tears. My lips tingled from Cahill's kisses, a little memory of our few stolen moments something I loved. It was as if I had a secret.

That thought pulled me up short. A secret? I had plenty of those. Too many. They just kept piling on, dragging me down with the weight of the responsibilities they brought with them. Don't tell this, act like this, never forget that. It was exhausting. And poor Cahill was stuck in the middle—knowing there was a secret but not knowing the details. I hated it, hated that the next few days could hurt him. I wanted to be with him, to get to know him, to explore our bond. But I couldn't. Not here, not now.

Not until Piers won that last fight.

"Hey, Trin, where've you been?" Piers walked up with a smile on his face. Another fighter I recognized walked by his side, one who liked to leer at me a little too much.

I forced a returning smile. "Just went for a walk. It stinks of sweat and male in here."

From the corner of my eye, I caught sight of Cahill as he walked in the door. My wolf whined for her mate, but I fought the instinct to turn. I stayed focused on the men in front of me, not wanting to give anything away. Not wanting to give in to the need and the hurt and the ache for the one I couldn't be with.

The shifter next to Piers gave me a lecherous smile and leaned closer, sniffing me in a way that made my inner wolf slink forward, ready to defend. "It may smell like sweat in here, but you smell like another shifter. You running around on our boy here? When's my turn?"

Piers' throaty growl rumbled loud enough to stop all the chatter in the area. "What did you just say to her?"

I lifted my chin, refusing to let this animal get under my skin. He may have smelled Cahill on me, but there were a million reasons for that. A million beyond him and me kissing by the river.

A crash from across the aisle stopped the fighter from saying anything else. We all turned toward the sound, watching as a metal table settled against the concrete, top side down. Cahill stormed away from the area without looking back.

"That guy's going to kill someone," the fighter beside Piers said.

"Yeah, he's a definite hothead." But Piers wasn't watching Cahill, he was eyeing me. He cocked his head, looking at me with a question. I couldn't lie to him, never had been able to, so I pinched my lips together and held his gaze. Holding my ground even though it felt like quicksand under my feet.

Knowing he'd get it out of me eventually and terrified of what he'd do when he found out Cahill was my mate.

SEVEN

Cahill

I snuck into the gym after Trinity, doing my best not to look her way. Something was wrong in her life, something that scared her. I saw it in her eyes. Felt it in the way she clung to me. I wanted to be the one to help her, but instead, she went to Piers. The guy who currently had his arm wrapped around her.

What the hell was going on?

I couldn't understand the situation I found myself in. Mating bonds were sacred, blessings from the gods and creators. I'd seen them go wrong and I'd seen mated pairs unhappy, but I'd never seen a mate choose someone other than their match. It just wasn't done. And yet there was Trinity, ignoring me and letting Piers wrap himself around her like some sort of shifter blanket. Just the fact that her fingers were clutching the back of his shirt made me see red, and the fucking pheromone cocktail in the air wasn't helping. I took a deep breath, tamping down the fire within. Calm, I needed to find my calm.

But because I was apparently a masochist when it came to Trinity, I edged closer, just enough to listen to the conversation.

I had to know, had to figure her out. I needed to understand why she was so committed to the bastard at her side when I knew she felt the mating pull as I did. She'd shivered in my arms, had responded to my kiss with her entire body. She wanted me, but she refused to let herself take what she wanted. There had to be an explanation.

As I watched, another shifter leaned over Trinity, sniffing her. My wolf howled in my head, ready to attack the man he saw as a threat. I reined in my animal side and slipped closer, edging along one of the stainless-steel tables used to hold water and tapes, needing to hear what the bastard said. Wanting to be close in case she needed my protection.

I missed the first bit, barely hearing what seemed to be a question. But then I moved closer, and the fucker asked Trinity something again.

"When's my turn?"

My roar was loud enough to turn a few heads. Unwilling to rush in and start swinging in case I scared her again, I grabbed the closest thing I could—the metal table. I upended it with ease, creating enough of a racket to turn everyone's heads, including Trinity, Piers, and the fucker who dared to proposition her. If I couldn't jump to her defense, I could at least make enough noise to distract the fucker. I made sure to memorize his face, then turned and stalked off. Trinity was protecting Piers from something; well, he'd better be man enough to protect her as well since I couldn't. At least not yet.

"Yo, Appalachia."

I spun toward one of the handlers, ready to rip body parts off if necessary. Doing so gave me the perfect shot of Trinity... walking down a hallway toward the sleeping bunks with Piers. At least that other fucker wasn't near her anymore.

"What?" My word came out on a snarl, so I coughed, hoping

the guy would think I had a dry throat or something. "Sorry. What do you need?"

"Against my better judgment, the powers that be want to put you in the ring tonight." The handler looked me up and down, assessing, probably worried I was about to snap. "You think you're ready to fight yet?"

I looked down the hallway again, no longer seeing Piers and Trinity. They were probably tucked in a room together. Alone.

My shoulders sank, defeat and confusion a heavy burden to bear. One I had no idea how to cope with.

"Yeah, I'm ready to get this over with."

———

The arena where the fights were held in front of human crowds was huge. A ring with metal fencing all the way to the ceiling sat in the middle with a small walkway of concrete around it. Then came the stands. They rose from the floor almost to the roof on all four sides. Rows upon rows of wooden benches for the humans to sit on. Not that any of them was. Sitting, that is.

When the handler led me into the room, the crowd was on its feet. The room was packed full of humans, and all of them were here to watch us fight, not knowing the supernatural side of the men they cheered for. The sound of their screams nearly deafened me, made me want to shift, to prepare to defend myself. I fought it back, but it took a lot more of my focus than I'd expected. The smell, the energy, the noise—they all melded together to create an environment that drove my wolf mad. With every step closer to the chaos, my control slipped, and I had to divert my attention to yank it back into place. There was no way this could end well.

"There're only two rules here, kid," the handler said as we waited for the signal to take the ring.

"What's that?" I bounced on the balls of my feet, keeping my blood flowing, throwing my arms out loosely every few bounces.

"Don't shift, and do your best not to kill your opponent."

That stopped me cold. "Do my *best*?"

The handler shrugged. "It happens. Even we can't heal if our heart stops or we lose all our blood too fast to replenish it."

I shuddered and shook my head, resuming my warm-up bounces. But my head wasn't in it. Bleed outs...that's how those fuckers who'd attacked our pack had killed so many. That's how they'd murdered my sisters. A claw to the throat was all it took, a half-assed beheading, really. Both the girls had been facedown in the mud, left in pools of their own blood like trash on the side of the road. As much as I wanted to win so I could get back home, I couldn't see doing that to someone. In self-defense? Sure. To avenge my sisters and my pack? Absolutely, already done it. But for sport? No. I wasn't that fucking crazy.

The crowd roared louder, apparently happy with the end of the first fight. I couldn't tell who'd won or lost, as both shifters seemed to need assistance to leave the ring.

The handler turned to me, double-checking my hand wraps as he spoke. "Your opponent's mean but not quite as big as you. Use your size to your advantage, stay light, and give them a good show. You'll be fine."

I nodded, following him down the walkway as the announcer screamed my name over the loudspeaker. Well, my name for here.

"In black, we have one of our newest cage fighters. He's a beast, an animal raised in the wild and brought up on good, clean, mountain air. Give a welcome to...Appalachia!"

I scowled as I set my mouthguard. Idiots. These humans were practically salivating at the chance to watch us fight, throwing money around as if it were nothing. I pictured my home, my pack, the sad faces and air of mourning that covered us. The grief we'd experienced over the last year. We needed to pay off the security team, and I needed to go home to help my friends heal. To give myself time to grieve the loss of my family. That had to be my focus. Them...not me. And definitely not Trinity. Though that would be hard considering she was sitting in the third row with that motherfucker Piers draped all over her again.

My mountains...my pack...my grief...not my mate. Not my one chance at something more.

My opponent stepped into the ring looking tough and ready. And wouldn't you know, it was the guy who'd propositioned Trinity earlier in the day. That didn't bode well for me keeping my control, not shifting, and not killing him. Not well at all. I could feel the energy coming off him, the rage and the aggression. He was completely pumped up, something that worked in my favor. I'd let him wear himself out coming after me and wait for a time to knock him down. Easy enough. Just avoid being hit...and *do my best* not to kill him.

The second the bell rang to start the fight, the guy in the ring came out swinging as I knew he'd do. One punch, two, six... he was wild in his movements and his attack. Chasing me around the ring, using up all his energy trying to keep up with my dodges. Meanwhile, I feinted and hopped, staying light, moving simply. *Eyes on him, always eyes on him, watch his arms, the motion comes from the shoulder, don't let him win because you blinked.* Killian's words stayed in my head, all the times we'd sparred and fought having taught me a number of lessons. I didn't need to be the biggest, the baddest, or the toughest. I just needed to be the smartest and have more endurance than my opponent. With the way this guy was rushing hard at me, that wouldn't be a problem.

On a turn around the backside of the arena, Trinity caught

my eye. I tried to refocus, but there was something in the expression on her face, something sad and scared that snagged my attention. It was a moment, barely more than a second. A tiny spot of time shared between Trinity and me as hundreds of people screamed for blood.

And then Piers broke our stare by leaning over Trinity and...

Was he kissing my fucking mate right in front of me?

EIGHT

Trinity

I kept my hands clasped in my lap as my eyes followed Cahill around the ring. He wasn't attacking in any way. Instead, he moved and dodged his opponent's punches, simply avoiding being hit. Bouncing back and forth, weaving around the other fighter. It was a beautiful display of his athleticism, and yet terrifying.

"He's so fucking smart." Piers sounded impressed, so I leaned closer, trying to hide my knowledge and interest.

"Who?"

"That guy...Appalachia. He's running on defense right now, letting that fighter Asylum wear himself out. I've seen him hit—the guy's a beast and could have knocked his opponent to the floor already, but instead, he's waiting. The bosses are going to love him."

"Why would they love him?" I glanced at Piers for a split second, too worried about Cahill to turn away for any longer. Piers was completely focused on the fight, his eyes dark, an expression close to obsession on his chiseled face.

"The bosses like longer fights, remember?"

I did remember. Longer fights...more money...more blood. I bit my lip, wishing Cahill would hit the other guy already to end this. "Well, I hate them."

He leaned over me, his lips close enough to mine for me to practically breathe his words. "What's got you all nervous, Trin?"

Before I could answer, the crowd roared. Piers spun away, allowing me to watch as Cahill leaped across the ring. He raged at his opponent, quickly throwing three fierce hits before the other man seemed to know what was going on. Asylum fell to the floor like a rag doll, unconscious. The crowd screamed and stomped their feet, all excited over the violence. Over the blood.

The whole spectacle made me sick.

Cahill stood in the center of the ring, breathing hard, staring down at his opponent. His handler rushed to him, grabbing his arm and holding it up in triumph. Cahill didn't react, barely moved. But his eyes found mine. Darted to Piers then came back again. My heart stuttered at his tormented expression. Pain and confusion—and so much anger. I knew what was in his head, knew what had made his switch flip. And it was my fault. All my fault. He didn't understand about Piers, and he needed to. This charade couldn't last for much longer.

Piers leaned closer, but instead of curling into his side as I'd always done, I pulled away. I couldn't pretend...not with Cahill watching me. Not knowing how much my actions hurt him.

"What's up, Trin?" Piers asked.

I shook my head, my eyes still locked on Cahill. On my mate. "We need to talk, but not here."

The tension around us increased. I could feel Piers' stare burning my cheek, but I didn't care. Cahill needed my attention. He needed to know what was happening. He needed me, but there was nothing I could do. Not without risking everything.

Piers stood and grabbed my hand, pulling me after him without another word.

"Where are we going?" I asked, finally losing sight of Cahill.

"Somewhere not here." He gave me a concerned look over his shoulder before yanking me behind him. I caught one more glance of Cahill before we exited the arena and headed for the bunk rooms. My mate stood in the cage a champion but looking completely enraged. He must have thought I was leaving him, but my trek to him was only just beginning. This was it. Time to make my move. Time to break character.

When we reached the door to our room, Piers held it open for me. I walked into the space we'd shared for the past few weeks, pacing the length of it. Wringing my hands.

"Tell me," Piers said as he leaned against the dresser in the corner.

I shook my head, my eyes burning. Shit, this was such a mess. But I couldn't live the lie anymore, not after I saw...not after I knew.

"Trin, we don't keep secrets. We trust each other, remember? Only us...always us. Together," Piers said. His words hit me hard, almost knocking the wind out of me. *Together. Only us.* The words we'd said to one another a thousand times. The ones we'd whispered as we'd run from the only home we'd ever known. As we'd left behind the hate brewing against us.

I stopped pacing, turning his way, meeting his wary eyes with my watery ones.

He frowned. "What is it?"

"That guy...the fighter who won."

"Appalachia. The new guy. What about him?"

I stepped closer, too afraid to say anything out loud. Knowing this was a moment that could destroy what we had.

When I was close enough to touch him, I rested my hands on his shoulders and leaned into him, brushing my lips against his ear so I could whisper my truth.

"He's my fated mate."

Piers went stiff under my hands. I stepped back, watching him. Waiting for some sign of his emotion. Would he be angry? Sad? Betrayed? Happy for me? I had no idea. We'd been together for so long in our current situation that it wasn't anything I usually thought about. It simply was. But now... Now, we needed to think. Things needed to change.

Piers stared at the floor, his brow furrowed, silent. And then he raised his eyes to meet mine.

"You need to go. You don't have much time."

Cahill

I stormed into my room, sweat-covered and shaking with adrenaline. Fuck, I'd pounded that guy. I hadn't meant to, not really. I knew I'd win, but not like that. I hadn't been prepared for Trinity. Hadn't known what seeing her and Piers—

The snarl I let loose was uncontrollable. It shook the shitty little mirror over the chest of drawers. I grabbed my head, knowing I needed to hold myself together. The anger at seeing my mate with another, the rage from her rejection, the fucking smell of blood and sex always on the air... It was all too much.

Raindrop.

I paced like a caged animal, which I guessed I was. Owned and collared by the powers that be in this place. My handler had told me the bosses were thrilled with my fight. I'd gone in as the underdog, and the bets had rolled in favoring my opponent throughout the match. That was, until I lost control and knocked his ass out with a few well-placed hits. Still, they'd made a lot of money on me, and that thrilled them. It scared me, though. The anger, the violence...I'd had enough of that over the last year. I wanted quiet, I wanted to stop fighting, and I wanted my mate.

I snarled low and deep, again shaking the mirror. I had no control over that last one, a fact that incited my rage instead of calming it. Fuck, what was I supposed to do about Trinity?

Without warning, my door opened. I spun, crouching, ready to attack whoever dared to enter my room without knocking. As if my thoughts had somehow called to her, Trinity slipped inside. She closed the door and pressed herself against it, eyes wide, looking determined but hesitant. My mate was nervous...perhaps even afraid. Of me. That was enough of a jolt to pull me up short, sort of. The last thing I wanted to do was scare her, but it was all too much. My control could only stretch so far, and her walking in the door smelling like another male was definitely not helping the situation.

"What the fuck are you doing here?" I eased back a step, retreating from her even though I wanted nothing more than to move closer. The scent of her washed over me, all natural and earthy. It called to me, teased me, made me hard for her. Made it difficult to resist her.

She frowned but didn't drop her eyes from mine. Instead, she raised her chin, almost challenging me. My brave little warrior. "I came to see if you were okay after the fight."

Oh, hell. I stalked closer, unable to stand my ground. Needing to feel her heat, bathe in her fresh scent. Needing her to erase the memories burning in my mind of blood and cheers and pain. And Piers.

"You checking up on me, Trinity?"

She nodded, slow and smooth. Eyes staying locked on mine. Not backing down. When close enough, I extended my arm and placed my fist against the door just above her shoulder. She could still escape, edging out to the other side of me, but my position gave us both the illusion of a trap. A cage. I was boxing her in, and she knew it.

I ducked down and brought my face to her level. "Why?"

"I was...worried." She stumbled over that last word, her voice suddenly softer.

"Worried." I cocked my head as my vision sharpened, my wolf side edging forward. "Did it look as if I had a rough fight?"

She shivered and shook her head no.

"So then why are you here...really?"

A lick of her lips, a flash of pink against red. Fuck, that was hot.

"I needed to see you," she whispered. I leaned closer, letting my body meet hers, pushing her against the door. So warm, so soft. Nothing between us but the sparkly fabric of the dress she wore, the sequins harsh against my bare chest.

Breathing her in, I brushed my nose along the shell of her ear. "Where's your friend, Piers?"

She froze, her body going completely stiff. "He's not my friend."

"Could have fooled me." I huffed and moved to back away, but her little hands grabbed me. The heat, the draw, the feel of her skin on mine. All of it locked me in place. She had me in her trap, and she knew it.

She stared right into my eyes, not blinking, not looking away as she said fiercely, "He's not my friend...he's my cousin."

I felt my whole world go sideways. "What?"

"He's my cousin. We were raised together in a pack outside of Denver. When they forced him to leave, I went with him. We pretend to be mates for a lot of reasons, but we're not. We're related."

I shook my head, trying to make sense of her words. "You smell like him."

"Of course I do—we share some of the same blood. Plus, we

spend a lot of time together. No one questions us that way." She lifted her hand to my face, running one finger down the side of my cheek in a move that made my entire body shiver. "We're not together, nor have we ever been."

I swallowed hard, fighting back the urge to press my lips to hers. Words were good, words were fine, but I wasn't ready yet. I still didn't understand. "Why do you lie?"

"Partially for my protection while here, but mostly for his. We've been pretending to be mates since we were forced out of the pack. It was the only way to keep people away from me and to protect him. If people knew..." She trailed off, her eyes dark and filled with fear.

"If people knew what?"

"Not now, not here." She leaned closer, her lips brushing my skin. "Too many ears and eyes around this place. But I had to come. I told Piers about us tonight, about you being my..." Closer yet, her cheek fully against mine, her body practically crawling up me to reach my ear so she could breathe, "Mate."

There it was...the word I'd wanted to say and hear and scream. My mate.

My hands curled into fists, clutching at her, something completely outside of my control. Trinity responded with a soft moan, arching her back to press her body to mine.

"He told me to hurry here so I could talk to you before the next fight ended. We can't risk the other fighters overhearing. No one can know about any of this. They'll make me leave if they find out, but they'll kill Piers. "

I ran my nose along her cheek, drinking her in, unsure if lying about being mated was worthy of a death penalty but not willing to argue about it. Too thankful not to take advantage of this moment. "Let me help you both."

She nodded, clinging to me. "Soon. But not now. Not tonight."

I closed my eyes as her hands came up to cradle my face. Such soft hands, smooth and gentle. I wanted to feel them all over. Wanted to spend hours learning her body as she learned mine. On a sigh, she leaned forward, pressing her lips to my brow.

"You are my mate, Cahill."

A whiny, whimpering sound escaped my throat. "Why'd you kiss him at the fight?"

"Is that what you thought happened?" She shook her head, running her fingers through my hair. "No kiss, not ever. He leaned in to whisper to me. Like this."

She turned her head, her lips so very close to mine and yet not. Even being a participant, I could see how such a position would give almost anyone watching the impression of a kiss. It was close, intimate, something others wouldn't doubt without reason. A move I'd fallen for myself.

"See?" she asked, backing away.

I nodded, my body shaking with restraint. She was still so close, right in front of me.

"You don't have any reason to be jealous," she whispered, pulling on me, keeping us pressed together. "I'm yours, Cahill. My wolf is certain of it, and we want to be yours. We just have to be patient."

I gripped her hips hard. My cock practically wept at the feel of her soft stomach trapping him. I wanted her, needed her, but I knew I couldn't have her. Not yet, she said. Not yet.

And then she rolled her hips against me, making me see stars.

"Fuck, Trinity," I hissed, clutching at her flesh with a grip too tight not to hurt. "You're making this so hard."

She smiled, pressing a soft, wet kiss to the corner of my mouth. "What would make it better, my mate? What do you need?"

TEN

His big body nearly collapsed into mine, pressing me firmly against the door. I had one second to truly feel him, every single inch of him, before his lips were on mine. All thought disappeared, leaving me in a haze of *damn* and *yes* and *want* and *so, so good*. The friction of our lips moving together, his tongue sliding against my own, the weight of him nearly on top of me. Perfection.

He edged back, his nose brushing mine, chuckling as I mewled at the loss of him. "How long do I have you?"

I sighed. "Not long, four of the fights are over. There're only two more, I think."

He growled, the sound breaking something within me. Something that felt much like the last shreds of my control. I stretched to meet his lips again, needing another taste of him. He met me halfway. One kiss, small but wet.

"So glad you're here."

"Me too. I missed you today." I pressed my lips to his chin, biting softly for a moment. Teasing him.

"Shit." He punched the door behind me, an explosive heat blasting between us. "When can I have you for real?"

"What's your contract? How long are you here?"

"Three fights." He moaned, pressing his hips into mine, the long, hard ridge of him making me want. Making me yearn to be filled by him, to touch and taste and envelop him in my body. To be ruined by him. "This was my first. I fight tomorrow night. So not long, Trin—"

I kissed him again, silencing the word before moving my lips toward his ear. "Don't say my name," I whispered, barely more than a breath. "They might hear you."

He snarled his unhappiness. That just wouldn't do, so I bit his bottom lip and hissed, "*Mine.*" He jerked and attacked my mouth, kissing me roughly. Overpowering me completely. Still perfect.

His hands slid down to the backs of my thighs, so I jumped, wrapping my legs around his hips. Giving myself over to him the only way I could. He pressed me into the door again, pushing against me in a way that made me claw at his shoulders and gasp. That made me look forward to when we could finally leave here and be alone. When I could have all of him.

"You like that?" he asked, his voice more grit than not. "You like feeling me so hard between your legs?"

"Yes." I rocked over him, panting against his lips. "Where will you go when your contract is up?"

He grunted, dropping his head to my shoulder as he kept thrusting, kept teasing, kept driving me mad. "Back to my pack in the mountains. They don't call me Appalachia for nothing."

"The pack where women aren't made to be servants." I dropped my head against the door, nearly lost in the haze of how much pleasure he was giving me while still dressed. "Will you take me with you?"

"Fuck yes. I'll take you anywhere you want to go if you're

willing to be by my side." He groaned, his hands grasping my ass hard.

Eyes closed, body building toward something amazing, I grabbed him around the neck and groaned. He was just so big against me. There wasn't a single space he didn't occupy. It was as if he was everywhere all at once. Surrounding me... smothering me in his scent.

And I loved it.

"Want to," I murmured, running my teeth along the muscle in his neck—something he definitely enjoyed if the harder thrust of his hips was any indication. "But I don't want to lose my cousin. He needs me."

"I need you," Cahill murmured as he twisted his hips, making me melt. Nearly making me scream. "But he can come, too. We don't kick out adult males like other packs. He can find a home with the rest of us."

"You might change your mind when you know everything, but I certainly hope not." I clenched my legs around him, wanting him closer, wanting him inside. "That's what I want. Someplace safe for us. All of us. I want to stop running and lying and living with so many secrets."

"No more." He licked the length of my neck, a gentle warmth that made me shiver. "I'll keep you safe. I promise."

I nodded, letting him take over the movements. I couldn't think, couldn't make my muscles work properly. All I could focus on was Cahill and heat and the tightening low in my gut. On a slow press up with his hips, one that almost made me see stars, he nipped at my neck. I jumped in response, which made him snarl and shiver. We were feeding the needs we shared, the actions of one a catalyst for the other. And it was so damn hot.

I licked my lips, not wanting to say the words but needing to. Knowing they were a necessity. "You can't claim me yet. I'll smell like you, and then—"

"I know." He pressed harder, his arms shaking, his hips moving faster. "Two more fights. A few more days."

"Yes," I hissed, that low burn glowing brighter in the bottom of my gut letting me know how close I was to falling apart. "I have to pretend with Piers still. I'm sorry. I don't want to hurt you."

"I know. I'll try to handle it."

As I hit that ridge between pleasure and pain, I pushed my nails into his shoulder and pulled down, unable to hold back. "We'll be okay. Gotta be careful."

He grunted, almost leaning into the claw marks I was surely leaving behind. "Careful, yes. Fuck, Raindrop."

His teeth touched my neck again, barely more than a shadow of a bite, but I still lost it. I came with a yelp, squeezing him, head back against the door with my mouth hanging open. Fireworks exploded behind my eyes as every muscle in my body seemed to pulse with the pleasure only he could give me. Cahill followed right behind me, thrusting hard and jerkily as he breathed into my neck. As he whispered words like *want* and *raindrop* and *mine*.

Finally, we stilled, the sounds of our heavy breaths loud in the otherwise silent room. Sweaty and disheveled with cramping leg muscles and a burn in my abdomen from the strength needed to hold myself up, I'd never felt better. The fates help me, I was going to explode into a million pieces when he finally got inside me. I could barely wait.

"Raindrop?" I asked once I caught my breath.

He chuckled and kissed my collarbone. "You smell fresh, like rain."

I pulled him closer, nearly purring. "I like it."

"Good," he said, groaning. "When is Piers done fighting?"

I sighed, wiggling against him to ease the ache in my legs.

"Two more bouts, but he probably won't fight for a few days yet."

"So I'll be done before him." His voice was rough, his worry obvious.

I swallowed hard, my stomach knotting. "Maybe...we can meet you somewhere?"

He tucked his face into my neck, rubbing his nose along the length and planting soft kisses. "I won't be able to leave you behind."

Clinging tighter, I closed my eyes and wished for things that were beyond my control. For safety and a quick end to the nightmare I was living. "We'll figure it out."

ELEVEN

Cahill

I spent the morning punching heavy bags and trying to work off a little post-dry-hump energy. Not that physical exertion seemed to be working to quiet my mind. Ever since Trinity had slipped out of my room to head back to the one she shared with Piers, my thoughts had been solely focused on her. Was she safe? Was she missing me? Was she as obsessed with me as I was with her? Did she wake up in the middle of the night with an ache inside to come together again?

I had, my hard cock practically weeping with want. Having a room to myself, I'd simply taken things in hand and rubbed one out each time, though I missed the feel of her against me. The smell of her around me, the taste of her on my lips. My own hand was a sad imitation, but it was the best I could do. Poor Trinity shared a space with her cousin, so taking care of her needs alone wasn't really a possibility. At least, I didn't think it was. Of course, the picture of her with her hand between her legs, biting her lip to stay quiet so Piers wouldn't hear her.

Yeah, that'd do nicely for later.

I shifted on my feet, trying to keep from getting hard at the thought of my mate pleasuring herself. I couldn't deal with that now, here, in the middle of the training facility surrounded by other fighters. They'd wonder, and I didn't want to bring any attention to Trinity and me. For whatever reason, she didn't feel safe here without Piers, something that rankled hard. Still, at least she was watched by him. Piers. Her cousin...not a lover or competition for me. A blood relation.

Thank fuck for that.

As I switched from hitting with my right arm to my left, my handler came up with his ever-present clipboard.

"Appalachia, you ready to fight again tonight?"

I nodded, still hitting the bag, still thinking about Trinity.

"This opponent will be harder than last night. You're moving into the big time now, kid."

I grunted, mixing things up, hitting the bag harder to hide my excitement. A fight tonight, then just one left. I'd be free of my pack debt soon, and then I could take Trinity and run. Though we'd have to wait for Piers. Maybe I could delay the next one, or add on a fourth for good measure. Or maybe—

I grabbed the bag, holding it still as I finally gave the handler my full attention. "What happens if someone doesn't want to fight?"

"You backing out, kid?"

"No, just curious, I guess."

He grunted. "Not all guys come here with debts, but for the ones who do, each fight is currency to pay it off. Debt is debt, no matter who pays."

I perked up. "Debt is debt. So let's say I finish the fights to pay off my debt but feel bad for someone who has a longer time here. Could I fight for their debt?"

The handler shrugged. "It's not unheard of, but the money draw of each fighter would need to be similar. We wanted

Killian for one fight to pay off your pack's debt, but you came in his place. For you, the cost is three fights. Anyone weaker, the cost would be higher. So the balance still has to be kept. If you decided to fight for someone weaker, there would be fewer fights needed to pay off the debt. Which also means, if they're stronger—"

"There'd be more." I nodded, not wanting to ask about Piers in particular but wondering if there was some way to help get him out of his contract sooner so Trinity and I could leave. So we could all get the hell out of here and back to my mountain.

The trainer looked me over, one eye squinting a bit. "Anything you need to tell me?"

"Nope. I'm all set." I shook my head, pushing the bag away from me. My thoughts wandered with every punch, a future I dared not hope for playing behind my eyes. Trinity and I could leave together. Maybe I could take on another fight for someone. Maybe there was a way to delay so Piers could leave at the same time.

"Hey, Appalachia."

Speak of the devil... I turned to see Piers leaning over the ropes of a ring. The man seemed arrogant, grinning in such a cocky way even my wolf took notice of what looked an awful lot like a challenge. "Come on over here and give me some target practice."

I chuffed low but tossed my towel over my shoulder and headed his way. Trinity's cousin and I needed to have a few words anyway. "Sure thing, kid. So long as you don't mind missing every shot."

Piers laughed, his eyes darker and warier than his bright smile let on. I climbed into the ring slowly, keeping him in my sights. I didn't think he'd pull any tricks on me, but one never knew. Better to stay safe than be sorry later.

Piers approached slowly once I was standing on the bouncy base, offering his fists in a sign of respect for the start of a fight.

"Don't ever drop your guard," Piers said, voice quiet, eyes hard. I nodded, understanding his words were for more than our current bout. I rocked back and forth, arms up, ducking my head as he did the same.

"Anything else you want to tell me?"

He swung left, practically flying across the floor. "She likes hanging out in the woods behind this place."

It was my turn to grin. "Already knew that one."

"Breaking the rules already, huh? Not smart."

His first hit came as a surprise. I barely stepped out of the way in time, his glove brushing my chin as I leaned back. A glancing blow, but still...contact. I snarled in response and brought my hands higher.

That cocky grin of his grew. "Told you not to drop your guard."

We sparred for a few minutes, both of us dancing around the other, neither landing any good punches. Not that I thought that was the goal of the exercise. Hopefully the rest of the guys in the gym didn't see anything unusual.

"She hates it here," Piers whispered as we circled closer. "She hates the violence."

I nodded once, jabbing with my right. "I'm not a fan of it myself."

"Really? That's surprising. You seem to know your way around a fight."

"Knowing how to fight is a requirement in this life. Doesn't mean I have the heart to beat other shifters to a pulp for no reason."

He threw a solid punch, catching my forearm as I blocked. "Money's a reason. Fame."

"I'd rather have peace. I've seen enough violence for this

life. Besides, it's too fucking loud here. My wolf can't settle in this place."

He stopped, feet planted and arms dropped as he huffed a laugh. "Your fates don't fuck around when they pair people up, do they?"

Before I could ask what he meant, another fighter stepped to the edge of the ring. "Yo, Piers. Where's your eye candy?"

My growl was low and quiet but enough of a warning for the guy's eyes to widen. Piers spun in the direction of the interrupter. His shoulders tensed, fists clenched and ready to fight, but then he fell back a step. Eyes hard but that damned cocky grin back on his face.

"Sorry, man," he said, shaking out his arms. "She's back in our room recovering from last night."

"Get her ass up next time. We need our morning dose of tits and ass." The man laughed before walking off to join a group of shifters at the other end of the room. Piers' grin had fallen, a sickly smile left in its place as he glared after the shifter.

"Fucking place makes everyone a ball of testosterone," Piers grumbled, ducking low again.

I kept my eyes on Piers, biting back the instinct to defend my mate. Knowing now was not the time. But still...

"That's just an excuse, asshole." I edged closer, eyesight sharp and animalistic. Piers zeroed in on me, responding to the anger in my voice. Smart boy... I was about to teach him a lesson, and he knew it.

He dropped to a crouch, ready to go again. I stayed loose and watchful. I needed one spot, one moment of...and then, there it was. An opening. Piers took a single step back, dropping his eyes to my right shoulder. I swung hard and wide with my left, knocking him in the side of the head. The bones in my hand crunched in a sickly way, but it didn't matter. Piers fell like a brick to the floor of the ring.

I leaned over his prone body, offering a hand, pretending to help him up. When I had him in a sitting position, I yanked him forward to speak directly into his ear so the others wouldn't hear me.

"You ever let these fuckers talk about her like a piece of meat again, and I'll rip your fucking arms off."

Piers stared, eyes wide. I glared right back, letting him know how serious my threat was. I didn't like the way other men were allowed to leer at her, to undress her with their eyes, or to talk about her. It made Trinity into an object, which wasn't acceptable. I especially didn't like Piers laughing off their sexist remarks.

After a moment to catch his breath, Piers smiled and shook his head, taking my hand and letting me pull him up. "Yeah, those fates don't fuck around with you wolves. You two really are a perfect match."

I didn't reply, too wound up after what that other guy had said to deal with this shit. I needed my mate, wanted to be sure she was safe. Sparring was over, and luckily, Piers knew it.

"She's out in the woods by the river," he whispered, heading for his water bottle in the corner of the ring. "I'll back you up if anyone comes looking for you, but they won't buy my bullshit for long. You've got about an hour before you'll be missed. Go."

Without a backward glance, I took off for the door. My mate was outside, and I wanted to be close to her. To guard her...and maybe find a little time to be alone together. I stripped as soon as I hit the tree line and took off in wolf form through the woods. Screw their rules. My wolf needed to run, and I was going to make sure he got a chance to. The air was cleaner out here, no longer filled with scents that drove a man wild. The rocks bit into my paws in a way that was familiar, a slight ache that made me homesick for my own mountain. Trees and sun and a cool breeze that blew through the treetops with a soft rustle, those were all things natural. That building against the mountainside, those men pumped up on hormones, was pure wrong. I wanted to be done with wrong. I wanted the one thing in my life I knew was decidedly, perfectly right.

It was time to track my mate.

TWELVE

Trinity

The sun blazed bright in the sky, bringing with it a blanket of heat. The air was humid, almost sultry in its thickness, causing sweat to trickle down the back of my neck where my hair hung heavy. The river rolled by not far away, sparkling and bringing a soft, sensual sound to my ears. A quiet, peaceful background noise to the brushing of the leaves above me. I sat in the shade under a tree, enjoying the tickle of the breeze against my skin. Finding peace in my solitude with Mother Nature and the sounds of nothing but the wind and the river.

This was the time of day when the men were training, bashing each other's heads in and calling it practice for the real fights later. I hated the sounds of fists on flesh, hated the grunts and the smells and the cursing. The unnaturalness of it all. So I stayed outside by the river where I could be alone. Where it was quiet and peaceful.

Or at least relatively so.

Because for only the second time since I'd been coming out here, I heard footsteps approach. Soft, with a four-part pattern telling me they were wolf and not man. Definitely not Piers. Someone approaching who'd already broken the rules. I sat as still as stone, staring into the woods, my heart racing. Unsure whether to be excited or terrified...or maybe even a little of both.

But then he appeared, a large, dark gray wolf, almost black along his topline. He crept through the shadows, his head lowered in a way that said he wasn't going to attack, his eyes on mine. Deep, bright eyes in the most unusual color of light brown. Nearly amber. I'd know those eyes anywhere, had been dreaming about them, actually.

"I heard you coming," I called, waiting for him to show his human self. The wolf rose to his back legs, the body morphing from fur to skin in one smooth movement. So much skin.

"I didn't want to scare you, so I circled around and gave you a warning." Cahill moved out of the shadows and into the sun, his skin so much darker than mine. A deep golden hue that seemed much more at home in the wild than my own. And while he kept a hand in front of his groin in a rare display of modesty, I still saw. Still knew. He was half-hard just being this close to me, and that fact started a low fire inside of me.

"You're very naked," I breathed, the words barely more than a whisper.

"I left my clothes by the gym. I know it's not allowed, but my wolf needed to track you. He felt...compelled."

"My wolf feels much the same." I looked him over again, dragging my eyes over all that gorgeous tanned skin before meeting his. "My human side does, too."

His lips turned up in a sly grin. "Aren't you supposed to avert your eyes or something? Some pack rule about not seeing each other naked until the Alpha has given his blessing to the mating."

I snorted a very inelegant laugh. "I'm no longer in a pack, so

I don't need to follow anyone's rules. Besides, I don't know a single mated couple who followed that rule."

"Yeah." He moved behind me, dropping down to sit with his legs on either side of me. "I don't think anyone in our pack followed it either. Though we hadn't been blessed with a mating for a good twenty-year stretch. Only recently has anyone found their fated match."

"That's so sad." I surrendered to my need for more—more skin, more warmth, more contact—and leaned against his chest, letting his scent surround me. "Lucky you then for finding me."

He kissed my neck and squeezed me closer. "Very, very lucky me."

We sat that way for several long minutes, watching the world go by as we took comfort in one another. It was lovely, silent and calm in a way my world tended not to be. Most men, Piers included, would have tried to fill the quiet, blathering on about something and making my head spin. Not Cahill—he sat behind me calm and sure, confident enough to give nature its chance to shine while he watched. But time passed and my mind began to spin off into what was coming. Even the peaceful river I loved couldn't drown my worry.

"You have a fight tonight," I whispered.

Cahill squeezed me tighter, burying his face in my neck as he sighed. "Yeah, I do."

I rose to my knees, swinging around him so we reversed positions. So I could be the one supporting him. His worried eyes met mine as I moved, but I simply shook my head. This was what I craved, a chance to give him my strength. To support him here while we were alone...since I couldn't support him once we were back inside the gym.

"I hate the fights," I said once I settled behind him on the grass. I wrapped my arms around his chest and buried my head against his shoulder, squeezing him. One of his large hands covered mine, pressing into his muscles. Capturing me even though I was trying to capture him.

"I'm almost done with my contract."

I slid my free hand down his chest, touching, feeling, learning every dip and ridge. Every scar. Discovering what made him relax, what made him sigh. What made him shiver in my arms. Lower, along the curves of his abs, spreading my fingers over his stomach as if I could protect him somehow.

"I do worry about you," I whispered, my voice shaking. "A lot."

"I know."

"I can't show it, though. Not in front of the others."

"I know that, too."

Breathing deeply, taking in the smell of him, the warmth of his body against mine, I surrendered again. He was my mate, and he would be in a ring tonight battling some other shifter. I would have to watch silently, hiding my fear and my attraction. I would have to lie with my entire body and play the role of someone else's mate. Something I'd been doing for so long but that seemed nearly impossible since I met Cahill. A feat that had gone from a stroll through the hills to climbing a mountain with a single glance.

But at that moment, as we cuddled under the tree with no one else around, I could be *his*. All his. And I wanted to.

"We're all alone out here."

He groaned as my fingers raked over his hip bones, leaning into me, giving me more room to touch and feel. "I noticed that."

I nipped his neck, dragging wet kisses down to his shoulder, tasting him. Taking him into my body in any way I could.

He made a noise like a whine, a needful, desperate sound that fueled my own fire. I slid my hand from under his, letting it join the first, both trailing fingertips up and down his thighs. "Whatever should we do to pass the time?"

Hard muscle clenched and relaxed as I teased higher, closer to where we both wanted me to go.

"Pretty sure you have a plan."

And I did. I had a plan to make him relax, to claim him in the only way I could, to extinguish the fire I knew had to be burning him alive.

"I always have a plan."

I slid both hands to the apex of his thighs, one reaching between his legs to cup his balls, the other grasping his heavy dick and running up the length of him. He groaned again, head against my shoulder, surrendering to my touch. He let me take the lead, spreading his legs and sliding down my body, giving me the perfect view over his shoulder. Hot, hard, and thick, he filled my hand. I practically moaned at the feel of him, at the sight of my pale fingers wrapping around him. At the deep color of the head sliding in my grip. So pretty...so sensual.

My strokes started slow but with a solid grasp. I knew men didn't need gentle, but I still wanted to ramp him up. Wanted to make him gasp and shiver and beg. So I tugged and pulled, twisting my hand, teasing the head of him with my thumb on every other pass. Meanwhile, my other hand kept the same rhythm with his balls, massaging and gently working them. Cahill sagged against me, his hands on the ground beside my hips to hold himself up. Laid out before me like some kind of sensual treat just for my eyes.

He groaned and shuddered, hips jerking up now and again as he searched for more. As he chased his pleasure. "Trinity, I should—"

"Shhh." I moved faster, knowing he was close, certain he was just as turned on as I was. "Let me do this for you. Let me make you mine."

He growled low, his legs shaking in earnest. "Yours. Always."

Smiling, I leaned down and bit his earlobe, sucking gently before letting go. "Good. Now I want to see you come."

"Shit," he hissed. His hips jerked harder, thrusting into my hands. I followed his cues, watching him, knowing he was close. Feeling it in the tension of his body. I kept my eyes trained down his body, noticing the muscles tense and release as he breathed, as he jerked, as he took everything I could give him and lost control at my hands.

As he stoked the fire of my arousal simply by letting me be the one in control of his own.

"Raindrop," he gasped, his body locking down, his voice little more than a whisper. He came with a groan, spurting over my hand in long streams of heat and wet. Such a sight to see—his muscles flexed, ridges running across his abdomen, legs locked. Sexy, solid, and totally mine.

I didn't release him right away, instead softening my touch to tease the orgasm into lasting longer. To corral every bit of pleasure for him. He still moved with my touch, still rocked his hips. Hell, he nearly whimpered as I tickled under the head, shivering in the heat of the two of us wrapped up in each other under the sun.

"Feel better?" I asked as he relaxed against me in what seemed like an exhausted heap. He sighed his assent, lying quiet and still for a few minutes.

He rolled over so fast, I almost didn't see him move.

"It's my turn." He popped to his knees, knocking me over. I landed on my back in the grass with him looming over me, a fire in his eyes that matched the one inside of me. One I knew we couldn't put out, not yet. Not the way we both wanted. And by the gods, did I want to feel him smother those flames.

He pushed up my skirt and dragged my panties down my legs, keeping his eyes on mine the whole time. That look, that expression, was a question of sorts. I knew I could tell him no, could close my knees, and he'd stop. But I didn't want to. I didn't want him to stop at all.

My fingers scrabbled to find purchase on his smooth skin, wanting him closer, needing his weight on me.

"Cahill," I finally urged when I couldn't reach his shoulders to pull him to me.

"Shhh." He grabbed my knees and pushed them apart, spreading me before him. Tickling the insides of my thighs with his fingertips. "I woke up six times last night to jack off to the thought of doing this."

I nearly came from his words, gasping and turning my head to hide from the sight of him so turned on for me. But I couldn't look away for long. I needed to see, to watch, to know what desire looked like in his eyes. To prepare myself for what he was about to do to me.

With a growl, he wedged his shoulders between my thighs and lifted my ass off the ground, bringing my most intimate parts right up to his face. There was no lead-in, no teasing or gentle increase in touch. He dove in like a man possessed, like a man starving for me. And perhaps he was, because I knew I was starving for him. Knew I craved his touch more than anything else.

His hot mouth completely surrounded my clit, his tongue flattening against it in the most obscene, delicious lick. I yelped and arched off the ground, wanting less and more all at the same time. But Cahill knew, and he gave me what I needed. He licked me from front to back, sliding his tongue inside on every trip, coming to suck on my clit as he reached it. Even in his attack, though, he was gentle. His tongue building pressure, his mouth never passing that point between pleasure and pain. Never teasing me too harshly. Giving me time. Setting me up for an intense orgasm.

I lifted my legs and pressed my feet onto his shoulders,

purposely spreading myself wider for him. Begging for more with my body alone. With a groan, he moved one hand around so he could slide two fingers inside me, immediately curling them, searching out something that'd taken me years to find alone. Something deep and hidden. And find it, he did.

"Cahill," I gasped, grabbing his hair in both hands and yanking him closer as his fingers slid over a spot that set my body on fire. He moaned and sucked on my clit some more, letting his fingers press and slide and press again, focusing on that spot. Driving me mad with every push and slide. My legs shook, my breathing was ragged, but I was close. So close. The burn in my gut told me, the way I couldn't hold still, the deep, empty need of—

Before I could do more than moan, Cahill's body landed on mine, pinning me beneath him. I immediately wrapped myself around him, more instinct than thought. I was too far gone to worry about consequences, too turned on to even think about stopping.

Snarling in his urgency, he crept up my body, his eyes practically glowing as they met mine.

"Need you," he whispered as his dick nudged between my legs, his shoulders tense. A sign that he was holding back. Waiting for my permission, for my consent. "Tell me yes, Raindrop. I won't unless you say the word."

There was a split second of indecision on my part, a moment when my brain tried to stop my body from taking what it wanted. But Cahill held my gaze, tense and shaking, both of us needing, wanting, desiring.

"Yes," I groaned, clawing at his hips. He thrust forward, sliding deep and hard. He gasped into my ear when he was all the way inside, a sound that made my body clench. So simple, so soft, and yet it meant so much. Meant that my desire for him was mirrored back at me, that he craved me as much as I craved him. That he was just as desperate for this.

Shivering, my entire body on edge, I took all that he gave me. I wrapped my legs around his hips and bucked up into him, needing more. Wanting hard and fast and hot and now. And good lord, he gave it to me. Thrusting harshly, moving my body along the forest floor, his hands rough as they held me to him.

He wrapped his arms around my shoulders and yanked me closer, as if I were trying to get away, as if he couldn't get enough of me. Damn, *I* couldn't get enough. Every inch of him was buried deep inside me, his pubic bone pressing against my clit on the forward strokes, but I wanted more. I wanted deeper. I wanted harder.

And he gave it to me, over and over and over again, pushing me far past anywhere I'd been before. Making the entire world disappear until it was just him and me and sweat and sex. Until I couldn't resist a moment longer.

I came with a loud moan, curling my torso to the side as every nerve ending fired at once. Cahill slowed, rolling his body into mine in a way that made me keen. Buried deep, he flexed his hips and pushed against my clit to drag out my pleasure. Just enough to keep me on edge, to make me feel ready for more, never pushing me too far. Never making me want him to stop. Every movement a tease of what else we could do. Of all that was possible to experience between us.

His hips soon lost their rhythm, his movements becoming uneven and quick. Three slides, five...body locking in place. He came with a groan, holding himself inside me, every muscle hard and tense for one beautiful moment. Then he relaxed, grunting softly as his thrusts turned shallow and slow, filling me with heat and wet and right. Keeping us joined under the sun as he began to explore my curves with his hands and mouth. Pushing my dress all the way up over my chest.

"I'm going to claim you right here," he murmured, his lips trailing to my breast, just under my nipple.

"Soon," I replied, my hand in his hair, holding him to me. Wishing we could give in now, could do what we wanted.

He slid out of me with a groan, rolling to the side with his arms wrapped around my back. Holding me close. And though I missed him being joined with me, I loved the feeling of his body wrapped around mine. So I sighed.

"You smell like me."

He laughed softly, tickling my side with his wet fingers. "I taste like you too, I bet."

Laughing, I reached up to wipe the moisture from his chin, not at all embarrassed. The sight more turn-on than anything else. That was me, us...proof of our connection and attraction. Evidence of how he knew what I wanted, how I needed him. He grinned as my fingers slid over his bottom lip, eyes bright, seeming happy and at peace. If only for a second. Because really, that was about all the time we had. Stolen minutes and hurried seconds that brought me to the highest heights of hope and promptly dropped me back down into despair.

"We have to go back soon," I whispered, hating to break our little bubble but knowing Cahill would be missed if he disappeared for long.

His eyes darkened, his smile fading. "I know. Though I'd rather stay here with you—or rather, not here. On my mountain, where we can be protected by my pack and still find privacy." He leaned down, pressing his lips to mine in a soul-searing kiss before he backed away to place his forehead against mine.

"Come home with me, Trinity."

"Soon," I said, smiling. Wishing we didn't have to wait. Wanting him so much, my heart felt as if it were pushing against my ribs.

"Soon," he whispered back, giving me one last kiss. That

promise must have been enough for him. Seconds later, he hopped to his feet, not at all concerned by his nakedness. I wasn't concerned by it either, though I did take the opportunity to really get an eyeful. Not that anyone could blame me. The man was gorgeous, robust and stunning in his skin. And he was mine.

Reaching down, he helped me to my feet. I wiggled and tugged, making sure my dress was back in place and covering me, not even bothering to look for my discarded panties.

"Ready?" he asked, smiling as I ran my palms over my ass one last time.

"I think so."

"Good." He yanked me up into his arms and then over his shoulder, smacking my ass hard once I was basically hanging off of him.

"What are you doing?" I screeched with a laugh.

"Carrying you back." He took off at a jog, following the path I'd taken earlier.

"Well, aren't you just a mountain Romeo."

"Romeo was a tragic hero who died because of stupidity. I'm not about to follow in his footsteps." He smacked my ass again, leaning in to bite my thigh as well. "I'm not wasting our forever on a misunderstanding. Not a fucking chance."

THIRTEEN

Cahill

The arena was packed, humans yelling and screaming as the fight before mine came to a close. My stomach twisted, churning in an almost painful way. I absolutely loathed what I was about to do. Two more, just two more, and I'd have worked off the debt my pack had accrued. Two more, and then I could figure out how to get Trinity home with me. I could do this. I'd waited decades for her—a few more days was nothing. As long as we were in the same place, we'd be okay. I wouldn't leave her behind as she waited for Piers to finish his term. I'd fight as many battles as needed to stay put.

And I'd win them...for her.

My mate was standing at the back tonight, farther away from the ring but close to where I waited. I liked her near me, even though we couldn't touch or talk. Still, she was close enough to hear me if I spoke. Too bad we were surrounded by handlers and trainers.

Trinity was alone, something I wasn't comfortable with. This place, these humans and the shifters, were too out of control. She needed someone with her just in case. I needed someone with her as well. Otherwise, my attention would never fully be on the fight I was about to be involved in. And that was a dangerous situation. Hopefully, Piers would be joining her soon, then I could relax a bit. Though I'd be happier if I were the one standing at her side, holding her hand, wrapping my arm around her.

She must have felt my eyes on her because she turned, meeting my gaze. That moment, the tiny turn up of the corner of her mouth in a smile, was worth more than anything else at that time. I cared for her, and I knew I'd grow to love her. We definitely had a future together, one I'd honor and cherish forever. One I couldn't wait to begin.

But first, two more fights.

"Okay, Appalachia. You're up next."

I nodded to the handler, slipping my bite guard into my mouth and bouncing on the balls of my feet to keep my legs warmed up. I needed to get my head in the ring.

"We want a good fight with lots of time for people to bet. Do you hear me?" The handler grabbed my wrists, smacking my taped hands to make sure they were wrapped tightly enough. "I don't care how easy the fight is, you drag it out. Though this one might be tougher to win, kid. We're putting you up against one of our best."

"Doesn't matter," I mumbled around the bite guard. "I'll win."

"If it means anything, my money's on you." He glanced over his shoulder as the announcer called for me. "They bet when there's blood. Give me blood. Drag it out; I want to see your opponent in a lump on the floor when this is done."

I nodded as Trinity again turned to me. By the sadness and disgust on her face, I knew she'd heard the handler. My stomach sank, and I wished I could wrap my arms around her, tell her how much I hated this, too. Make sure she understood what was at stake. She should never have been exposed to this world. She was too sweet, too soft for this life. Soon, I'd get her out of here and home with a pack who would care for her as much as I would. She'd love the mountains, love the freedom and beauty that came with living there. And she'd definitely love the quiet our sheltered packlands provided.

After one final glance her way, I headed toward the ring. I couldn't think about her right now, not unless I wanted to lose the fight. I'd meet up with her later, talk her through what was said, explain how much I hated this and didn't want to live a life so violent. I'd calm her down. But right now, I needed to focus, to concentrate. Fuck, these guys were vicious, the crowd bloodthirsty, but I'd give them what they wanted. Two more fights, and my devil's due was paid. Two more, and I could begin a new life with Trinity. *Two more, two more, two more.*

I swung up into the ring and bounced around, throwing punches at thin air. With every beat of my heart, I repeated my mantra in my head. *Two more. Two more.*

"And going up against our mountain man is one of our winningest new fighters. A man without a past. Our very own Tidal."

I swung my last punch, almost losing my balance. *No.* It couldn't be. But when I turned, there was Piers, stepping into the ring. Mouthguard in place, hands taped like mine. Ready for battle. And looking at me like he wished I'd just disappear.

"What the fuck?" I hissed when he was close enough to hear.

He shook his head. "I know, man. But this is the draw. I didn't have time to track you down once they said who I was fighting tonight."

I looked over his shoulder into the crowd, spotting Trinity with ease. She stood in the back still, eyes wide and filled with fear. I couldn't do this to her. I couldn't hurt her cousin, and yet if I didn't, he'd end up hurting me. Blood would be spilled on the mat tonight no matter what...mine or her cousin's. I had no idea what would be worse for her to bear.

"At least it's not a fight to the death," Piers mumbled.

I nodded, keeping my eyes on Trinity. "She's not going to take this well."

"Understatement. Pretty sure we're fucked."

"Sounds about right."

The bell rang for the fight to begin. I tore my eyes away from my panicked mate, wishing there was something I could do to comfort her. But there was nothing. If I didn't fight, I'd have to stay longer. If I lost, I'd have to stay longer. If I beat Piers, he'd have to stay longer. It was a complete no-win situation.

Piers and I bounced and circled, neither taking the first swing. The crowd grew quieter, their cheers turning to yelled profanities and calls for blood. Even the handlers and trainers looked ready to blast us for not fighting. But I couldn't attack him, and he knew my fighting style well enough not to attack me. We were at a crossroads neither of us wanted to take.

Finally, Piers huffed and moved closer. "The bosses are going to make us fight more matches if we don't give them what they want."

Two more.

I glanced up at Trinity as we swung around the floor. "I know."

"So let's do this...for real." And then he swung.

FOURTEEN

The crowd erupted as Piers blasted my mate with a punch to the jaw. My stomach twisted at the sight of Cahill's head spinning to the side. As he wiped the blood from his jaw and zeroed in on Piers, my heart raced and I couldn't catch my breath. I didn't even know where to look, which man to focus on. The noise bouncing around the concrete arena only added to my disorientation. My mate and my cousin, in the ring. I was sure Piers had gotten the same message as Cahill—make it bloody, make it last.

I was going to be sick.

"Kill him! Knock his teeth out."

The humans screamed things made up of my nightmares. I gripped the wall, needing it to stay on my feet. I hated to watch, didn't want to see, but I couldn't look away. I hated to even blink. Piers and Cahill were at war, and there was nothing I could do to stop them. Nothing I could do to make it all end.

The fight seemed to last for hours. The humans around me grew louder and more violent as the minutes passed. With every punch, every kick, every speck of blood that flew in the air or dripped down skin, my temperature dropped. I was shaking, shivering from a cold emanating from within. One formed of pure and utter terror.

As the fight went on, the hits grew harder. The sounds louder and more sickening. On a turn around the backside of the ring, Cahill threw a quick jab with his left, then struck hard with his right. Piers stumbled back, spinning face first into the chain link fence caging them in from the force of the brutal hit. Even from where I stood, I saw the striations in his eyes go red, saw the edge of his hairline darken with the shadow of scales. As the crowd screamed, I saw our world begin to crumble.

"No," I whispered, stepping away from the wall. Not now, not when we were so close to escaping. Not in front of all these humans, for God's sake, and especially not when he was fighting my mate. But it was too late, the beast within had taken over. Piers roared an almost inhuman sound that reverberated through the arena. The crowd cheered louder, having no idea what was to come. Cahill took a step back, eyes locked on Piers, probably seeing the same changes I did. He was focused and attentive, but he didn't understand. He didn't know the truth. He couldn't possibly have any idea what was about to happen. How bad things were about to get.

With no warning, Piers leaped into the air. Black claws ripped through the tape on his hands, something I could only pray the humans didn't notice. The handlers and trainers raced for the ring, probably having seen the same thing and knowing they needed to end the fight. Not that I thought they'd make it in time. I'd seen my cousin shift a thousand times, knew what to look for and what was expected, knew his speed and strength. The spectators, trainers, handlers, and Cahill didn't.

Hopefully, none of the humans had any idea the man jumping at my mate was about to shift into a dragon.

Piers landed directly in front of Cahill, too fast for my mate to back away. The cold spread all the way through me, leaving me frozen in place, unable to approach the ring. I stood helpless as Piers brought his hands down and thrust them forward with the momentum of his jump, hitting Cahill square in the chest. The thud, the crack of broken bones, the deep, angry sound of what could very well be death would be a noise I never forgot. One that would haunt me, no matter the outcome.

I watched as Cahill's eyes rolled, as his entire body seemed to fold in on itself. As he fell onto his back on the ring floor. As he didn't move.

The crowd took a deep, collective breath, a single, odd moment of utter silence, before it erupted in screams even louder than before. But for once, I didn't care about the volume. I stood as still as a statue, staring at Cahill's motionless form, silently praying to the gods and the fates that he'd move. That he'd stand up. That he'd breathe.

As the medics rushed the ring, Piers turned to me, still fully human, his defeated posture drawing my attention. The sadness, the fear in his eyes was more than enough for me to understand. He'd lost control, he'd almost shifted, and his dragon had eliminated what he saw as a threat.

His dragon, a beast more powerful than any wolf could ever hope to be, had very possibly just stopped my mate's heart and killed him on contact.

FIFTEEN

Trinity

I rushed through the halls for the medical wing, leaving Piers in the ring, not caring who saw or what they thought. Our secrets were out, or they would be soon. Piers had nearly shifted in the ring, his red eyes giving away his dragon side. No more hiding. Besides, I wouldn't let anything keep me from my mate again, especially not if he needed me, not if there was a chance I could lose him.

Could have already lost him.

Surprisingly, Piers met me in the hall outside the medical ward, blocking a door I knew my mate had to be behind. How he made it there so fast, I didn't know. Didn't care, either. All I knew was he was in my way.

"Let me through."

He put his hands up as if to reach for my shoulders. "Wait."

"No." I punched him hard, left then right as he'd taught me to hit when we were children. Both fists making a satisfying thump as they slammed into his chest, forcing him to stumble back a step. "You lost control. You promised me you wouldn't, but you did. And you lost it with my mate in the ring."

Before I could hit him again, Piers grabbed my arms and pulled me against his chest. I resisted at first, wanting to hurt him as much as his actions had hurt me, but then I broke, sobbing, shaking in his arms.

"I'm sorry, Trin." He wrapped his arms all the way around me, holding me tightly. And I let him because I had no idea if this was it, if he was about to be all I had left.

"Is he—" I choked, unable to say the words.

"He's alive."

I sagged, crying harder, relief making me weak. "Oh, thank the fates."

The door swung opened, and the female doctor walked out, glancing from Piers to me in confusion. "Anyone here for Cahill?"

"I am," I said, pulling away from my cousin. I was done lying, especially when it came to Cahill. "He's my mate."

Her eyes widened, but she didn't say anything about my admission, simply directed me inside. "His heart stopped, but we were able to get it going again. He had a couple of broken ribs that are already healing. His heartbeat isn't quite regular yet, but I'm confident he'll be right as rain in a few hours."

"Thank you," I whispered, refusing to take my eyes away from my mate to give her my full attention. Cahill lay on a bed on the opposite side of the room, dwarfing it and yet somehow looking small at the same time. His eyes were closed, but his chest rose with every breath. His very bruised, very damaged chest. Dear God, what had Piers done? I couldn't move, was too afraid to take a step, but then he opened his eyes and found mine.

"Hey, Raindrop."

I was across the room instantly, not even thinking about

moving before I was there. I gripped his hand, bending to place my forehead on his shoulder as I sobbed. Wanting so much to touch and feel and make sure every single inch of him was okay.

"It's all right," he soothed, bringing one arm around my back to hold me closer. "I'm fine."

"I thought…" I shook my head. He shouldn't be soothing me; I should be soothing him. But there he was, taking care of me. Being the gentle, sweet man I knew he was underneath all that brawn.

"I know what you thought," he murmured, his voice quiet and a little weaker than normal. "I thought it too for a minute there. But the doc was able to get me back. I'll be okay."

"You'd better be." I clenched my jaw, my nails clawing their way across his skin as I resisted the urge to strip the sheet off his hips and make sure he was whole with my own eyes. Instead, I placed both hands flat against him, taking comfort in every pulse from within.

Cahill chuckled, his chest vibrating beneath my hands. "My heart's still there, Raindrop. I swear."

"And I'd like to keep that old ticker ticking," the doctor said, coming up on the other side of the bed. She put a stethoscope to Cahill's chest, listening for a moment as she frowned. "Still not quite steady, but getting better all the time. If you can walk, you can go back to your room for the night. You can stay here if you like, but I have a feeling it'll be a bit busy with all the fights scheduled."

Cahill sat up without pause, gently moving me back. "My room. I'm done here."

I shook my head. "What? How will you—"

"I'll take him," Piers interrupted, coming to stand beside us. "It's the least I can do."

"You should be running," I whispered. "They know now. You have to get out of here before they come for you."

"Too late," Piers said. "Besides, I'm tired of running. I've been hiding everything about myself for years, Trin. Using you to do it. It's time I come clean and deal with the consequences."

"Piers, no—"

Just then, the door opened and two of the bosses walked in with Piers' handler following. The older of the bosses took the lead, his face stiff and cold as he addressed the doctor.

"Jane, I'd appreciate it if you left. Now."

"Of course, Mick." The doctor nodded, glancing at me before she disappeared through the door and out into the hallway. The handler closed the slab of metal behind her with a hollow slam then leaned against it. Blocking our way out.

"Interesting fight, gentlemen," the man named Mick said, his voice making his displeasure clear. "I'm quite certain that's the closest we've ever come to revealing ourselves to the spectators. Well, not ourselves, seeing as how Piers isn't quite one of us, are you?"

He glared at Piers, who simply shook his head.

"And you—" he scowled as he directed his ire my way "—you seem to have found yourself a new beau. Or perhaps that's your true mate seeing as how I doubt a dragon shifter and a wolf shifter would end up in a triad."

I clung to Cahill's hand as he edged a step in front of me. His hands were shaking, his skin pale, but he was ready to fight. I could tell by the hard set to his shoulders, the intense expression on his face. He'd protect me, even though he may have been the one needing the protection. The two men I cared about most in this world were in danger, and there was nothing I could do about it.

"This is my fault," Piers said, making us all turn our heads. "It was easier to hide my dragon side with her as my accomplice. You wolves have strong noses; Trinity kept me smelling like one of you instead of like a dragon. I take full responsibility for almost shifting and for Trinity's part in my lie."

"As you should, boy," the other owner said, his voice harsh and growly. "If the wolf shifters knew there was a dragon to fight, they'd be here in droves vying for a shot to take you on. Do you know how much money you've lost us?"

I glanced at Piers, confused. "You're mad because his dragon-shifting would have made you more money?"

"Yes, of course." Mick shook his head as if scolding children. "Dragons are rare these days, but the legends remain. Too tough to be broken, too mean to be bested. They are the ultimate test for a wolf shifter. Beat a dragon, and you can brag forever that you're the biggest and the baddest. Wolf and bear shifters alike would have paid to be in my ring with Piers. But instead, you come here on a lie, hide what you really are, and dare to bring an unmated female into our midst."

"I'm not unmated." The words escaped me without thought, without care for what my place was in this mess.

Mick growled, puffing up in a sign of aggression as he glared in my direction. "I've heard about enough from you."

"Well, I haven't." Cahill grabbed my hip, pushing me farther behind him. "She's not unmated, and I'm not about to let you speak to her like she's nothing."

Mick's growl turned harsher, louder. "Now, look here—"

"What'll it take?" Piers asked, distracting all of us.

Mick cocked his head, looking over my cousin in a way that sent chills down my spine. "What is it you're asking, dragon?"

Piers lifted his chin and took a step forward, brave and ready to do battle. "What'll it take to get these two out of here... alive and uninjured?"

I gasped. "Piers, no."

I took a step toward him, but Cahill held me back. Mick noticed and smirked, his eyes dropping to Cahill's injured chest.

"You think you can take me, boy?"

"I know I can," Cahill said with an arrogant tilt to his brow. "I'm the only shifter who's ever come close to besting Killian O'Shea. I fought beside three witches and a tiger shifter to destroy not just a mob of shifters trying to stage a coup, but two werewolves. And I walked away without a scratch. You want to come at me? I'll fight back, and I'll win. And I'll tell everyone I see that the owner of The Pack House fell to a tired, injured shifter. But if you dare to come at her?" Cahill crept forward, a throaty snarl leaving his lips. "I'll fight, and I'll win. But the difference is, you'll be dead when it's over."

Mick glared at Cahill, the two exuding more power than I'd ever been around in my life. For several tense moments, I thought for sure I'd have to watch my mate battle one of the leaders of The Pack House fighting ring.

But then Mick sighed. "She's free to go. You still have one fight left with us to pay your debt."

Piers looked at Cahill, something unspoken happening between them. "I take his last fight."

"Piers," Cahill said as if in warning, but my cousin refused to be deterred.

Piers stepped forward, back straight and chin up. "You want my dragon in your ring? Fine. But I take Cahill's fight so he can leave with Trinity. My cousin and her mate deserve a new start away from the noise of this place."

I held my breath, anxious and scared and hopeful all at once. Piers was giving us a chance to go, to start a new life. One away from this place. I didn't want to leave him behind, not for a second, but he fit here. We didn't. And we never would.

The two owners looked to one another, saying nothing. I waited impatiently, clinging to Cahill's arm. Time seemed to slow as we all watched, wondering what was next. How this would all end.

"Fine," Mick said finally. "You still have two fights to fulfill your contract, yours and now Cahill's. You fight those two fights, plus give us two extra—all with the shifter opponents knowing you're a dragon—and the Southern Appalachia pack is free from their debt. We can work out a mutually beneficial payment agreement for more fights at that point if both parties are so inclined."

Piers looked to Cahill and nodded. "Deal."

Mick extended a hand, shaking Piers' then—reluctantly—Cahill's to solidify the agreement. He ignored me, but I couldn't say I expected more from him. The man never would see me as more than an annoying woman who got in the way of his fighters' concentration. Still, Cahill kept his arm around my waist, holding me close, refusing to let me disappear into the background. Something that made me respect him all the more.

Mick sneered, running his hands over the lapels of his dark suit. "Piers, we'll see you in the morning. Appalachia, you and your mate get the hell out of my building."

As the owners turned and left the room, Piers glanced my way, giving me a goofy smile. That expression, the contentment and excitement I saw on the face I knew so well, soothed something inside of me. Piers liked it here, he wanted to fight, he wanted to stay. And now he could without worrying about me. I had a place to go and someone to go with. But my God, I would miss him.

Cahill wrapped his arm around me, tucking me into his side and kissing the top of my head as if sensing my conflicted emotions. "So Trinity and I are free to go? We can just leave?"

"I guess so," Piers said with a shrug. Casual, sort of surprised, it seemed. But *that* wasn't it for me. I'd been by his side since I was a child, had left my pack behind for him when they found out his father was a dragon shifter, not a wolf shifter as they'd always thought. I'd brought him food when they'd caged him like a beast as they waited to see how he would shift. I'd helped him escape before the Alpha could kill him once he shifted to his dragon form. And I'd followed him across the country as we tried to find a place of safety to call home, as we hid and lied and conned our way through life. He was my family, my friend, and I couldn't just leave him behind.

Tears falling, I rushed to him, wrapping my arms around his neck. "I don't want you to stay."

"Hush, Trin. I like it here, remember?" He held me tightly for a moment, then pulled back, ducking down to look me in the eye. "But you don't have the stomach for this place, and that's okay. You deserve more than living a life you'll never be happy with."

"What if you get hurt?" I whispered.

"That doc was kind of hot. I'll just snuggle up to her until I feel better." He dodged my playful slap, grinning before focusing on Cahill. "You take care of her for me, okay?"

Cahill nodded. "I'll make sure you know how to reach us for when you're through here. There will always be room in our pack for you."

"Even though I'm not...like you?" Piers swallowed hard. "Your pack won't think I'm too dangerous or a mutt?"

Cahill's face grew serious, his fingers sliding along the handprint burns on his forearm. "I made the mistake of calling a man a mutt once, but I don't intend to do that ever again. If there's one thing this past year has taught me, it's that your character is way more important than your genetics."

I grabbed Cahill's hand, smiling up at him. He sighed and shrugged, a sly grin sliding across his face.

"You're my mate's kin, and that makes you my family. No one will judge you while I'm around. Besides, you're tough, smart, and have a hard time controlling your temper. You're *exactly* like the rest of the men in my pack. You and our Alpha will fit right in together."

Piers laughed, stepping forward to give me another hug. "Sounds perfect...for someday. I'm not ready to be tied down to one place yet, though. Plus I've got a few fights left to win."

I hugged him back, wishing we didn't have to be separated but knowing it was for the best. For now. "Call us if you need help, or if you change your mind. We'll come get you. And don't be gone forever, okay? You come join us soon. Who knows? You may meet your mate there."

Piers chuffed a sad little laugh. "Dragons don't mate like wolves, Trin. You know this."

"What do you mean you don't mate like wolves?" Cahill asked.

"Dragons don't do the whole insta-mate thing," Piers replied. "There's no immediate knowledge of a match or soul-mate magic. We simply choose a mate and mark them."

"So you're almost humanlike when it comes to love?"

"Sure," Piers said with a shrug.

I shook my head. "It's more intense than human love and way more" —I paused, my face growing hot— "uh...sexual. Their attraction becomes intense once the dragon chooses a person to focus on. Sex becomes nearly...unavoidable."

"Sounds familiar," Cahill murmured low, his eyes on mine, his look so intense, I knew he understood where my mind had gone. "Lucky dragons, though the whole instant-attraction thing has its benefits."

"I bet." Piers grinned, interrupting our heated stare. "And now I get to celebrate kicking the ass of the toughest competitor I've ever seen. Let's get you two the hell out of Dodge. I'm sure my cousin here would like to put you into bed so you can heal, and there're a few human females who'd I'd like to do the same with now that I get to be single again."

Cahill glared. "You've always been single."

"True," Piers said as he hurried toward the door. "But I didn't get to act like it. Having your cousin sleeping in the same bed as you sort of puts a damper on your love life."

"Looks like you're staying with me tonight." Cahill leaned on me, leading me out of the room even as I shored him up. "I bet I can get one of these humans to take us to the nearest hotel. It might take a few hours for someone from my pack to get here to pick us up."

I bit my lip, nearly squealing as his hand dropped to grab my ass. "Don't go getting any ideas, mister. You are officially out of commission."

"No, I think I could—" He winced and ducked to one side, obviously in pain.

I raised my eyebrows. "You were saying?"

Lips pursed, he avoided my eyes as he grabbed hold of Piers and let my cousin help him down the hall. "Maybe one night to heal wouldn't be such a bad idea."

"Told you so."

EPILOGUE

Trinity

"Damn it," I hissed, pressing my hands against the headboard of the bed to stop the banging of my skull on the wood. Cahill laughed breathlessly from behind me, easing off his thrusts.

"Sorry, Raindrop." He grabbed my hips and dragged me down the length of the mattress, sliding back inside me once we were settled and I was no longer in danger of a sex-acquired concussion. "Damn, you feel so good."

I nodded, unable to speak, too close to coming to form words. For three months, we'd lived in Cahill's little cabin in the mountains. We'd taken advantage of every inch of space, every counter and chair and table. We'd learned so much about each other. He was like a kid in a candy store the day he figured out I could make him come almost instantly by tugging on his balls as he pressed all the way into my mouth. As for me, the best surprise was finding out how much of a dirty-talker he was. He hadn't been able to let loose when we were at the fighting compound, but once we were back in his cabin, the words had sprung forth. I swear, there were times when I thought he could make me come without touching me if he said the right things. And he always said the right things.

"Damn, baby. You're so soft and wet. I can't get deep enough."

But this—this time in our mating bed on a rainy Sunday afternoon—had to be the best we'd had, the longest and most intense. Or maybe that was just because we knew it'd be our last for a couple of days so we were taking advantage.

"Fuck, spread your knees for me. Need to open you up," he said, groaning. I did as he told me to, my entire body shivering at the new angle the position put me in. Loving how deep he was. "That's it. Fuck, so close. Gotta get you there. Want to feel that pussy come around me again."

"Almost," I said, pushing back against him. His hand snaked around my hip, fingers finding my clit with ease. Another thing I loved about the man—he never, ever, left me wanting. Three rubs of his magic fingers, and I broke, coming with a keening moan. Cahill followed right after me, shoving into me hard, going still as he roared his release.

We finally collapsed in a heap, sweaty and tired and blissfully happy.

"When did Piers say he would get here?" I asked, wrapping my body around my mate's. I loved these moments. The quiet ones after sex, when we would rest all skin on skin. When it was just us.

Cahill kissed my forehead and wedged one leg between mine. "Later this afternoon. He said he didn't want to come up the mountain after nightfall."

"Can't blame him. That road's hard enough to follow in the day."

Cahill didn't answer, instead sliding down my body to press kisses along my neck, my collarbone, my sternum. He lapped at his mating bite, the one in the exact spot on my breast where he first said he'd put it. He'd claimed me two days after we arrived on pack land in a beautiful, peaceful moment. No big buildup or showy gestures. Just us, together, alone and joined as one.

I'd wanted us to officially claim each other the night of his fight, the night I thought I'd lost him. I had been terrified still, completely on edge about leaving and missing Piers and Cahill's heart stopping again. Luckily, he'd refused. He'd wanted to claim me at home, in a safe place where we could be relaxed. So we'd waited, and I was so glad we did. He'd professed his love to me the night he claimed me, had made me promises that he'd always be by my side before he sank his teeth into my flesh and joined us forever. That sweet moment was one of my absolute favorite memories between the two of us. His too if the way he was obsessed with my mark was any indication.

"We should take him to see the memorial," I whispered. Cahill stiffened underneath me, but only for a moment. We'd been dealing with the loss of his packmates and sisters slowly, sometimes painfully so. He'd resisted going to the hand-carved stone the pack had installed on the highest ridge overlooking packgrounds for weeks when we finally made it to the mountain. Not that I could blame him for his resistance. He needed time to come to grips with the brutality the fates had shown him. Only recently had he agreed to accompany me to the ridge. I found the spot full of peace and hope, a beautiful spot in the wilderness. He saw it as a final resting place for two girls taken away from him far too soon.

"Think he could fly up there?" Cahill asked, his almost joking words not hiding the catch in his voice.

I stroked a hand over his chest, wishing I could take all his pain away. "Maybe. He's been known to fly a time or two."

Cahill kissed the top of my head and pulled me in tight, almost clinging to me. "Now that's something I'd like to see."

"Then you shall."

We lay quiet for long moments, him staring out the window, me watching him. Waiting. I knew he'd untangle his feelings soon enough; he always did. It was just so raw for him still.

"They would have loved you," he finally whispered.

I smiled. "And I bet I would have loved them, too."

For the next hour, he regaled me with stories of his twin sisters. I'd heard most of them before, but I didn't interrupt him. He needed this. He wouldn't heal if he hid the pain of his loss away. As the words flowed, we stayed cuddled under the quilt. My body wrapped snugly around his, offering the only kind of comfort I could give. And when the stories moved from his sisters to the witches, the mood changed as well.

"I'm telling you. This little slip of a woman had me almost on my knees."

"That little slip of a woman with fire in her blood."

"Yeah, she did." He raised his scarred arm, smiling as he checked out the handprint. "I nearly gagged at the smell of myself on fire."

"Well, that's a lovely visual."

He chuckled. "Sorry, but it's the truth. There was a guy at the denhouse named Klutch who had to take me outside to deal with the burns. He actually did gag."

"Poor guy," I said with a laugh.

"He was cool about it all, even though I'd been a total ass." He grew quiet, but not the heavy sort when I knew he was thinking of his sisters. This was a calm silence, one of anticipation more than loss.

"Maybe we'll go see them sometime," he said at last.

"See who? The witches?"

He shrugged. "All of them. The Feral Breed guys, the witches... I need to apologize for...everything."

His words were simple, but the conviction behind them was

fierce. This was more than a simple apology, and I knew it. "You want to atone?"

He sighed, staring at the ceiling. "Yeah, I sort of do."

"Then we'll go."

His head whipped in my direction, his brow furrowed. "Really?"

"Sure, why not? If you say we can trust the witches, then we can." I inched up his body to place a soft kiss against his lips. "I trust your judgment, Cahill."

He wrapped his arms around me, deepening the kiss. Stoking a fire inside me that would never be extinguished.

"You're the best thing that's ever happened to me," he whispered.

I ran a hand down his cheek, holding his gaze. "Back atcha, Appalachia."

One last kiss and we went back to our quiet little bubble. Heads together, legs tangled...his hands firmly on my ass. Such a peaceful moment. But eventually, I grew too excited to sit still any longer.

"Should we get out of bed?" I asked, anxious to see Piers again after so long apart. His call saying he was done with the fighting had come as a surprise, but my mate had told him he was welcome with our pack at any time. So Piers was on his way, and he was staying with us until the pack found a spot for him to get settled. Alpha Killian was already looking forward to having a dragon to spar with.

Cahill sighed and dragged his fingers between my legs...the tease. "I suppose we should, considering our guest is on his way."

His voice killed me, and he knew it. Knew exactly what would happen when he dropped that tone down deep and let it get all gravelly. When he spoke in that voice, I practically stripped no matter where we were. Luckily, I was already in bed with him and naked. Time-saver.

I rolled on top of him, pushing him onto his back and wiggling down the length of his body. "You know, we probably have another hour or so before he arrives."

Cahill chuckled deep, fisting my hair as I licked from his navel down. "Maybe more than that."

"Maybe." I took his dick in hand, letting my fingers slide up and down the length as I rested my head on his hip bone. "Maybe we should take a shower."

His eyes lit up. One thing I'd learned about Cahill, he liked shower sex. Said the steam increased my scent and drove him mad. Made his wolf come out. He would get so rough, be so aggressive with me, I'd end up screaming his name or falling into his arms as I came, unable to keep my feet. I'd walked away with many bruises from our time spent in the stone shower stall of the master bath, and I loved every one of them.

"We probably should shower," he said, raising an eyebrow. "Though, we don't have much time."

I sat up, letting my fingers trail over the head of his dick. "Just a quick one?"

"Am I ever quick?"

"No, and thank the fates for that."

He grabbed my hand, dragging me up the length of his body so he could press his lips to mine. "I thank the fates for a lot, most of all anything having to do with you coming into my life."

I melted against him, but my sweet Cahill had a naughty side that couldn't be hidden for long.

He smacked me on my bare ass and jumped out of the bed, pulling me along with him. "Now come on, let's get dirty. I want to feel you come on my cock at least one more time before Piers arrives."

I giggled as I padded behind him. "Whatever you want, my mate."

He spun, dragging me into his arms. "Fuck, that still sounds good."

Kissing me hard, he led me into the bathroom and under the hot water, pressing me against the stone with the weight of his big body.

"Mate," I said as I hopped into his arms. My legs around his hips, my back to the wall, he slid inside me, strong and fast and sure. Making my eyes close, my body shiver.

"My mate," he growled as he bit down on my mating scar for what had to be the hundredth time. "All mine."

"Always."

CLAIMING HIS PRIZE

Dragons don't play well with others...

Dragon-shifter Piers has been fighting at The Pack House—an underground MMA-style fight club—for months. He's bested every opponent, won every prize, except the attention of the hot human doctor he can't get off his mind.

Doctor Jane patches up shifters to keep her father safe, a fate she was forced into by the owner of The Pack House. She'd be okay with her lot in life if it weren't for the handsome dragon shifter with the charming smile she can't stop thinking about.

When another dragon claims Jane as his mate, Piers will have to fight to the death to save her from a fate she didn't choose. But the biggest obstacle in his way isn't the fire-breathing dragon set on claiming what isn't his but the doctor herself who might choose duty over everything else. Maybe even him.

Scales will fly, hisses will sound, and dragons will take to the sky, but only one will end up with the ultimate prize: love.

ONE

Piers

Pain exploded across my rib cage. The bastard landed a halfway decent punch, but there wasn't enough strength behind it. Kudos for me. I curled my body, exaggerating the strike and moving with the hit to avoid any serious damage. I may have been able to heal quickly, but a broken rib would put a kink in my form for a solid two minutes. Not ideal when you were in the middle of a no-holds-barred cage match.

The crowd responded to my show with cheers and hisses, growing louder as I pushed the other man away from me. I brought my hands back up, ready to take him on again. I didn't attack, though. I waited and watched. One second, two. I let the crowd and anyone tracking the fight think this douche had a shot. That he'd actually be able to get one over on Tidal, that he'd mar my perfect fight record. That suspense and possibility of an upset added to the drama of the match. It made the humans in the stands bet a little bit more. Risk their hard-earned dollars on the dream of someone being a better fighter than me. That risk meant money, and money made the bosses real happy with me at the end of the night. So I faked like this kid had a shot at beating me, and my opponent was just dumb enough to think it was real. Sucker.

As the other guy in the ring came at me again, I purposely stumbled back. Yeah, I could put on a show with the best of them. A little wincing, a little wobbling. A little hiding out until I had this guy right where I wanted him. I'd call myself a wolf in sheep's clothing, but that would be too far from the truth. I was a dragon in wolf's clothing, and this guy was about to find out what that meant.

My opponent hit the wall of his own patience in a decidedly obvious way. He dropped his left arm, swinging with all he had on the right. But I was faster than this schmuck, and I'd learned a hell of a lot from watching guys fight. I dodged right and down, practically ducking under his fist, then came up hard. I didn't go for a punch, though. Didn't need to—this was no boxing ring. I clutched his shoulders and pulled, then brought my knee up into his gut. His sternum cracked against my thigh, the snap more felt than heard. Not nearly a fight-stopping blow, but enough to get his attention. And by the way he growled an inhuman rumble as I shoved him back, I'd say I pissed him off.

Pissed off wolf shifters made bad decisions.

"You're fucking mine, Tidal."

I grinned around my mouthguard and gave him a wink. Dumb bastard.

There are moments in every fight when, as a fighter, you see the end clearly. You can spot the trajectory of a run or the angle of a hit. You can tell by the way your opponent limps on one side or slows his swings that he's reached the end of his endurance. I saw the end of this particular match right as my opponent took a single step toward me. One step, and the rest of the fight played out in my head. Every angle, every attempt to beat the best. He was going to rush me, but in his haste and rage, he'd forget to guard his body. He'd leave me the perfect opening for an uppercut to his chin. A knockout shot. If I hit him hard enough and at just the right angle, I'd scramble his brain for a few hours. If I missed... Shit, I couldn't miss.

Time slowed in my reality. I leaned into his attack, dropping into a fighting stance to give myself room to maneuver. The man moved with purpose, each step precise and planned, each circle of his shoulder screaming his intentions. He was going to swipe left then hit hard with his right to fake me out. Thinking he could get my focus on the wrong hand. I was too good a fighter and had been through far too many matches to fall for that old trick, so I tucked my right arm in to block the body shot I knew he'd take and balanced my weight on my toes. One more step—he only needed to take one more step.

He took that last step, and he came up hard with his right straightaway. No left.

I reacted with a dodge, but I wasn't quite fast enough. My inner beast raged at the pain as that right fist connected with my ear. The world wobbled around me, my equilibrium thrown off from the blow. I stumbled back for real and grabbed the cage around me to stay on my feet. Motherfucker, that was a cheap shot, and the bastard knew it. He came at me harder, faster, swinging without a plan and not using the rest of his body for the attack, taking advantage of my dizziness. Of my need to figure out which floor I should attempt to step on. There were three, after all.

I took four more solid hits before I said fuck it all and rushed him with my eyes closed. There was no way I was going down like this; no way he was winning from a goddamned hit to the ear, of all things. I barely stayed on my feet, but I still managed to move in on his body and use proximity to get a couple of jabs to his ugly mug. And when he stumbled back, when he lost his balance and fell against the cage, I took advantage. Fuck this clown, I was winning this fight. I won every fight.

I beat him down with a procession of hits that left him trapped against the cage with his arms up and his head tucked behind them. But this wasn't boxing—this was all-out war. Something this dude needed to remember. Boxing experience was good for the ring and to make the fights last longer—it was a fucking art form at times—but wrestling, martial arts, and street fighting were what made the difference between an opponent and a threat. He was no threat.

Gripping him by the shoulders, I pushed down again and brought my knee up into his chest, cracking a few ribs this time. He growled and curled to one side, leaving me the perfect shot. I brought my knee up harder, aiming for his face. Knowing this was the end of the fight. The snap of his chin hitting my kneecap was loud enough to hear over the screaming spectators, as was the sound of his body hitting the mat. He was breathing, though, something that couldn't be said for all fighters who lost in this ring.

"And the winner is...*Tidal!*"

The crowd roared, and a team of trainers hurried into the cage to look after the loser. He'd need their attention, for sure— probably end up spending the night in the medical wing. Not that I gave a shit about him. He wasn't dead, and that was all I needed to know. I was more worried about my own self and the fact I still couldn't keep my balance. The blow to the side of my head must have knocked something loose or snapped something within my ear, something that wasn't healing as fast as I'd like. Let the second-string medical team deal with the loser on the floor; I was going to see the best. And the prettiest, by far.

"Great job, Tidal," my trainer Laudon said as I exited the cage.

"Gotta see the doc." I ripped the tape off my hands with my

teeth, fighting off chills as my sweat caused my body to cool below ambient temperature. "Fucker caught me right in the ear."

"I'll make sure he's waiting for you."

"She. I want Doc Jane." I stepped as if to head for the locker room, but the floor tilted. I lunged for Laudon's arm to keep from falling over, nearly knocking him to the ground with me. He turned with a questioning look, to which I rolled my eyes and pointed at my head.

"Ears?" he asked. I nodded, swallowing back the nausea that was threatening to make me spew all over the damn floor. Without another word, Laudon pulled my hands to his shoulders and hurried toward the back, jumping around as if he were celebrating. And thank fuck for his quick thinking. If the others figured out a weakness of mine, they'd take full advantage of it. I'd have bastards knocking me in the side of the head in every match. I knew, because I'd have done the same thing if it meant winning.

I let go of Laudon once we reached the back, holding on to the wall instead to stay upright. The man didn't comment, simply stayed by my side as I fought my way along the hall. I wasn't about to appear weak in front of anyone on staff if I didn't have to. But the closer we got to the medical ward, the harder it was for me not to want to run, which wouldn't have ended well. She was there... Jane. The human doctor. The woman I'd been flirting with for months. The woman who started off as a simple distraction but had grown into something so much more in my head. The woman I'd become completely obsessed with getting into my bed. The only woman I'd run into in this place who wouldn't give me the time of day.

And yes, it was completely ridiculous that her refusal to see me as more than a patient made her epically hotter. But I'd been chasing her for months, following her around like a damned puppy. And she shot me down every time. I liked that.

"Who died?" Jane asked—her back turned to the door—as I struggled into her exam room. Laudon snickered behind me, though I ignored him. I was too busy trying to use some sort of magical energy to get the woman to turn around while holding myself up against a cabinet. Stupid fucking ears.

"Good to see you, too, Doc." I gripped the counter as the room spun hard. Shit, I couldn't drop now. Not here. Even if she was my doctor, I didn't want to fall on my face in front of her.

Jane barely glanced over her shoulder at me before going about whatever she was doing at the back counter. "What is it this time, Tidal?"

I swallowed hard and pasted on my most charming smile. "Are you ever going to call me Piers?"

"I treat fighters for Mick and the other owners of The Pack House. You're a fighter, so I'll use your fighting name." She shot me an irritated look, her dark eyes sparking as she lit an acetylene torch. "I have work to do. Are you coming in here for some sort of care or what?"

Grinning, trying hard to cover up how queasy moving made me, I stepped away from the counter.

And promptly fell face first to the floor.

"Shit." Jane's shoes squeaked as she rushed to my side. Her hands were warm against my skin when she turned me over, hot even. Blessedly so. The blood in my veins felt ice-cold, and the room refused to hold still.

I held out a hand to keep her away and swallowed back the sick that was definitely about to make an appearance. "I'm fine."

Laudon completely ignored my attempt at shoving him away, the bastard. He grabbed my arm and pulled me to my feet, manhandling me toward the gurney in the middle of the room. "He took a big hit to the ear during a fight. Hasn't been stable since."

"I'm fine." I grabbed my head when the room spun again, trying to hold my vision together while not vomiting all over the pretty doctor's shoes. "I just need to lie down for a few."

"You need a bit more than that," Jane said. "Thanks, Laudon. I'll take it from here."

I groaned and clutched my midsection, willing the room to just stop spinning. There was no way to feel balanced, no place to spot for reference. I was a fucking dragon shifter; I flew loops through the air and dove at speeds humans were unable to comprehend, but this dizziness was completely new to me. New and slightly terrifying. Fuck, if hitting me in the ear could put me out of commission, my fighting days were close to over.

The door barely had time to close behind the trainer before Jane jabbed me in the thigh with a needle.

"What the hell?" I grabbed the table as a growl rumbled through me, the animal side of me a bit too close to the surface. Sharp claws ground against the metal, and my vision exploded into a rainbow of colors. Struggling, I yanked hard on my inner dragon to pull him back into place. I couldn't shift in here. Not now, not in front of Jane. She'd never want to be near me again if she saw that side of me.

Jane leaned over the gurney and pushed my shoulders back down. Her long, dark hair was caught up in some kind of bun thing, but there were wisps floating around it. As if they'd escaped, like they couldn't stand to be contained. Those strands mesmerized me as something like warmth flowed through my veins and fuzzed out my brain.

"Ow," I murmured, still captivated by dark hair, by the roundness of her face. The light freckles I'd never been close enough to notice before. She was so fucking beautiful, it hurt.

And she was looking at me like I was some sort of specimen to be examined. Shit.

Jane raised her eyebrows—drawing my attention to the honeyed brown of her eyes—as she pulled the needle from my leg. "Hurt, big guy?"

"No," I huffed, though the word came out a little higher than I'd planned. A little too dragonesque. "You surprised me is all."

Jane hummed and turned away. "Stay still for a bit. That'll help with the nausea until the anti-inflammatories kick in. Hopefully, your metabolism won't burn through either before whatever your opponent probably broke in your ear repairs itself."

"He didn't break shit," I mumbled, my entire body relaxing as the sick feeling began to recede. Even the claws and colors faded, the dragon side of me taking a back seat. Jane just laughed. At me. The woman I was obsessed with seeing naked was laughing at me. "Mind telling me what's so funny?"

"You." She shook her head, her smile lighting up the room in a way I rarely got to see. She tended to scowl more when I was around. "You're such a Neanderthal. God forbid you admit that an opponent got the better of you for a single punch."

She was looking at me in a way she never had before, as if she were truly seeing me. That stirred something within me. For the first time, it seemed I had her attention, and I wasn't about to lose it. Trying to appear tougher than I felt, I grabbed her arm and lifted myself onto an elbow. "That's not me being a Neanderthal, Doc. It's me being a survivor. If I admit—even to myself—that one of these chumps is better than me, I open the door to lose. I give them the chance to take me down."

"You have to win." Jane pulled her arm away halfheartedly, but I refused to release her. If she'd wanted to get away from me, she could. I wasn't one to force a woman to be close to me. But she was barely trying, only tugging on my hold a bit. I could tease her with my strength. Maybe.

Daring it all, I pulled her a little closer, leaned up a little more so I could be in her face as I whispered, "It's not that I have to win, it's more that I refuse to play by someone else's rules. I never lose, Doc, because I don't want anyone lording their control over me. I can't live that way. It's against my nature."

"So dragons are competitive and independent?" she asked, her voice a little breathy. She was staring at me in a way she never had before. Truly seeing me. A fact that made the man in me hopeful.

"Dragons aren't just competitive." I sat up, no longer dizzy. Jane placed one hand against my bare chest, her flesh so fucking warm compared to mine. The heat and the touch dragged a low purr from deep within. A sound of lust and desire for my kind. A sound that made her eyes go wide and her pupils darken.

"No?" She took a step back, but this time, I let her go. I could see the flush of her cheeks, the way the blood ruddied the skin along her chest. She was warm. Excited. The beast within sat up and took notice, too. He was too close to the surface after the match and the injury, too hard to wrangle back into his cage within my mind. Too interested in this human woman to be quiet.

I shook my head to her question, practically salivating over the fact that Jane was obviously affected by me. "We're territorial and demanding. We like getting our way because we're too damned independent to do what others tell us to."

Jane bumped into the cabinet, grabbing the top with both hands and leaning back as if to escape me. "You choose your own fates."

I slid off the table and stalked closer. There was something almost needful about the way she spoke those words, something wanting. I ran a finger down the side of her face as I whispered, "Always. One should never be subject to another's wants and desires. You're so warm, Doc."

Taking a chance, I leaned in, staring at her lips. That distraction was my downfall, because I missed the look of rage that passed over her face until it was too late. She hauled back and swung her arm, hitting me square in the ear. The same one that bastard had gotten in the ring.

"Fuck." I fell back with a squeal, curling into a ball on the floor. My stomach rolled as the room wobbled, and I dry heaved a couple of times. Fucking balance issues.

Jane just huffed and stepped over me, totally ignoring the pain she'd caused. "Next time you touch me without my consent, it won't be your ear you have to worry about."

Oh, I'd made her so mad. That hadn't been my plan, not at all, but it was too late. I'd made a bad decision and lost this match. But I'd be back, which meant I needed to make sure she knew I accepted this defeat.

"Understood," I said as I rolled to a sitting position. The room spun again, though not as badly as before. My dragon pushed forward, his heat-sensing eyes taking in the landscape. Jane was hot. Physically, way hotter than she should have been, though whether that was from exertion, fear, or something else, I had no way of knowing. As much as I wanted to chase her a bit more, my ear was throbbing, and my stomach ached with the need to be sick. It was time to retreat. Graciously.

Or perhaps almost childishly, if I had to be honest about it.

"Damn, woman. You really pack a punch."

Jane didn't even flinch. "My dad was a boxer. He taught me well."

"Way to go, Dad." I pushed myself to my feet, still a little wary of moving too fast. "I swear, I won't touch you again until I get your consent."

Jane grabbed that same torch she'd been playing with when I walked in from the back counter. "You won't get my consent."

"Oh, Doc. Didn't you hear me when I said I was competitive? You just gave me one hell of a challenge." I shot her a sly grin and stumbled for the door, ready to head back to my room and lick my wounds. Or jack off. Whichever.

Jane laughed again as I hurried out the door. That sound made me grin. My dick was half-hard, my ear throbbing, and my vision totally stuck between human and dragon, but Jane laughed. Sort of a win. Still, the world was a Technicolor rainbow of heat and shadow brought on by my dragon forcing me to look through his eyes. A fact that really wasn't helping my balance issues.

"Hey, Tidal?"

I spun at Jane's voice, hurriedly leaning into the wall to keep from wobbling. "What's up, beautiful?"

"Want to pay me back for that move?"

I shrugged. "What did you have in mind?"

"I heard a rumor about dragons, and I want to know if it's true."

My throat tightened, the natural fear of others finding out too much about us long ingrained in my body. But this was Doc Jane. For some reason, I trusted her. Perhaps more than I should have.

"Ask, and if I can, I'll answer."

She paused, staring at me, weighing my truthfulness. "Can dragons really *see* heat?"

I cocked my head, letting my dragon come forth. Really letting him out as much as I could without shifting. I knew she'd see the red of my eyes from where she stood, knew she'd spot the scales as they appeared along my hairline, but that was okay. She was the team doctor, practically a shifter herself, and I wasn't about to go full dragon in front of her. This would be okay.

"I can tell you're slightly aroused—which I like, by the way—because you're quite warm between your legs. And the top of your head and tips of your ears are downright hot at the moment. Good to know your anger signs, Doc, and that I turn you on."

She blinked, silent in her surprise. So I shrugged.

"Dragons see heat and taste scent." I flicked my tongue out, nearly collapsing as the heady scent of her overtook me. "And my God, Doc, you smell delicious."

TWO

Jane

I waited until I could no longer hear the dragon's footsteps in the hall before I allowed myself to relax.

"Stupid, handsome reptile." I tossed the spent syringe in the hazmat box and slammed the lid. So he was hot. Big deal. Dark hair and light eyes were sort of a weakness of mine—and Tidal's black curls and soft green eyes definitely fit that bill—but that didn't mean I had to fall for them. And yes, he was built. But every guy here had muscles upon muscles. Beginners walked in with six-packs and trained fighters often sported eights. Tidal's lithe, lean body went against the bulkier wolf shifters in the rings, but he was still just one of the fighters. I'd been dealing with that damn dragon and his cocky flirtiness for months without falling prey to his tactics. I still hadn't, technically, but that was a close call. He'd almost gotten me to break, to let go of my control and allow him to... I don't even know.

One should never be subject to another's wants and desires.

"Stupid, handsome, independent reptile."

I sighed and headed for the back exam room. My

workspace, one aspect of my life I actually had control over. Well, sort of. Because in those dark hours when I was completely alone, I had to admit, my control was just an illusion. A forced vision I clung to with everything I had because, deep down, I knew—it could all be taken away in a heartbeat.

"Stupid wolf shifters," I mumbled, reaching into the cabinets in exam room four to inventory the torches. One never knew when we'd need to use the things to hold skin together. Claw marks didn't heal as fast as most damage that could be done to wolf-shifter skin, but cauterizing the skin helped. Of course, to cauterize such fast-healing skin, you needed serious firepower. Hence the acetylene torches in every exam room and doctor bag. We liked to be prepared for cataclysmic damage.

I counted and straightened as I let my thoughts wander, let the visions of dragons flying through the air dance in my mind. Piers—or Tidal, as I forced myself to call him—was so different from the wolf shifters who tended to dominate The Pack House. More inquisitive, smarter in some ways. Whether that was him or his dragon, I'd probably never know. No one did. Unlike wolves, dragons were extremely secretive, even among other shifters.

Still, I liked his style, the calculating way he sized up his opponents before taking them on. I always had found men who fought with their brains attractive, especially when all that cunning was in the muscled body of a street fighter. But Tidal was also one of the fighters in The Pack House, a position that was most certainly off-limits, considering my employer. That just made him all the more intriguing to me, if I was being honest. Forbidden fruit and all that. But I could never let him know about my attraction. He'd use it to his advantage, find ways to garner my attention and risk...everything.

"Something wrong, Jane?"

I turned as Mick walked into the room, schooling my

features on autopilot. Mick demanded smiles from his employees, along with respect. Neither of which he deserved, in my opinion. The old wolf shifter wasn't my favorite person, but I owed him a lot. More than my own life, really. And he never let me forget it.

"Evening, sir." I kept my voice even as he walked closer, refusing to allow him to intimidate me.

His eyebrow winged up, a sure sign that I'd done something wrong. I quickly scanned my words and actions since he'd walked in, cursing internally. Without another second's pause, I dropped my gaze to the floor, hoping to appease the man who pretty much owned me. The things you forgot when you had dragons on the brain.

Mick wasn't a dragon—he was a man with a wolf inside. Things like body position and direct eye contact indicated dominance and pack order. I knew better than to look him in the eye, but my thoughts about Tidal had distracted me. Something I couldn't risk happening again.

I coughed and lowered my voice, doing my best to sound meek and frightened by the old bastard. "How can I help you this evening, sir?"

"I think I'd like to turn up the heat."

My stomach dropped at his casual comment. The heat in The Pack House was the system Mick and his partners used to send pheromones through the air. The whole thing had been Mick's idea back in the early days of the business. I'd warned him then that keeping male shifters in pheromone-laced air would be trouble, but he'd disregarded my advice. Just as he'd disregarded it every time he'd told me to increase the amount of hormones released.

Not that I stopped trying to get him to see reason.

"Sir, we've already seen rage problems with some of the fighters. And the new recruits aren't—"

"How's your father?" Mick turned his sharklike smile at me, cutting me off.

I swallowed the fear his question incited and kept my eyes locked on that evil smile. "Good, sir. Finally getting over that bug he caught last month."

"Ah, excellent news. And at such an opportune time. Wouldn't want any sort of stress to make him fall ill again, now would we?"

I squeezed my eyes closed, breathing deeply to try to get my heart rate back under control. "No, we wouldn't. I barely get to see him as it is. Another sickness would cut into that time."

"It would, wouldn't it? Be a good girl, Jane, and you'll be rewarded." He turned, heading for the door. "Three degrees higher should do the trick. And thank you for being so accommodating."

The click of the door closing behind him was like a cut to the thread holding me up. I slowly sank to the floor and pulled my knees into my chest, doing my best to hold back my tears. I'd spent too many years with Mick not to see this side of him grow. He'd been a nice enough man when we started The Pack House, when he agreed to pay off my medical school loans if I came to work for him. When my father was still healthy and oblivious to Mick's dual nature, when he and Mick would go fishing together on the weekends.

But that was a long time ago.

Resigned to do as I was told so as not to cause trouble with my dad, I struggled to my feet and trudged to the locked box on the far wall. There—behind a metal door even wolf shifters couldn't break through—lay the key to Mick's bastardized air system. The key to his ability to keep the men he conned into working for him rough, mean, and ready to fight.

It also kept the very pack-oriented shifters from forming

bonds with the other males, something no one outside of Mick or I knew.

In the early days of The Pack House, fighters sometimes had a hard time going all out on the men they'd bonded with. Mick couldn't have that, so he figured a way to cut pack ties would be to introduce women into the mix. Males fought for female attention in packs every day, so adding that mating factor to The Pack House should have worked to snap those connections. But some of the men found their mates, which led to shifting at the wrong times and couples running to escape possible separation. So Mick went back to the drawing board. Eventually, he figured out that introducing the scent of a shewolf in heat, but without the actual woman in the building, would keep those pack bonds from forming minus the drawback of actually introducing mated couples together. And it'd worked.

But over the last few years, as he'd upped the amount of pheromones and played with the chemistry even more, I'd noticed problems. Lung issues, uncontrollable rage, excessive dominance of even the most docile shifters, hormonal shifts—symptoms more in line with steroid use in humans. Problems Mick refused to acknowledge or deal with.

And it was time to turn up the heat and wait for the fallout again.

My hands shook as I turned the wheel, adding more of Mick's hormone cocktail to the forced-air mix. Thinking about Tidal, about all the men out in The Pack House who would have no idea why they'd wake up with an erection later this evening, who'd struggle to control themselves over breakfast, and mop the floor with their opponent if they were the lucky ones. And I thought about the ones who would end up on my table if they weren't all that lucky. The ones I would help bury in the caves below us while Mick lied about fighters with contracts completed or missing home too much to stay.

The ones Mick would drive insane...just like my father.

———

The next morning, I walked the training floor to observe the few fighters who were up as early as I was. The effects of the pheromones were already apparent. Men who would have normally given me a smile or a head nod in greeting scowled instead; others who would have ignored me leered and made inappropriate hand gestures as I passed. All signs I'd grown accustomed to over the years. They'd settle eventually, growing used to the hormones and reining in their hypermasculine side once more. If they lived. Violence was a definite threat between the fighters during this unstable time. Case in point, I spotted two fighters embroiled in a heated argument along the back wall. While I watched, the bigger of the two swung, knocking the smaller to the floor. The trainers jumped into the scrum to pull the two apart, but I knew it was too late. The smaller shifter was bleeding all over the floor—he'd probably end up in the medical ward within a few minutes. I wasn't on for the day yet, so I ignored the mess and turned down another aisle between rings. The trainers would call for help if it was needed, and there were two other doctors who could handle such things. It would take a few days for the fighters' systems to even out in the new environment, which meant I'd be busy enough without jumping into every scuffle on the training floor. Besides, unstable wolf shifters were dangerous.

"Morning, Doc."

Dragon shifters, on the other hand...

"Tidal." I nodded as I passed him, my hands clenched into fists in my pockets. Even though I so desperately wanted to stop and look him over, see how he was faring, I kept my head up and my feet moving. I would not let him bait me into anything like last night. I would not let him know how much his presence affected me. I would not fall for his charm and risk what little of my former life I had left.

But damn, did he smell good.

"So," he said as he walked along beside me, ever the demanding dragon. "Did you have a nice evening?"

I shot him a look out of the corner of my eye. He was close, but not too close. Leaving enough room between us so we didn't even brush shoulders. I appreciated that, though I doubted it would last long. Tidal was nothing if not persistent.

"It was fine. And how was yours?"

I knew I'd made a mistake when he chuckled. The sound was lower than human, darker. Filled with a sensuality I'd never heard from another man or creature before.

"Oh, Doc. I had a wonderful night. Would you like to ask me why?"

Would I? Hell yes, but I knew better than to fall for that one. "No. I don't think I would."

He hopped in front of me, blocking the path but still not touching any part of my body. "Ask me anyway."

"Tidal—"

"Piers." He grinned as I glared. He wore such a childish expression, one filled with glee. A handsome, charming, gleeful dragon. What world was I living in?

With a roll of my eyes, I sighed and asked him the question he was waiting for. "Why was your night so wonderful, *Tidal*?"

His smile faltered a tiny bit when I stressed his fighting name, but it returned with a vengeance just as he leaned in to whisper to me. "It was wonderful because I could smell you on me. Between that and the pheromone increase, I was practically chafed this morning."

I jerked back, more concerned that he noticed the hormones

than that he used my scent to feed his spank bank. "You can smell the pheromones?"

He cocked his head and licked his bottom lip. "Not smell so much. Dragons don't have the sense of smell that wolves do, remember? They're more a taste on the air than a scent."

He licked his lip again, slower this time. I nearly gasped when I saw the fork at the end, a tiny separation most people never would see.

"Your—"

He shook his head, his face growing darker and more serious. His eyes scanning the room around us as if for threats. "My dragon wants to come out and play in the tasty air, is all. It'll be fine in a few hours."

"Hours?" I grabbed his arm and yanked him closer, practically hissing to him to keep my voice low. "The wolves take days to get used to the hormone increase."

A sly smile crept across his face as he looked down to where my hand rested on his skin. "Dragons are better than wolves, Doc. You should know that by now."

I yanked my hand away, his calm confidence throwing me off-balance. It would be so easy to lose control with this man. To let go and be a woman with him, to give in to my urges and see where things went. But I couldn't. Mick had made sure I'd never be free from this place, and Tidal wouldn't be around forever. Our hooking up would be a temporary distraction that could lead to permanent problems.

"Tidal," Laudon yelled from one ring over. "Get your ass in the ring now."

"On it." Tidal gave an irritated grunt, then grinned and jogged to a ring, leaving me without a backward glance. Not quite what I'd have expected, though neither was his forked tongue. That was new.

"Yo, Doc." A shifter named Docket was leaning over the

ropes of the far ring, practically hidden from the rest of the room behind huge storage lockers. "Doc, c'mere. I've got a problem."

I sighed, pushing all the inappropriate thoughts of Tidal out of my head. Another lifetime, perhaps.

"Coming." I weaved in and out of piles of training equipment as I headed down the deserted walkway. The farther toward the back I went, the more my heart pounded. It was darker here, completely out of the main area. No one would be able to see me back here, and there was a small group of half-naked men watching me. Half-naked men breathing air that made them dangerous and sex-fueled. A bad combination for the only female in the building.

"Doc," Docket said as he hopped down from the ring.

I stopped a good ten feet back, not willing to get too close until I knew what I was walking into. Yelling at myself for being led to this deserted area in the first place. "What's the problem?"

Without warning, Docket dropped his shorts, letting his very hard and very large dick spring forth like some kind of jack-in-the-box. "It hurts, Doc. How about you kiss it and make it better?"

I rolled my eyes and turned to leave, but another shifter blocked my way. He grabbed my arms and held me still, pressing himself against me.

"Let me go," I hissed, keeping my voice low. I kept my eyes on Docket's, staring him down. I couldn't appear afraid, could never show an ounce of weakness around these guys. Especially not when I might actually be in danger. They'd eat my fear up with a spoon and come back for more.

Docket sauntered closer, a growl backing up his words. "Aw, can't you fix it, Doc?"

The men chuckled and stepped closer as a pack, but then their heads whipped up and to the side almost in perfect, freaky unison.

Tidal hopped over the ropes of the ring to my right, looking completely casual and at ease as he jumped between the pack and me. The shifter holding me let go and took a few steps back while growling at the new addition, but Tidal didn't seem to care.

"Why don't you have one of your buddies here take care of that for you?" Tidal blocked Docket without apology, something I was seriously grateful for.

"Aw, c'mon, man," Docket said as he pulled his pants back up. "We were just having a little fun."

Tidal huffed a laugh. "Little is the correct word, that's for sure."

All the men laughed, except Docket. The shifter scowled our way, causing the hairs on the back of my neck to stand on end. He was angry, and angry wolf shifters were irrational and dangerous. But Tidal didn't seem worried. In fact, he stood there facing the other shifters as if they were all just shooting the breeze or catching up on the latest water-cooler gossip. The only sign of his acknowledgment of the situation was the way his fingers flexed. He didn't form fists, just kept his fingers slightly curved in. Whether that was to be ready to clench them and throw a punch or to hide his claws, I couldn't be sure.

As Docket leaned forward, his growl growing louder, Tidal edged in just close enough for me to hear him as he whispered, "Consent to touch you, Doc?"

I nodded, a bit wary but way more comfortable with him than with the rest of these guys. Tidal took me by the elbow and gently tugged me back. Then he followed. Retreating. Bringing me with him. His hold on my arm was strong, the pressure welcoming. He wasn't going to leave me behind.

But of course, he couldn't leave without opening his mouth. "Next time you want to shake that thing in someone's face, Docket, you might want to consider who you're bothering."

"Why's that, snake?"

Tidal chuckled, a little darker than before. "Snake? That's the best you got?" He pulled me farther back, putting himself between Docket and me. "You really need to think of who you're bothering before you start harassing anyone around here because this lady happens to be the best doctor on site. Piss her off again, and she won't be too happy to treat you when I set your ass on fire."

"Ooooh, I'm scared." Docket scoffed, laughing to all his friends. "The doctor's single, which means she's up for grabs. And I'm ready to do some grabbing."

Tidal stopped, a hiss sounding from within as he cocked his head. "Not happening."

Without warning, Tidal threw his arms back, roaring into the warehouse in a way that nearly shook the rafters. Smoke poured from his mouth, and sparks danced in the air on his breath. The wolf shifters dispersed, all running in different directions. Even Docket rushed off, practically falling as he turned the corner at the far end of the walkway.

When he finished, when Docket and his friends were off causing trouble somewhere else and the smoke was no longer rising, Tidal turned to me, looking slightly sheepish. His normally green eyes were still red, his pupils elongated in a reptilian way. The sight enthralled me, the fact that he did all that to protect me making me feel something for another person I hadn't felt for years. Safe.

"You roared," I said, my voice soft. Still unable to get the picture of him in that moment out of my head.

Tidal's forked tongue slipped out to lick a piece of ash from his bottom lip, and he shrugged. "Sorry about that."

He was apologizing? I was practically ready to bow down to him in thanks, and he was saying sorry? What was it about this man? And why did he have to come into my life at a time when it was not my own?

Giving in to temptation, I approached Tidal slowly, carefully raising my arm. He watched me, still and almost nervous, the prey to *my* predator. But he had no reason to be.

I touched a finger to his lip, brushing over a tiny burn where an ember must have fallen. Holding back the shiver as our flesh met. "Does it hurt?"

"Not anymore." He took a deep breath, his fingers wrapping around my wrist. His body calling to me in ways no one else's ever had. Making me want things I couldn't have. I was lost... falling...and so very screwed.

THREE

Piers

The struggle to contain my dragon was real and getting harder with every passing second. As was I. Fuck, I'd never been so close to Jane before. And I'd never wanted a woman as much as I did her in that moment.

"Tidal," she whispered, her hand resting on my chest.

"I'm gonna need some consent here, Doc. Or do you want me to stop?" I leaned forward, letting my lips brush over her wild, dark hair. Closing my eyes as the taste of her passed over my mouth. So fucking perfect.

"We shouldn't do..."

I waited, but she didn't finish her sentence, so I leaned closer. Breathing her in and tasting her scent again. Wishing I could do more. Could touch and feel and explore. But this was it—this closeness, this hand on my chest, my fingers around her wrist. This might be all she gave me, and while I was beginning to think no amount of connection would ever be enough, it was still more than I probably deserved from her.

"Shouldn't what, Doc?" I asked when I couldn't wait any

longer. "What are we doing here?"

Her eyes dropped to my mouth, and her lips followed. It was a kiss I hadn't been expecting but welcomed nonetheless. Hell, I devoured it. Fiery and hot, her little tongue joined with mine as I plunged into her mouth. The taste, the feel, the heat of it all had me grasping her hips to pull her closer. Had me yowling low in my throat as my dragon drank her in. As my body lit up from within in response to her.

One kiss quickly became more. My hands grasped her ass and yanked her body closer. Every taut inch of her pressed against me, every inch of me craving more. And by the gods, the heat rolling off her was positively addictive. I reveled in it, sought more of it. My hands slid under her top without thought or direction from me, my body craving that warmth. When I had her wrapped in my arms, she groaned and yanked on my hair. My yowl grew, the burn of a smoky fire roiling in my chest. Yes, this was it. This was what I wanted. Her...this...fuck yes. The pain was good, the press of her skin better. I wanted more, wanted to feel again. Wanted her always.

But without warning, she broke away from me and stumbled back.

"Shit," she hissed, bringing her hand to her mouth. She looked so shocked, as if she hadn't expected to kiss me. I totally understood that. I hadn't expected it, either. Loved it, wanted more of it, craved her body more than ever...but I hadn't expected it. Still, I had enough sense not to tell her that.

"Wasn't quite the reaction I was going for there, Doc." I grabbed her hand gently and pulled it back to my chest, pressed it against the bare flesh that was now heated from her touch. "Feel how warm I am. That's because of you. That's your body and mine, together."

She shook her head, looking panicked. "Tidal—"

"What's all this?" Mick appeared over the ropes of the ring

to our left, his glare firmly in place. "Jane, I thought we were working under a don't-touch-the-merchandise policy?"

My dragon roared within me, furious that this lesser being interrupted our time with Jane. The man side of me was more worried than angry. Jane looked...afraid. She was hiding it well behind that bland, doctor expression, but there was fear in her eyes as they avoided mine. Something that didn't sit well with me.

Jane didn't pull away from me, though. She stood tall, fighting to hide that fear as she changed the position of her hand on my chest. "Your dragon was feeling a little overheated after a scuffle with a couple of other fighters. I thought it best to do an immediate exam before moving him."

Mick turned his attention to me, his head cocked. "That so, Tidal? Well, we did turn the heat up yesterday. Perhaps he's feeling the effects."

Something in Jane's expression cracked, her shoulders sagging. I had no idea what Mick was talking about, but whatever he meant by *heat*, my feeling the effects upset her. I wanted to calm her, to pull her into my arms and soothe her, but that bastard was still fucking there and Jane... Well, Jane let me go.

She dropped her hand from my chest, breaking what little connection we had, and nodded at the wolf shifter. "I believe that's a likely possibility."

Mick grunted. "Take him back to the medical ward and do a full work-up. I've got a new fighter coming in soon, and I want to make sure Tidal is in the best shape before they step in the ring together. A sick dragon does not make for a good fight."

"Yes, sir. Of course." She glanced at me, looking decidedly uninterested, her eyes flat and empty as they met mine. "It'll be difficult, though. We don't know enough about dragons to make a comparison."

Mick laughed. "We know all we need to. They're cold-blooded, they fight like hell, and they have no loyalty to the ones they take as their mates. What more do we need to know?"

"Just...physiology and immune system information. But we'll get by without it." Jane walked past me, avoiding touching me as she did. "Come with me, Tidal."

The way she said my fighting name cut as hard and sharp as claws could. I still had no idea what the hell just happened, but something Mick said had made Jane shut down. That wasn't okay with me. I finally got a response from her, and I wasn't about to go back to the doctor-patient relationship we had before.

I followed her through the warehouse and down the hall leading to the medical wing, my mind spinning with options. It was quiet back there with all the fighters either sleeping or training; quiet and cold. Too cold. In such a short amount of time, I'd gotten comfortable with Jane's body pressed against mine. I'd absorbed that heat and my body had warmed in response. But not touching her led my skin to cool once more, something uncomfortable and oddly foreign now that I'd experienced Jane's heat. I wanted more of that warmth. Immediately. But if the set of her shoulders was any indication, there would be no more touching today.

"We should do a blood panel," she said as soon as we walked into her exam room. Her words were stiff, clipped almost. Doctor mode. *Shit.*

"Something wrong, Doc?"

"I'm fine." She ignored my look and headed for the cabinets. But as she pulled on a pair of gloves, my heart sank.

"Stop."

She jumped at my demand, turning to finally—*finally*—look into my eyes. I hadn't meant the word to come out so forceful, but seeing those plastic sheaths cover her hands made me almost panic. I wanted her touch. I needed her heat. And those gloves would deaden that for me.

"Can we..." I licked my lip, tasting her on the air. Recentering myself on her presence. "Your hands are so warm. Can you not use the gloves?"

Her eyes stayed locked with mine even as her eyebrows furrowed. "You're cold?"

"Dragons are cold-blooded, like Mick said. We take on the temperature of the air around us." I hesitated, a bit uncomfortable admitting the truth but willing to tell my secrets...to her. "I prefer hotter temperatures than what The Pack House is kept at, so I'm usually a bit chilly. Being so close to you in the training center warmed me through, so now the cold is extra cold." I shrugged, unable to hold her eyes as I whispered, "Cold after warmth hurts. It makes my skin feel tight, and I don't like it."

Jane took a step toward me, looking quizzical and concerned. "The cold hurts?"

I shrugged. "Once I've been warmed, yes. After a fight, after a shower." I met her eyes again, trying to put all my want into that look. "After absorbing the body heat of a beautiful woman."

"Perhaps you need to find a beautiful woman to keep you warm," she said, her voice soft, barely more than a whisper.

I kept my eyes on her, refusing to look away from such a moment. From such a truth. "I'm trying, but she keeps putting up roadblocks."

Jane looked down, her lips twitching with the need to smile. I wanted her to smile, to be happy. I wanted a lot for Jane, things that didn't even quite make sense.

"Please, Doc?"

With an exaggerated sigh, Jane pulled the gloves from her hands. "Okay. But I'm putting them on when I stick you."

"Protect it before you inject it?" I grinned, especially when she looked at me with that exasperated expression. "Totally understood. I'm all for safety."

"On the table, mister funny man."

I hopped up on the exam table and lay back, completely comfortable being under her inspection once more. Jane hovered over me, running her hands over my bare chest and stomach. Pressing, palpating where organs would be for a regular human. Her brow furrowing when she didn't find them in the so-called *right* spots. But when her hand slid down along my hip bone, it was I who reacted.

"Sorry." I coughed as she ran both hands down my thigh, my cock responding to her in a way that had to be noticeable. "You do realize I'm perfectly healthy, right?"

Baseball, think of baseball. Pitches, strikes, outs, batters, balls... Yeah, I want her to touch my balls.

Shit.

"Of course. But Mick gave me carte blanche to run tests on you. I'm taking full advantage."

I stared at the ceiling, willing my soldier to stand down. Sort of wishing Jane would show him a little attention at the same time. A thought that didn't help the stand down request. "So you're using my body for science? Such a disappointment."

Jane moved to my feet, bending my ankles and pressing her fingers against my bones. "Perhaps we'll be more prepared for the next dragon."

"There won't be a next dragon. My kind aren't exactly fans of dogs." My leg twitched as she moved back up my calf. Something that only made the problem in my groin worse. Jesus, I was hard as stone.

She hummed, her eyes unfocused as her hands ran over my knees, completely ignoring the tent in my shorts. "No dogs, no mates. Got it."

"Oh, we mate." I glanced down the length of my body,

pulling up my lips into a half smile at her wide eyes. "We like to mate as much as possible. Multiple times a day, if possible. The heat from the friction of two bodies writhing together is delicious."

"That sounds like sex, not mating. If there's one thing working with wolves has taught me, it's that mating is on a whole different level than dating, marriage, or...coupling." Jane rolled her eyes, grabbing another pair of gloves from her pocket. "All right, Tidal. I'm going to take some blood just to check a few things."

"Consent?"

She froze, her head cocked, an adorably confused expression on her face. "What about it?"

"Well, if I'm not allowed to touch you without consent, I feel it should be reciprocal."

"But I've been touching you."

I raised an eyebrow and waved a hand over my hips. "And I liked it, obviously. More than I think you want me to. But this is different. This is my blood. And when it comes to dragons, our blood is sacred. We don't spill it for just anyone."

She was quiet for a long moment before she finally gave me a nod. "May I have your consent to examine your blood, Tidal?"

"Piers." I refused to look away even as her eyebrows winged up in surprise. "If you want to see the inside of me, you should at least use my given name. I'm Piers."

Another pause, but her eyebrows had dropped back into place and her eyes were still on mine. All things I considered good signs of progress between us.

She raised her chin, looking so damned fierce as she asked, "May I have your consent, Piers?"

"Of course. For anything."

Jane stared into my eyes for an extended moment, seeing something there that made her smile. "This won't hurt."

"Doc, I have a feeling anything you do to me is going to hurt. It just depends on if it's the sort of pain I like or not."

She smiled wider, looking far too pleased with herself. "Trust me. I'm a doctor."

Her hands on my skin were no longer as warm with the plastic gloves in the way, though I understood her concerns. Humans were much more susceptible to diseases than shifters were.

The process of bloodletting took less time than I would have liked. As soon as Jane was finished, she tucked the tubes of thick, dark red liquid into a holder on the counter and spent a few minutes labeling each one. So precise in her movements, her attention to detail intrigued me. As I sat there waiting for her to finish, I took a good look around the exam room. The entire place was clean and organized, not a single thing out of place. Orderly...like Jane.

When she was done and the tubes were standing in a rack in perfect lines, Jane crossed her arms over her chest and leaned a hip against the cabinet. "You can go now."

The dismissal hurt more than it should have, but I faked my way through it. "I was hoping for another kiss to make my boo-boo feel better, Doc."

Jane's smile fell, her eyes dropping from mine. "That can't happen."

I was on my feet and in front of her in a blink. Not touching. Assuming the consent I'd received earlier had expired. "Why not?"

"We just...can't."

My dragon rumbled within me, making my voice drop deeper. "I'm not really one to follow rules, Doc."

"No, you're not. But I am. I have to." With that, she spun and walked out of the room, leaving me in the cold. Literally.

FOUR

The morning after the blood draw, I woke up shivering, thinking of Tidal alone in his room and wondering if he was as cold as I was. Though he might not be alone. Bringing women back to your room was against the rules for the fighters, but everyone knew Tidal didn't follow all the rules. He didn't have to. Success in the ring and the money he brought in kept the bosses happy and gave him a free pass.

Most of the time.

I'd dreamed of the dragon shifter all night, had woken up twice gasping as the desire from my naughty imagination had taken me over. But dreams and reality didn't always mix. Still, after the second time, I'd needed to break out the toy I kept tucked away in my nightstand. It was small, a little finger vibe I'd snagged at a drug store, but it helped take the edge off so I could go back to sleep. Nothing like what I really wanted.

Stupid, handsome, charming, protective dragon with the impressive...package.

Frustrated with myself for many reasons, I threw the covers

off and stumbled from my bed. Within fifteen minutes, I was showered, dressed, and on my way to the medical ward. I'd been up late helping patch up fighters who'd brawled in the training center, just as I'd expected from the heat raise. I wanted to stay in bed and sleep more, but there were fights tonight, which meant I'd be even busier. I needed to make sure all the supplies were organized and the rooms cleaned before the walking wounded started trickling in. The dead ones never cared if I had gauze handy or not.

I was working in exam room three, triple-checking that each acetylene torch was functional and close at hand, when Mick sauntered through the door.

"There you are."

His voice made the hair on the back of my neck stand up. I wasn't ready to deal with him, was still too distracted by thoughts of Tidal to face the man. But I had to. No one kept their back to Mick for long if they were smart.

"Here I am." With shaky hands, I placed the torch on the counter before turning his way, my fake smile firmly in place. "How can I help you, sir?"

"How's Tidal?"

I shrugged even as my blood went cold. There had to be a reason why he was asking about Tidal. He never asked about a fighter unless he was worried they'd died. "Fine. Bloodwork shows nothing abnormal from what I can tell."

He hummed and nodded, closing the door behind him. "So, you think you understand dragon physiology?"

I looked from him to the door and back, my instincts flaring bright. My answer was more cautious, my words specific. "I understand as much as I can considering I've only ever had Tidal to study."

"Good, that's good." Mick strolled around the room, his eyes unfocused, his hands clasped behind his back. He reminded me of a tiger in a cage. Threatening. Bored. Psychotic. "Jane, I'm going to need you to keep a secret."

"Of course," I said, though the words made me sick to my stomach. Mick and secrets meant trouble. Lots of trouble. I'd been the victim of his secrets for years, but he just kept piling them on.

Mick glanced at the door, his movements growing quick and jerky. Something I would have guessed as nerves showing in his body language. Something I'd never seen from him before.

"We've got an off-site project that needs extra attention. I've been handling it on my own to this point. The other owners aren't involved."

The speed of his words, the almost babbling manner in which he spoke made chill bumps rise on my arms. What the hell was all this? "Okay."

"I'd like for you to consult on the project for me."

I wanted to say no. I wanted to say hell no and run for the door, to be honest. I wanted out of this place, out of this life, and away from The Pack House, too. But Mick would never allow that. Any of it.

In fact, Mick gave me a harsh stare as he turned the screws just that much tighter. "I bet your father would be so proud of what you've become, Jane. He always wanted you to be a doctor."

And there it was. The noose around my neck. The Achilles' heel to my entire future. The reminder that, no matter what I wanted, I had to bend to Mick's will.

"I'd be happy to, sir." My voice surprised me. It was low, crackly even. Lifeless in its tempo. It was the voice of someone who had given up.

Mick grunted, his eyes again darting around the room. "You cannot breathe a word of this to anyone. Ever."

A shiver of dread raced down my spine. He'd said those

words to me once before, about a minute before I practically fainted when he shifted to his wolf form. That one promise had kicked off the free fall into what my life had become. One shift, one moment that wasn't as private as we thought, resulted in my father losing his mind and me being trapped working at The Pack House. Forever.

"Of course," I whispered, wishing there was some way I could say no. That I could escape to another reality where I was free to do what I wanted and not stuck being enslaved by the beast before me. "Whatever you need, sir."

Mick's smile spread in a slow and calculating way. "I think you're going to bring a lot to this project, Jane. Now, come. Let's go play with my new toy."

It didn't take long for Mick to drive us to the location of his special project, though it certainly wasn't what I'd expected.

"This is it?" I asked, staring out the window at the mountain rising from the grass.

Mick grunted and pointed. "The entrance is behind that brush."

I squinted, trying to see past the shrubbery and dead branches. "Is that—"

"A cave. Yes. Very observant. Come, Jane."

I swallowed down the fear the place instilled in me and grabbed the door handle.

"A word of warning," Mick said, dragging my attention back to him. "Whatever you do, don't run."

He was out of the car and moving toward the hidden mouth of the cave before I could fathom the meaning behind his words. Don't run? Like...how you're not supposed to run if a dog threatens you? What the hell was in there, and why was running something to avoid?

Resigned but wary, I sighed and followed Mick. One step inside the cave, and a fear unlike any I'd known slammed into me like a brick. Terror even. Something was very wrong in this place. I felt hunted, watched...like prey. A feeling that refused to leave and, in fact, grew stronger as we walked deeper into the low-ceilinged space.

When the darkness finally overpowered the light, making it nearly impossible for me to continue, I stopped.

"Keep going. We're not there yet." Mick said, his voice harsh.

"I can't see."

There was a sigh and the sound of movement before Mick turned on a large, torch-style flashlight. The heavy piece of equipment did little to dispel the shadows and even less to calm my nerves.

"Better?" Mick asked, sounding more irritated than concerned. I nodded, feeling chastised. Mick turned and strode deeper into the slowly widening tunnel. I hurried after him, my blood pounding in my ears, my skin cold. The tunnel was horrible, a long, dark road leading to something I didn't want to know about. But it was nothing compared to the cavern at the end. It was in that moment, as we ducked through a small opening in the stone walls, that every instinct I had told me to do one thing.

Run!

I clung to the rock wall to the right of the opening, denying my instincts and working to keep my feet still. There was something dark in this place, more so than just the lack of lights. A shadow among the inky black. Darker than dark. Something breathing in the quiet, still air.

I swallowed hard, willing myself to stop shaking. "Mick?"

He shushed me, taking a few more steps into what I was finally able to see as a large, natural chamber of some sort. Stalactites hung high in the air, the sheer size of them something amazing to behold. But it was the shadow moving between the mineral formations that truly stole my breath.

"Don't run," Mick whispered when he heard my gasp. I swallowed hard and pushed my back against the wall, needing something solid to hold on to. Mick glanced over his shoulder, the look in his eyes only making my fear grow. It was not the expression of a confident man. But he turned to face the slithering shadow up above, then took another step into the dark.

"I brought the physician I told you about, Saern," he called, his voice echoing in the cavernous space. "Please come say hello."

A deep, dark chuckle sounded from above, just before a cold wind blew through the chamber. With a crash, a huge beast landed before me. Tall and wide, with scales the color of a moonless sky and even darker eyes, he dwarfed me. I whimpered and pushed myself against the wall, my fingers scraping against the rock.

The beast sniffed, his forked tongue nearly touching my skin. I recoiled, biting my lip to keep from screaming. A dragon. Another fucking dragon. One that instilled more fear in me than Tidal ever had. One that set my instincts to flight with no option to fight. One I wanted nothing to do with.

With a huff, the dragon shimmered, twisting and shrinking until he reformed into a dark-haired, humanoid man. A very naked man.

"She's lovely. A treat." The dragon shifter took another step toward me, his movements far too slithery to be human. He was nothing like Tidal, who could easily pass as human without seeming to try. This thing was all...animal.

"She's here to help us." Mick stepped closer, a growl in his voice. The man—Saern, if Mick was correct—whipped his head around, his movements extraordinarily fast, almost as if it was disconnected from his body.

"You promised me a treat." Saern's voice made me shiver, made my stomach plummet.

But Mick shook his head. "She's not your treat."

Saern sighed, looking me over with a covetous gaze, raising his hand as if to touch me. "Pity."

I edged to the side, trying to avoid Saern's clawlike fingers, unable to stop myself from retreating. The shifter cocked his head in a way that spoke of a hunter examining his prey, a look I'd never seen on a human face.

"She's skittish," he hissed, almost sounding excited. And, oh God, was he right. I was skittish. I was fighting every instinct I had to stay put. Don't run, Mick had said. A nearly impossible command.

Mick growled again, the fierce rumble reverberating in the cavern. "She's protected."

"Another pity." Saern slipped closer, his footsteps nearly silent. "I have a feeling she'd give me a good chase."

I bit back a scream as he raised his hand again, inching closer. Those black eyes were locked on my chin, hungry eyes. Filled with evil and want and arrogance. Hissing, he ran a finger down the side of my face, his rough skin leaving a burning trail along my cheek.

"You'd make me work for it, wouldn't you, my treat?"

"Mick," I whispered, looking for help from the only person I thought might be strong enough to give it.

Mick growled long and deep, nearly making the room shake. "You will keep your distance, dragon."

"Or what?" Saern smirked, not even bothering to turn

toward the wolf shifter. "What exactly do you think you're going to do to me, dog?"

Mick didn't answer, though his growl turned harsher, fiercer. Saern stood before me for a moment, staring into my eyes, completely unaffected by the other shifter. Moving closer instead of retreating. His pupils were long and oval, more reptile than human, the fork in his tongue more obvious than Tidal's. His beast was stronger. His humanity deeper within him.

Shit.

"Are you worried, treat?" Saern's smirk grew as I turned to escape his fingers.

I shook my head, unable to look him in the eye. Trying my damnedest to simply keep breathing.

Saern chuckled. "Your blood flows faster when you lie. Did you know that?"

"That's enough, Saern." Mick's command made the dragon shifter pause. His smirk dropped to a scowl, and his eyes darted to the side where Mick stood for the briefest of moments. But then they were back on mine, and he was leaning closer. Whispering in my ear. "Your dog thinks he's in control, doesn't he?"

Before I could ask what he meant, he swung back, kneeling a few feet in front of me. Bowing, it appeared. I looked to Mick, expecting some sort of response, but he seemed as confused as I felt.

"Saern?" Mick questioned, taking a step closer.

"My name is Mesaern Thundairous of the Vontruiler clan. And I choose you, Treat, as my mate."

FIVE

Piers

"You lost your balls in that last fight, Tidal? You're hitting like a girl."

I slammed my fist into the heavy bag and shot a look over at Beadan. "I know a number of girls who could kick your ass, man, so I'll take that as a compliment."

He laughed and went back to working the small bag while I started a high-low kick sequence on the heavy one. As much as I was training and working, Beadan was right. I wasn't hitting as hard I normally would be. I'd become obsessed with thoughts of Doctor Jane. I'd fallen asleep thinking about her, woken up in the middle of the night thinking about her, and ended up jacking off in the shower thinking about her. The woman wouldn't leave me alone. And it was no longer just an I-want-to-get-her-in-my-bed obsession; it had grown into the I-want-to-get-to-know-her kind. A truly dangerous kind. The kind that would get me killed if I couldn't knock my own head back on straight in this crowd.

Though perhaps it wasn't my obsession with her that was so

distracting. It was the lack of her at the moment. I hadn't been able to find her this morning when I'd gone to the medical wards. Someone mentioned she'd left the site with Mick, which had soured my mood. It shouldn't have. Before that last fight, before the ear and the shot and the rescue the next day, I could go a couple of weeks without seeing her and barely notice. Now, I'd been separated from her for what amounted to a matter of hours, and I felt as if I were missing a part of me. Even my dragon was silent about anything other than her as he waited to catch another glimpse of the good doctor. But she was gone, and I had no idea when she'd be back. So I'd come to the ring for practice. That had been hours ago, and I was still stinking up the joint with my shitty moves.

Trainer Laudon hopped into the ring and stood behind the heavy bag, a frown on his face. "You're out of sync."

I growled and tried to kick without the bag coming back at me, only to fail once more. "Shit."

"You okay, Tidal?"

"I'm fine." I struck with my fists, giving up on lower-body training and going back to working my arms.

Laudon grabbed the bag and leaned into it, holding it in place. But after only a handful of hits, I knew this wouldn't work. My mind was too scattered, my body too far on edge. My dragon was practically pacing on my last nerve. I needed a break.

I stopped hitting and doubled over, breathing hard. Laudon came running as I knew he'd do.

"You okay?"

I shook my head. "Yeah, man. I need to use the bathroom, though."

The trainer took two steps back and gave me a sympathetic frown. In a building full of men, there was one thing everyone understood. Sometimes, you had to drop a load alone.

Laudon nodded and smacked my shoulder. "Find me when you're done and we'll try again."

I nodded and left the ring, trying not to move too fast. Once I was out of the training area, I headed for the service hallway that ran the back length of the building. At the end was an emergency door leading outside, one I hadn't used in a long time. We weren't allowed outside, and we certainly weren't allowed to do what I was about to. But if there was one thing I'd learned about the difference between wolf and dragon shifters, it was that the wolves were easier to control. My beast refused to be tethered. I could either get outside and shift or suffer until he tore through my mind and took over. The former seemed the better option.

I rushed through the door without looking back. As soon as I hit the tree line, I shifted. Skin became scales, wings pushed through the flesh of my back, and my eyesight sharpened. The world became a sea of colors—red and blue, orange and yellow. All denoting the temperature. All showing a rather cool day on the mountain. Spots of brighter colors scurried through the undergrowth, animals moving about their business. They ran from me as prey tends to run from predators, but they were no concern of mine tonight. I needed wind, I needed space. I needed to fly.

My wings unfurled behind me as I took two steps and jumped, taking to the air smoothly. This was what I'd been missing since I'd been fighting my way through The Pack House. The freedom, the feeling of letting go that came from soaring above the trees. I couldn't fly for too long or go too high, but I could take a few loops around the mountain. Just enough to clear my head and settle my dragon. Enough to figure out what was going on with the good doctor.

But as I arced over the river and beat my wings to go higher, the irritation from my dragon didn't disappear. It was a weight on me, a tether around my neck, tying me to the ground. It grew and pulled tighter the farther away from The Pack House I flew, drawing me back, refusing to let me escape. Irritation sizzled under my skin, and smoke trailed from my nose. For the first time in my life, flying wasn't enough to calm the billowing currents inside of me.

I swung back around, heading for The Pack House. The weight I felt as I flew away lessened, the direction the right one. But the reasoning behind the sensation was something I couldn't understand. So I stepped back, giving more mental space to my beast. Letting him take over our thoughts. It was something I rarely did, as the loss of my humanity scared me, but this time, it was needed.

Digging deep, trying to see what my dragon saw, I gave him as much control as I felt comfortable letting go of. And he took it, practically singing his joy at having the reins hang free. At first, it was almost as if the beast was blocking me, as if he didn't want me to see what he wanted and needed. Why he was so focused on staying at The Pack House. I could only see red and orange, fiery hot colors that made the dragon needy and demanding. That blocked everything from his mind but whatever was behind the wall of color. But then the focus changed, moved back, and out of the fire came understandable shapes and shadows. And I knew.

The dragon had chosen Jane as his mate.

I landed on the riverbank with a thud, not even shifting human once more like I normally would. My tail swished back and forth as I paced the rocky shore, my yowls, hisses, and grunts peppering the forest with sounds rarely heard. How had I missed this? While I knew I was definitely attracted to Jane, I hadn't expected *this*. Hell, I hadn't expected to ever find a mate. My father had told me the stories of our kind. I knew the legends that followed us, the ones we let the other shifters believe. That we chose mates at random, that they weren't fated, that we could leave them and choose others if the whim hit us.

All lies, sort of.

The truth was our dragon chose their mate. The connections took time, took getting to know someone. It was much like how humans chose a spouse, except that once our dragon had chosen a mate, that was it. The dragon chose once in their life, tying their soul to the one they wanted for their remaining days. No, it wasn't a fated connection; it was one we had to work to build and nurture. There was no instant attraction, no understanding that the two belonged together. There was only the feeling of rightness that came when you realized they were the one for you. When they proved their loyalty. When you claimed their body, mind, and spirit as a part of your own.

And blessings to anyone—human or otherwise—who stood in your way.

"Shit," I hissed as I finally shifted human. For about the millionth time in my life, I gave thanks that dragons shifted with their clothes, unlike our wolfy counterparts.

Sitting on the bank of the river, I grabbed the neck of my T-shirt and pulled it over my head. I was too warm for once, too worked up from flying and figuring out what my dragon had done. So I balled up the fabric and rested it behind my head as I lay back on the cool ground. The sky was a field of color, clouds hanging high above in fluffy counter to the sleek blue. I stared for minutes or hours, waiting for guidance. Letting my dragon settle so I could figure out what to do.

When he finally did, when he sat back and gave me the ability to work with him once more, it was with one thought in mind.

Mate.

"She might not want us," I said out loud, even though he

could hear my thoughts. But I knew, even before the dragon laughed inside my head, that it didn't matter. I'd still be chasing her. I'd still crave her. There was no turning off the mate switch once the dragon had chosen. No second chances or do-overs. Jane was it for me, for my dragon, forever.

I just had to figure out how to make her feel the same way about me.

SIX

Jane

"I'm not your mate."

Saern laughed, the sound echoing coldly through the chamber. "Of course you are, Treat. But we'll get to that. First, do your job."

His order practically dripped with arrogance, and I bristled in response. "Excuse me? My job—"

"Jane." Mick's voice made me jump, made me squeak, something that had the dragon cocking his head with interest. "Our friend here is going to join The Pack House soon, but he needs medical attention first."

My stomach plummeted. This animal was coming to The Pack House. The wolves could be bad enough—rough and strong and filled with testosterone to the point of overload—but this guy would be a train wreck. He'd slaughter his opponents. The only one he could possibly fight and lose to would be Tidal.

Oh God, Piers.

"Jane," Mick barked again, looking irritated.

I shook off my thoughts and focused on Saern, no matter

how much I didn't want to. "Medical attention. Right... For what?"

"Ignorant humans stealing the sky again," Saern spat. "I clipped one of their wind machines, and it caught my wing. I can no longer fly, my treat."

"I don't—" I licked my lips, still worried about Tidal, still too terrified to move closer to the beast voluntarily. "I have no idea how to fix that."

Saern roared a displeased sound, making the rocks shake all around me. I clung to the wall, curving in on myself. Forget The Pack House; this guy was going to kill us all here. But Mick didn't cower. He just waved a hand in the dragon's direction and waited until Saern had grown quiet again. Apparently, this was old hat to him.

"Examine the wing, Jane," Mick said, the order clear in his tone. "His other wing is fine, so you can examine it as well to look for abnormalities and differences. Or you can examine Tidal's when we get back."

"Tidal isn't going to shift in front of me." I knew that, felt it with a certainty that infused my words. There was a barrier there, something between us that kept his dragon side from me.

"He will if I demand it." Mick growled, deep and thick; a warning. "Now do as you're told, girl."

My body, my mind, and my heart sagged as one. This was my lot. Do as Mick told me to do, and be grateful for the chances he'd given me. I'd been his faithful servant for years, had done his bidding no matter how much I disagreed with him. I couldn't start to refuse him now when we were in such dangerous company. Besides, it could be worse. Mick could have killed me already.

Fortifying myself with a deep breath, I took a single step forward, my legs feeling as heavy as concrete. "May I...examine your wing?"

Saern smirked, an exceptionally lascivious expression on his angled face. "By all means."

He shifted directly in front of me, nearly knocking me over with the force of the transition. My heart pounded, my entire body growing cold and covered in goose bumps. Jesus, Mary, and Joseph... What the hell was I supposed to do with *that*? Taller than any man ever born, wider than three of them, the black-scaled beast sat blocking my path. Watching me. I tried not to look the animal directly in the eye in case they had domination hierarchy like wolves, but that didn't stop me from seeing him. From noticing the details. The glistening moistness of his scales, the way he almost seemed to absorb the light. The near-constant hiss he released. This was a nightmare, a total and utter nightmare. And it was one I couldn't just wake up from to escape.

As I edged around the side of the dragon, I slipped farther and farther into shadow. Saern blocked the small amount of light Mick's torch lamp offered. I couldn't work in that darkness.

"Light," I said, holding a hand out to Mick. "Can you bring the light back here so I can see?"

He paused, his eyes flicking to the dragon. I knew that expression, though I'd never seen it on *his* face before. Mick was afraid of Saern. I couldn't blame him; in fact, I almost pitied him. It had to be difficult going from the biggest predator to prey.

"Mick." I nodded once when his eyes met mine. "Light? Please."

Mick nodded and followed me, lighting my path. Saern didn't move, didn't turn or adjust his position one inch to make things easier on us. An act that struck me as telling. If Mick thought he was somehow in control of this situation, he was wrong. Dead wrong. And it was likely that I would end up paying for his miscalculation.

As I passed Saern's tail, I stumbled over a pile of rocks. My arms flew up to stop my fall, my hands landing on the scaly back of the dragon. I recoiled at the feel, at the hard, cold, rocklike pattern etched underneath my palms. Saern sighed, though. Curving his back as if to elicit more touching. The move reminded me of Tidal craving the warmth of my hands. Of the fact that Tidal and Saern were one in the same. Both beasts inside. Both dragons.

Tidal just had more charm than this one.

As I finally reached my destination, I noticed the angle of the wing in question. The bone supporting the structure certainly looked broken, but I'd need to do a physical exam to be sure. Something I was dreading. I had no gloves with me, no barrier to keep between my flesh and his. But I had a job to do. I crawled up a pile of rocks to be able to reach Saern's wings, and I let my years of medical training take over my thoughts.

With trembling hands and a sick feeling in my stomach, I ran my hands over the leathery flesh of the healthy wing. Saern didn't move at first, just held stock-still as I gingerly sought form and function. Used my fingers to declare normalcy. When I was finished, I moved on to the damaged wing. Saern went stiff as my fingers made contact, so I paused and gave him a moment to collect himself. When he seemed calm once more, I tried to follow the outer support skeleton—the one with the definite angle where it should be straight—but jerked my hands away when the creature moaned.

"Am I hurting you?"

Saern dissolved before me, morphing into something from a nightmare. Half man, half dragon, some kind of dark, reptilian thing with patches of skin showing through scales. I swallowed down the gag his appearance brought on, trying to remain calm. To not be terrified by the...thing.

"Not at all, Treat," Saern said, his voice a chilling

combination of growl, hiss, and human. "The heat feels amazing."

I nodded, my thoughts spinning off to Tidal once more. To how much he enjoyed the heat from my hands as well. To how cold he was compared to the wolf shifters at The Pack House. Saern felt even colder to me—chilled, almost—the ambient temperature in the cave probably the cause.

"Getting back to it, Treat?" Saern looked over his shoulder, his bugged-out eyes making me feel the need to bite back a scream. I swallowed and nodded, doing my best to stay professional. To stay brave. To ignore the instinct still yelling at me to *run*.

Saern continued to moan and groan through the exam, sighing when I placed my palms against him. I was diligent in my examination, if not a little quick. I wanted away from him and out of this cave. I wanted to be back at The Pack House with beasts I knew how to handle...and a dragon shifter who didn't terrify me. I wanted all kinds of things I couldn't have, but thinking of those wants kept my mind from focusing on the way Saern was obviously drawing a pleasure I wasn't intending to give him from my touch.

When he shivered as I placed my hand at the base of his wing, releasing a purely sexual moan at the same time, I surrendered to my need to leave and cut my exam short.

"All done," I said, hurrying away from him. "Definitely broken, though it appears to be knitting together slowly. Perhaps you should eat more protein and rest to encourage your body to repair itself."

"How long?" Mick asked, staring at me, his face ashen even in the low light.

"I have no idea."

"A few weeks," Saern said, still in his half-human state.

"Wings are not like other parts of me. It'll take time to heal well enough to pull me through the air."

Mick scowled. "You'll fight in human form, though, so there should be no delay for our deal."

Saern glared at Mick, his voice thick with hate when he spoke. "I will not fight without my wings. I understand your silly rules about not shifting, dog, but I will be whole before I purposely take on one of my own."

Mick huffed, obviously not liking this development. Not liking it, but not giving up on his silly notion either. "Fine. You heal. We'll be back tomorrow to bring you protein packs and to check on your progress. Let's go, Jane."

Saern smiled, the expression near horrifying on his current face. "Just one thing."

Without warning, Saern shifted to his full dragon and grabbed me, pulling me right off the floor. His tongue flicked out, the forked end running all over my face and neck. I screamed and tried to wiggle my way out of his hold, but he was too big. Too strong. Even Mick just stood at the dragon's feet, staring helplessly.

Saern hissed in my ear, and I whimpered in response. Something about the sound seemed to encourage him, though. He ran his scaly cheek against mine, hissing, his hands bruising me wherever he grabbed. His fingers spread wider, teasing areas he had no right to touch, making me scream again as I kicked and fought against his hold. But I was no match for him, for a dragon of his size and strength. No match at all.

Eventually, Saern shifted back to human with me still in his hold. We ended up with my body pressed against his humanesque one, with his arms wrapped around me in some sort of perverted lover's embrace. He ground his hips against mine as he buried his face in my neck. Assaulted me with his arousal as his tongue left a wet trail along the curve to my shoulder. Enjoying himself, obviously. Making sure I knew exactly what my touch had done. Making sure I knew who had the power in this arena.

"Saern." Mick's sharp yell gave Saern pause, though he didn't let me go. Not at first. But at least he stopped pressing himself against me. I was a shivering, nauseated mess, terror making my blood cold and my eyes fill with tears. But I was also filled with a rage hotter than a thousand suns. How dare Mick put me in this position? How dare this animal put his hands on me? For years, I'd worked by Mick's side because he held the safety of my father over my head, but he'd always protected me. I was an asset to him. An asset he was apparently willing to sell off if it meant a good return in the ring.

Not anymore. I needed to figure a way out of this before Saern went further. Before he took what I would never offer him.

"You've made me hard, Treat." Saern rocked his hips into mine one more time, chuckling as I squeezed my eyes shut and tried to pull away. "You'll learn to like it, mate. Women always do."

He set me down on my own feet, leering as he stepped back into the shadows. "I believe I shall take advantage of the warmth I feel from your touch to relieve my problem. You two may go. I will expect time with my mate daily until this ridiculous fight is over."

And with that, he shifted to his dragon again and scrambled up the stalactites, hidden in the darkness once more.

Without waiting for Mick or his torch lamp, without heeding the one piece of advice he'd given me, I ran for the tunnel leading to the exit. It was dark, and I fell over the uneven floor repeatedly and banged into the walls, but I kept going. Kept heading for someplace safer. Kept trying to get away. The incline told me we were close to the mouth of the cave, though there was still no light. I ran anyway.

Finally, I stumbled out of the cave into the deep night blanketing the area, running through the shadows until I found the car. Mick was right behind me, lighting his own path.

"Are you insane?" I shouted as soon as we were away from the mouth of the cave. "You think dealing with that...thing...is a good idea?"

Mick growled sharply. "I'd remind you to mind your mouth."

"And I'd remind you that you're going to have an arena filled with humans, many of them women. That animal is...uncontrollable."

"You worry about fixing his wing; I'll worry about The Pack House."

I sighed, desperate to find a way to reason with the man. Why couldn't he see the issues Saern presented? "Sir, I just don't think—"

"I didn't ask you to think," he spat. "Fix the goddamned wing, Jane, or I'll drive over to that nursing home where your father is stashed and shift in front of him again. I already gave him two strokes. I can certainly influence a third. Do you understand?"

I recoiled as if I'd been slapped. Mick had never outright threatened my father, had never even brought up how my dad ended up needing twenty-four-hour care. I knew, of course. I'd been there when Mick had lost control and shifted to his wolf, had watched my dad's eyes go wide, had seen his hand come up to his heart. I'd watched my father disappear as shock and fear caused a heart attack that led to a stroke that killed off a large section of his brain. Been by his side when the second stroke took almost all of what was left of him, leaving a shell of a man behind. I'd been there, and I'd done nothing to help him.

Ducking my head to hide the tears flowing freely down my cheeks, I backed toward the car. "Yes, sir."

"Good." Mick ran a hand through his hair and blew out a breath. "One dragon in the ring has been amazing for revenue. Two fighting against each other? There is no limit to what we can make."

"And if he kills Tidal?"

"So be it," Mick said with a shrug. "The arrogant bastard needs a good beating anyway."

Resigned but still hopeful Mick would do the right thing, I asked, "And what about me?"

Mick paused, looking uncertain for the first time since I met him. "We'll figure out a way to break his claim. Dragons don't mate like wolf shifters, Jane. They're not as set. Perhaps we can entice him to leave you alone."

I crawled into the passenger seat and turned my head toward the window, shivering. I pulled my knees up to my chest and wrapped my arms around them, needing to be small and hidden. Refusing to voice what I knew to be true. There was no limit to the damage that thing would do. Especially to me. Mick had basically sold me to the dragon shifter, and there'd be no dissolving that deal.

SEVEN

Piers

I slammed my fist into my opponent's chest, knocking him almost completely off his feet. The guys lined up around the ring hollered their approval like the animals they were. They loved a vicious fight, and I was not in the mood to hold back. I'd been sparring with Beadan for almost an hour, both of us jabbing and floating as we tried to avoid getting hit by the other. He'd failed too many times to count, but I was pulling punches to keep from really hurting the wolf shifter. I'd probably kill him if I went full out right then.

Beadan looped to my left. His steps were messy, and he was obviously winded. This spar had been going on for too long, but the stupid wolf wouldn't give up. He was the quintessential dog with a bone, and the bone was apparently trying to beat my ass. Unfortunately for him, I was getting bored going easy on the fucker.

He spat to the side and shuffled his feet, pretending to be ready for more than he could handle. "C'mon, lizard. Gimme better than that."

I smirked. "You can't handle better than that, pup. Why don't you head out of the ring with your littermates before you get hurt?"

Beadan laughed and danced closer. The move sparked a bit of territorialism with my dragon, and my control slipped. I circled wide, every move sharp but forced. I needed to stay focused, to hold back, to not let the beast come out. This kid wasn't really trying to hurt me, didn't even have the power to do so in my opinion. But with the way my dragon was on edge, it wouldn't take much for him to lose control and go for a deathblow.

"You've been cranky this week, lizard," one of the other fighters yelled from the ropes. "Is it that time of the month?"

The crowd laughed, some of them clapping. I didn't take my eyes off my opponent, though. One, that would be stupid, and two, the guy was right. I had been cranky. Downright pissed off, to be honest. I hadn't seen Jane in over a week, not since the day I accepted that she was my chosen mate. I tried tracking her down whenever I could sneak away, but the trainers were keeping me on a short leash. I was in the ring for hours upon hours every day, and if I wasn't sparring, I was being questioned about training methods and tested for muscle mass. And Jane was never here anymore—she was always off-site with Mick, working on some project no one seemed to know anything about.

Something was up.

The energy of something big coming and loss of all contact with my mate was a bad combination. My dragon was restless, needing to be let out. He wanted to take to the skies, to fly around this mountain range and find his mate. To claim her. That fact alone was enough to sour my mood. Add to it that I didn't have a match scheduled for the foreseeable future but was basically stuck in training hell and I was seriously not in the mood for anyone's attitude.

Cranky was an understatement.

Beadan charged me just as the entrance door swung open behind him. My eyes immediately locked with Jane's when she walked in, a mistake my opponent took advantage of. His fist connected with my chin in an uppercut that jarred my teeth and sent me stumbling back. The crowd around the ring roared and jeered, the wolves cheering on one of their own. I didn't care. As soon as I had my balance, I rushed out of the ring, tearing off the tape on my hands.

"Hey, Tidal," Beadan yelled with a laugh as I dropped to the floor. "Don't run away."

"It was a good hit, man. Own it." I kept my eyes on Jane, following her hurried steps toward the medical wing. "I think you knocked a tooth loose."

The wolves howled and joked about dragons, but I ignored them. Let them think I was weak—I'd show them the truth when I got them in the ring. But at that moment, I had more important things to worry about. Specifically, the doctor racing away from me.

I found Jane in an exam room I'd never been in before. It was more storage than most, neat and tidy but filled with supplies I barely recognized. Jane was leaning on a counter with her head in her hands, every inch of her body screaming defeat. Something that riled me in ways I hadn't thought possible.

I slipped inside, not wanting to alert anyone in the area, but desperate to talk to her. The snick of the door closing behind me made Jane jump and spin, and my heart dropped.

"Are you okay?" I asked. Her terrified eyes met mine, the bags beneath them ones I'd never seen on her before. She looked beyond tired, beyond scared. Jane looked wrung out, worn out, and terrified. My dragon raged inside of me, ready to defend our mate. Ready to shift and fly her off to someplace safe.

Unable to help myself, I took a step toward her. Her eyes widened and her face paled.

"Stop." She stumbled back a step. "You can't be in here with me."

"Why not?"

Her eyes danced around the room, as if she were looking for an escape. "Tidal, please. I need you to leave me alone."

"That's not going to happen, Jane. You're important to me, and that means I step up when you need something." I took a single step in her direction, slow and deliberate. "You obviously need something. Tell me what it is, and I'll help you get it."

She shook her head, retreating again. "You're not allowed to know what I've been doing. If you found out, Mick would—"

She cut herself off, her voice shaking along with her hands. The redness of her eyes broke my heart. She looked ready to cry. I couldn't have that. Not if there was something I could do.

I inched closer and put my hands up, surrendering. "I won't ask what's going on. Just...tell me how to help."

"You'll smell it. You need to leave."

"I'm not a wolf, Jane. My sense of smell isn't the same as theirs."

She didn't retreat this time, standing firm as I inched forward. Still nervous, but relaxing slightly. "But you can smell things more so than a human."

I shook my head. "Smell, no. Taste, yes. I bring air over my tongue and absorb the scents. But that's not an automatic thing in my human form. I'd have to pull my dragon forward."

She gasped and a shiver ran through her, one even I could see. "Please, don't. And don't...taste. Don't smell."

I blinked. The absolute terror in her voice left me cold

inside. If she couldn't accept my dragon, she couldn't accept me as her mate. And while I knew my dragon form could be seen as scary, he cared for her. He would never hurt her.

I edged closer, keeping my eyes on her. Wishing she would stop shaking so hard. "Jane, what's going on?"

She shook her head. "I can't tell you."

I took a deep breath, purposely not tasting the air. Keeping my promise to her.

"Okay," I murmured, creeping closer yet. "I won't ask. I won't get you in trouble. But know that I'm here, and I'll help you."

She laughed, a harsh, brittle sound. "Right. *You'll* help me."

"Jane, I—"

"How do you kill a shifter?"

My head jerked back. "What?"

"You want to help me? Fine. Tell me how to kill a shifter."

"A human usually can't kill a shifter, Jane. They're not strong enough."

Her body sagged as if all the air within her evaporated at once. I rushed forward, wrapping my arms around her before she fell. For a split second, I feared she'd push me away, but she didn't. She clung to me as if her life depended on it, like I was some kind of life preserver in the middle of an angry sea. Like she needed saving.

"Consent?" I whispered, resting my cheek on top of her head.

She nodded, pulling me closer.

I sighed and held tight, relishing the heat of her. "Tell me what's going on, Doc."

She shook her head, her entire body trembling as she bit back what sounded like a sob. I wrapped her tighter, pulled her closer. Wishing I could use my body to shield her from whatever had her so upset. Desperate to get my hands on whoever had her so scared and rip them into pieces. But I couldn't, not if she wouldn't trust me to tell me what was wrong. And I'd promised her not to use my dragon sense of smell to figure it out. I wouldn't break that trust. I wouldn't lie to her.

After a few minutes of holding one another, Jane seemed to calm. Her hands loosened where they held me, and her body stopped shaking. I kept her wrapped up against me, though. Kept sharing her warmth, hoping my touch gave her as much comfort as hers did to me.

"It should be my choice," she whispered before leaning her head back to look up at me. "Your fate is your choice. This should be mine."

"What should?"

Without answering, she grabbed my face, pulling me down to press her lips to mine. Her kiss was brutal, wild, and full of a passion that almost felt out of control. And I wanted more. I grabbed her by the thighs, lifting her up with ease, groaning when she wrapped those legs around my hips. When I had her entire body pressed to mine. The taste of her on my tongue and the feel of her heat all around me scrambled my thoughts. She was my entire focus. All I cared about, all I wanted, was her. My dragon agreed, clawing inside of my mind, begging to be let loose. To claim her as his. But I held him back, wanting this moment to last, being selfish with it.

When she nipped my lower lip, I lunged forward, pressing her back against a wall so I could gain a little leverage. The woman was unleashing the beast in me, and I liked it. Hell, I loved it. I pressed my hips into hers, where I was so hard and wanting against where she was soft and wet. Rolled them. Shifted and moved and writhed until her head fell back and she gasped her pleasure. Until I found the right spot.

"Like that, Doc?"

She groaned again, her eyes closed, totally lost in the moment. I pressed harder, rocking her against me, making sure to hit every spot that made her body respond to mine. Working for every shiver, every moan. Every fucking breath.

"Good girl. Take it. Take it all."

So she did. She took and took and took, riding me hard, pulling me where she needed me to be. And I let her. Giving her everything I had, making sure she got what she wanted from me. What she needed.

She came with a sigh, quiet but intense. Her entire body locked down, her legs squeezing me. I bit my lip and kept thrusting, kept pushing for more, to give her enough. Teasing every second of pleasure from her body. I was still hard, still wanting, but this was about her needs. This was all about Jane.

When her body relaxed and her gorgeous eyes met mine again, I leaned in to give her the softest kiss I knew how to give. She kissed me back, still desperate. Still clinging to me. Like a safety net of some sort.

"What can I do?" I asked quietly, my heart breaking and my rage at whoever had her so afraid boiling over.

She shook her head, a sad sort of look in her eyes. "Nothing. There's nothing anyone can do."

"Jane, I—"

"I should get cleaned up," she said, looking to the ground as she pushed me away. I stepped back, giving her room, letting her drop her legs and put space between us. Hating every inch of it, though.

"I... Okay," I said uncertainly. Something had changed. She was shuttered off again, putting more than just physical space between us. "Jane, wait. What's going on?"

She moved to the counter, keeping her back to me. "I have to shower. Mick is going to need me to leave soon, and I can't go like this."

I walked up behind her, not touching, just letting her know I was there. "Like what?"

"Smelling like you."

My breath shot out of me as if I'd been punched, and I suppose I had. Jane had thrown a good blow, knocking me down with only a few words.

"So you can't let anyone know I was near you."

She spun, her eyes wide. "I can't let anyone know we just did...that."

"That?" I asked, cocking my head.

She leaned closer, whispering in my ear. "They'll smell me. They'll smell how aroused you made me."

"I like you aroused."

She snorted a sad little laugh before pushing off the counter. "I have to go. I'm sorry I can't stay to—" She waved her hand in the direction of my crotch where my hard cock had tented my shorts.

I shrugged one shoulder. "You needed me, so I gave of myself. There's no reciprocity required."

She paused, rocking slightly as if she were deciding whether to run or fight. Then she hopped forward and hugged me.

"I wish I could choose," she murmured into my neck.

"Choose what?"

"Anything. Everything." She shook her head and backed away. "I have to go."

I watched her leave, wishing I could understand what the hell had just happened. Desperate to protect her from whatever had scared her.

How do you kill a shifter?

"Jane."

She spun at my sharp tone, her eyes wide.

"Wolf shifters can't regenerate without blood. Other shifters will usually go for a punch to the chest because we're strong enough to stop their hearts, but humans aren't. Go for sharp things and arteries."

She nodded, her eyes wary. Cautious. "What about...other shifters?"

Fuck. Other shifters meant she wasn't dealing with what she was familiar with, which was probably why she was asking in the first place. "Each breed is a little different."

She paused, looking away, fidgeting with her coat. But then she took a deep breath, and she looked me dead in the eye.

"What about dragons?"

I took a step back, my brow coming down. "Are you... Is there another—"

"How do you kill a dragon shifter, Piers?" The use of my real name didn't escape me, nor did the haunted look in her eyes. *Double fuck.*

I nodded once and swallowed hard, wishing more than ever that she'd just tell me. Knowing she needed my help. That I had to tell her the truth.

"Fire."

She cocked her head, looking completely lost. "But...you can *breathe* fire."

"Some of us. But remember how I told you about seeing heat? When I'm in dragon form, I can see all the soft spots in a dragon's scales. See where to direct my flames just as they can see mine." I shrugged. "Fire is almost always our undoing."

For a moment, barely a second, she seemed excited. But then she practically collapsed in on herself. "Humans can't breathe fire."

"No, but you have weapons. Flamethrowers, torches... Hell, a Zippo and some hair spray would work. Put flame in the air, and we'll run." I ached to touch her, inching closer without thinking about it, afraid for her. "Fire is what scares us. If we can't control it, we fear it. It's instinct."

Jane stared, the wheels in her head almost visible through her big, dark eyes. Without preamble, she rushed into my arms and kissed me, a desperation on her lips that nearly made me grab her up and fly off with her. Made me want to protect her. Made me ready to die for her.

"Thank you," she said, and then she was gone.

EIGHT

Jane

As I'd done too many times before, I stumbled out of the cave like a woman running from a monster. Which, technically, I was. This time, though, I was also holding my arm. The bones didn't seem to be broken, but the bleeding was excessive. I'd need to bandage the cut and soon. Mick still hadn't said a word about how Saern had manhandled me, hadn't even attempted to help me while that...thing held me against my will and rubbed himself all over me. I was disgusted, angry, hurt, but most of all, fucking done.

"You have to do something."

Mick grunted but refused to look at me. He'd been slowly growing more agitated as I'd been voicing my fears and complaints. I don't think he liked my not bowing to his every whim, but I wasn't backing down this time. Saern could not be controlled. He was playing Mick like a fiddle, but the man was too stubborn and arrogant to see it. Unfortunately, I was the one stuck in the middle between the wolf and the dragon, with the dragon having a considerable size advantage. It wouldn't be long before Saern took what he wanted from me, and I wasn't going to stand around and let that happen.

Mick drove us back to The Pack House, silent the whole way. I didn't initiate conversation either, though. I was too tired, too worn down from a week's worth of being harassed and threatened, of being terrified of what might happen the next time I had to walk into that cave, to focus on anything else.

Except Piers.

It'd been two days since our...event in the exam room. Two days of me obsessing over him, wondering what was happening, wishing I could run to him for guidance. Wishing I could make a choice to be with him. Saern assumed he could take my choices away from me just as Mick had been doing for years. But while Mick would rule my life, I knew Saern would end it. I couldn't have that. I needed to keep my dad safe, and I wanted to spend more time with him. Plus I had another dragon stealing my attention away from my wretched life. For once, I hoped that maybe, just maybe, I had a chance at something outside The Pack House. Doubtful, but there was a chance. A tiny one. Minuscule even.

"We'll be bringing Saern to The Pack House tomorrow," Mick said as he parked his truck behind the building.

I whipped around in my seat, that tiny bit of hope extinguished with a single sentence. "You're insane."

Mick growled, threatening me with his wolfishness, something I was beginning to fear less and less. "I've put up with your attitude regarding Saern for too long, girl. He *will* be coming to The Pack House and fighting. I *will* have two dragon shifters in the ring."

I hopped out of the car and slammed the door. "He doesn't have control of his dragon, Mick. You can't just toss him to the wolves while you've got the pheromones in the building pumped as high as they are and not expect him to lose control."

"The wolves will be fine." Mick huffed and strode to the door. "Brush up on your dragon physiology, though. I have a feeling Saern might do some serious damage to Tidal. At least, I hope he does."

I froze, my heart dropping. "You're going to let Saern kill him?"

Mick laughed. "Not kill, child. Just knock him down a peg or two. The humans love a good falling-from-grace story. Tidal's fall will bring more bettors into the crowd, which means more money. And money solves everything."

"You're an idiot." I clenched my hands in my hair, pulling. This was a mess—an absolute mess—and it was only going to get worse.

"Saern will be fine," Mick said, almost to himself. "He made a deal with me. If he doesn't honor that, or if he steps out of line, well...we have firepower."

I shook my head and sighed. Firepower. Right. "Get a flare gun."

"What?"

"All the bullets in the world won't stop him. Find a flare gun and keep it on you."

Mick didn't answer. Instead, he turned and headed for the entrance to The Pack House. The door slammed behind him, the sound practically reverberating in my chest. He was insane. There was no way bringing Saern into the ring would solve anything, let alone letting him fight. I'd been slowly healing his wing, taking my time and not advancing his care to keep him out of here. But, apparently, my time was up. As was Tidal's.

Piers. His name is Piers.

I shivered as the reality of the situation wove through me. Piers and Saern were going to fight, and I couldn't stop it. If I opened my mouth, my father died. If I didn't, Piers likely would. I was trapped.

Tomorrow would be bad. No, horrible. Tomorrow could very well be the worst day of my career at The Pack House, and I didn't want to participate. I wanted to run. But that would mean leaving my father behind for Mick to do with as he pleased, and I couldn't have that. It would also mean leaving Piers here to fight without his knowing what was coming, something else I refused to do. The wily dragon had gotten under my skin, and I had feelings for him. Deep feelings. More-than-friend type feelings.

"Shit." I kicked the ground, letting my thoughts spin, trying to work out a plan. Mick's moratorium on telling the truth was my Achilles's heel. If I told and he found out, he'd kill Piers. Or worse, my dad. If I didn't tell, Saern would kill Piers. Either way, I was pretty sure I was dead—whether from a wolf or a crazed dragon was yet to be determined. Not that Piers' dragon was that much safer. Though I hadn't seen him yet. Hadn't been introduced to his other side. He may not be as scary as Saern, or he may have terrified me. Guess I'd never find out.

I kicked the ground again. Frustrated and completely unsure of what to do.

"What'd that dirt ever do to you?"

I was in motion before I could blink, racing toward the man I'd been craving. Piers stood twenty feet away, tall and dark and so damned perfect, I couldn't resist any longer. I never even slowed, simply ran right into him. Confident he'd catch me.

And catch me he did.

His hands slid immediately to my ass, holding me up as I jumped at him. As I once again wrapped my legs around his hips. My lips met his in a fiery kiss. Teeth and tongues mashed, hands slid under clothes, and within seconds, I found myself with my back against a tree and a very hard Piers between my knees.

"Jane, what—"

"Please," I hissed, biting his neck, giving in to the desire taking me over. "Please just be with me. Want me."

"Fuck, Doc." Piers growled and pressed his arousal against me, making me shiver. "I want you. Of course I fucking want you."

"Then take me."

Piers didn't wait for more. He raced through the trees, carrying me deeper into the forest and away from The Pack House. When he found what must have been the perfect spot for him to hide us, he pushed me up against a tree trunk and attacked. He had my pants undone and around my ankles in a breath, had my panties torn off in the next. I rocked and kissed and bit, trying to get closer, trying to take a part of him into me. Wanting to get all of him.

With one hand under my ass, he lifted me, his other fumbling with his shorts. Pushing them down his legs. His skin was cold but warming quickly, his movements jerky and rushed. But then he was free, and skin met skin. Wet and swollen against hard and velvety. I rocked my hips against him, cursing under my breath. Spreading my wetness from base to tip.

"Fuck, Doc. You sure?" His words came out on gasps, his desire plain. His lust a tangible thing. I nodded and pulled him closer with my ankles. Wiggling impatiently as I tried to line us up. Thankfully, Piers wasn't a patient man. He reached down and placed the head of his dick at my entrance, rubbing it back and forth just twice before he thrust up.

I nearly screamed.

The stretch of him inside me was more than I had imagined. And I *had* imagined this. In the dark of my room at night, when I was all alone and wanting. With my hand between my legs and my face pressed into the pillow to stay quiet. I'd imagined it plenty. But my imagination had been lacking.

"That's it," Piers said, hissing his words, moving his hips into mine. "Take it. Every inch."

My head fell back against the tree, my hand grasping at his shoulder. He was so deep. So thick and hard inside of me. Stretching me in ways no other lover ever had. I loved it. I needed more.

"Harder," I begged, yanking on his hair. "Fuck, Piers. Make me come."

"Yes." His word was a solid hiss, his movements speeding up as he responded. He moved his arms underneath my thighs, lifting me higher, spreading me wider.

"Look at me, Jane."

I met his heated gaze, my eyes half-lidded. I was so close. So ready to come. It wouldn't take much. Not long.

"I know, Jane. I know you're close. But trust me, okay? I want to make it so good for you. Will you let me?"

I nodded, unable to speak. Too strung out on the feel of him sliding in and out to focus on silly things like words. He pressed into me harder, keeping his eyes on mine, lifting me with each slide out. The rhythm was hypnotizing, the movements more extended and slow. He kept me right on the edge, kept teasing me with his hands on my ass and the pressure of his body rubbing against my clit.

"Piers," I whispered, biting him on the shoulder. I couldn't keep my teeth off his skin, couldn't resist egging him on. I was a writhing, desperate mess, needing him to just fucking pound me again. He seemed to understand my desires. With a grunt, he jerked forward, slamming into me, pulling me down with his hands on my waist. And my God, was it good. The pressure built, the tingling inside of me growing with every rock. With every curse. With every wet slap.

"I want to see you come, Doc. I want to feel you squeeze my cock. C'mon, love. Let me see it." His deep voice only accented his words. Making me crave them. Making me feel them. I wrapped one arm around his neck, the other dangling as my legs began to shake. As my entire world dropped to a pinpoint I could no longer avoid. Until I bit down hard on Piers' neck in a moment of complete abandon, breaking the skin. Sending shocks and sparks all through my body. I came with a shout, feeling something more than sexual satiation rocking my body. Feeling a complete bond with the man I was wrapped around, a closeness. Something I'd never experienced before.

Piers bucked and growled, practically shaking the tree with the force of his thrusts. Chasing his own bliss in a wild sort of way as I shuddered from mine. He found it moments later, pressing deeper and groaning out his pleasure. I loved watching him come, seeing the way his eyes closed and his lips pulled back in what looked almost like a snarl. Knowing I gave him that. That I was the reason for his release.

But reality didn't let me out of her claws for long. As our bodies cooled, as Piers leaned against me, holding me, supporting me, my situation stole my good mood. There were too many things wrong to truly enjoy the one right thing I'd found.

Hating myself for what I knew I needed to do, I pushed on Piers' shoulder. He backed up, and I wiggled out of his hold. It was time to stand on my own two feet again. To be alone.

"You should get back before they figure out you're outside." I bent to pull up my pants.

Piers chuckled as he grabbed me and lifted me off the ground. "Not that I don't love the fact that you're coming around to my charms, but what was that about? And what's with the kiss-off?"

I shrugged, avoiding his eyes. "We both know this can't be anything."

"Wow," Piers said, the jovial tone in his voice making me

look up. "You're a really bad liar. Quit trying, Doc. It won't work."

I tried to hold firm, but he was right. I was lying, to him and myself. And I didn't want to do that.

"Oh God, that was so bad, wasn't it?" I shook my head, snuggling into his chest. Trying to steal a few more moments as I hid my embarrassment. "It's been a long week, and I don't know what to do."

He hummed and held me tighter. "Can I help?"

I was about to say no when an idea struck me. I might not be able to save everyone, but I could try to save him. Perhaps that would be my penance for working with Mick for so long. Save the dragon, and Mick wouldn't be able to put on his fight. Saern would still need to be dealt with, but Piers would be safe.

I dropped back to the ground and tugged Piers by the hand. He stumbled, yanking up his shorts as he tried to follow.

"Where are we going, Doc?"

I ducked under some low branches, looking back to make sure he was keeping up. "You asked if you can help."

"Yeah?"

"Well, you can't really, but your dragon may be able to."

He stopped, pulling me to a stop as well. Forcing me to turn toward him. "You need my dragon?"

I nodded and held out my arm. The injured one. The one with a gash I knew he might recognize the origins of.

His face turned angry, his eyes cold. "Where'd you get that cut?"

I ran my fingers over the slice on my arm. "I'm not allowed to say."

He huffed, a small growl building in his chest. "Doc—"

"I can't tell you." I walked into him and rose on the balls of my feet so I could whisper in his ear as he growled louder. "I can't *tell* you, but your dragon would know. He needs to know. He needs to figure this out so he can leave."

"Leave?" Piers stared at me for a long moment. The heavy darkness around us gave me no indication of his expression, but I knew he'd listen. Somehow, I understood that he would do anything I asked. And right in that moment, I was going to ask him to fly away. To leave. To disappear so Mick and Saern could never find him.

I was going to save him.

Without a word, Piers grabbed my hand this time and dragged me deeper into the woods. His steps were sure, but unlike Mick, he kept a careful hold on me so I didn't stumble. It was a quiet moment of seeing what I wanted, wishing for it. Knowing I couldn't have it.

When we reached the riverbank, I backed away from him. Giving him room, even though I knew from Saern that he wouldn't really need it.

"Go."

Piers cocked his head. "Go?"

I waved my hands and huffed. "Do your thing. Strip. Shift. Bring out the beast."

He raised an eyebrow. "You want me naked."

"Yes."

"I mean, I'd happily get naked for you anytime, Doc. But I don't need to."

"It's going to be hard to explain why you're walking around the training area naked, don't you think?"

"Not really," he replied with a chuckle. "But I won't go back in there naked. I'll still be clothed."

I tried to make sense of his words, but I couldn't. Wolves shifted without their clothes, ending up naked at times. Saern never seemed to wear any clothes, not even the ones Mick brought him. How was Piers not going to be naked?

"Wait...what?"

Piers stepped closer. "My clothes shift with me."

"No, they don't."

Without answering, Piers shifted. A huge, dark dragon appeared where once there was a man. I screamed and stumbled back, my chest tight. But the image melted. It was only there for the briefest of moments before he shifted back human. And fully clothed.

It took me a few moments to catch my breath enough to speak again, but when I was ready, I asked the only question on my mind. "How'd you do that?"

He shrugged. "Dragon magic, I guess."

"Wolves can't do that."

"Nope."

I shook my head, going over every detail of my time with Saern. "But...he's been naked."

Piers growled sharply, the sound silencing the forest around us. "Who?"

And wasn't that the question of the hour? "I can't tell you."

"But my dragon will know?"

"Sort of."

"Then I'll shift and stay that way for a minute." He paused, watching me with nervous eyes. "Don't be afraid, okay? He cares for you as much as I do. He won't hurt you."

He won't hurt you. Don't run. I swallowed back the fear Saern had taught me and nodded. I knew Piers wasn't Saern, but I was unable to break them apart in my mind. Unable to see one without thinking of the other. They were both dragon shifters. Both unknown to me. Both very possibly dangerous. Still, I trusted Piers. If he said his dragon wouldn't hurt me, I believed him.

"Okay." I backed up another step. Ready. Mostly.

"Okay." With a grin, he shifted again, this time immediately settling down on the ground and watching me with dark, reptilian eyes. A dragon lying on the forest floor like a puppy wasn't nearly as scary as one lording over you, I found. I stepped closer, looking him over. Inspecting for a moment. His scales were a deep red fading to an orange. Like a living, breathing sunset. His head and wings were shaped differently from Saern's, the covering over his wings looking far less leathery. He was a different animal, a different breed perhaps. And he didn't scare me.

"Beautiful," I whispered as I took a step closer. He didn't move, didn't even seem to breathe. I approached cautiously, just in case. My experiences with Saern made me jumpy, but I knew Piers wouldn't hurt me. And I was growing more comfortable with that knowledge, even when he was in this form.

When I was close enough to touch, I lifted my hand. Delicately, carefully, I placed my fingers against his nose. He finally blew out a breath and inhaled. Almost as if he'd been as afraid of me as I'd been afraid of him. I smiled at the thought.

"Piers." I twisted my arm, letting him see the gash there. Knowing it was time. "You need to know so you can leave. Tonight. There's no time left."

His dark eyes held mine, almost as if he was trying to refuse me. But he had to. I pushed my arm forward, whispering a quiet, *please.* His tongue flicked out over my arm, particularly around my cut. The sight of it didn't scare me, a fact that made this moment even more bittersweet. But the rumble that came from him had me taking a step back. He shook his head, running his nose all over me, flicking his tongue out to taste the air. All the while, his growl grew louder. Stronger. More dangerous.

He knew.

Piers shifted without warning. One second, I was watching an angry dragon, the next, a furious Piers stood before me, clutching my arm.

"A dragon bit you?" He glared at me, but I didn't say a word. Just watched him, hoping he'd get it. That he'd realize what was happening.

"That's where you've been going with Mick. There's a dragon in the area." He huffed and ran a hand through his dark hair. "I was raised in a wolf pack, Doc. I was brought up to be more human. Dragons...they're not. At all. Do you realize how dangerous dragons can be?"

I nodded. There was no need for an explanation. No requirement for more words. This was it. I was about to send Piers away to safety. Did I know how dangerous dragons could be? Yes. Totally. I had one in my life that I *thought* was going to kill me—and one I *knew* would when he took my heart with him.

"Please, go." My whispered words wobbled, my throat tight.

Piers shook his head, looking from my eyes to the gash and back. His brow heavy across his eyes. "Are you in danger right now?"

"You're in more danger. You have to go."

Piers sighed. "Okay, fine. We can take off and head north. I can find a place for us in New England, maybe."

I shook my head, tears welling in my eyes. "You have to go."

"Jane, dragons are dangerous. If he's had his teeth in you, it's doubly so. There's a marking smell coming from the bite. He's claimed you as his mate."

I nodded, freely crying.

Piers' eyes widened, his face crumpling into a look of pain like I'd never seen from him before. "Do you want him?"

I choked on a sarcastic laugh. "God, no."

"Good. That's good." He paced a few steps, obviously irritated. "What *do* you want, Doc?"

Without thought or care, I answered the only way I could. "I want you. I want to choose who I care about, and that's you."

"Oh, thank fuck." Piers grabbed me in a brutal hug, yanking me off the ground. "You're my mate, Jane. My dragon wants you, I want you...but it's your choice."

I ran my fingers through his hair, pulling him in for a kiss. Stealing one more moment. "I choose you."

"Then we need to go."

A sob escaped me as my heart shattered. "No. We can't."

"Doc, he won't give up on you now that he's claimed you. You think wolves can be territorial when it comes to their mates, you haven't seen anything. He'll destroy this whole mountain."

"I know. But I can't go. You have to leave without me."

He recoiled as if I'd hit him. "I'm not leaving you behind."

"You have to," I whispered. "The dragon—he's crazy. There's no stopping him. And Mick is bringing him here tomorrow to set up a fight between the two of you. He'll kill you."

"No, he won't." He paced, practically brushing against me as he walked past again and again. "You're my mate, Jane. My heart."

"I know." The tears were falling harder, the burn in my eyes too painful to see past. "But Mick wants two dragons in the ring, and he won't stop until he gets it."

"Fuck Mick and what he wants. Let me take you out of here. We can run someplace where this dragon won't find us. I'll keep you safe. I promise."

"He has my father."

Piers froze, his eyes wide. "What?"

"My dad knew Mick for years. They were friends, but Mick never told him about his wolf side. He told me when I was accepted into medical school. Said he would pay for my education if I kept his secret and learned to treat his kind. And I did, for years. But one day, Mick and I were arguing at his house about the ethics of using mating pheromones without telling those exposed. I should have known it then, but I didn't put two and two together. I didn't know his plans."

"Jane—"

"Mick was really angry because I kept shooting down his ideas with arguments about ethics, and my dad showed up just as he shifted. He had a heart attack, and the second one caused two strokes. He's in a nursing home nearby. I was a mess of fear and guilt when everything happened, and I still trusted Mick to care for his friend. He promised me he'd take care of everything." Jane paused, shaking her head and sobbing into her hands. "I signed over my rights as my dad's only living relative. Mick has the power of attorney for his estate and makes all his medical decisions. He lets me visit once every two weeks, but that's it. He holds my father over my head, guilting me into staying with him. I can't move my dad without him finding out, and he'd never let my dad go, so I can't leave."

Piers sighed, looking up at the sky for a long moment. "If you stay, then I stay. I'm *not* leaving you behind."

I grabbed his arm and tugged, desperation making me bold. "If you stay, Saern will kill you. There's nothing human about him anymore. He's all beast, all animal. And as strong as you are, I'm not sure you would walk out of the ring in a fight against him."

Piers stood stock-still, staring down at me. But I could see the thoughts flashing in his eyes; I knew he was thinking things over.

"So Mick's bringing this dragon tomorrow?"

I nodded.

Piers licked his lips. "Then I've got a little less than twenty-four hours."

"Good," I said, sagging in relief. One down. Piers would be safe from Saern.

"I'm going to need your help with this, though."

"For what?"

"To break your father out of the nursing home."

I blinked. Blinked again. My brain not able to form words for what had to be a solid minute. "You can't. Mick won't let you take him."

He shrugged. "So I'll kill Mick."

NINE

Piers

Walking away from Jane so we could sneak back into The Pack House was one of the hardest things I'd ever had to do. I wanted her safe, I wanted to protect her, I wanted her by my side. But that wasn't possible yet. Not until I made my plan happen. Jane was against me killing Mick, a fact that didn't surprise me in the least, but I couldn't see another way around it. Mick had to go so Jane and her dad could be safe. Dragons dealt in death every day. This was a no-brainer.

Speaking of dragons...*shit*. A dragon in the area was bad news; a dragon having taken a bite out of Jane to claim her as his mate was the worst news possible. He wouldn't hurt her intentionally, but if she refused him, he'd probably lash out. Dragons weren't known for their patience or calm demeanors. We were killers, beasts of the skies, and we took what we wanted when we wanted it. I had those same instincts, but I'd been taught to control them. To let my human side lead. This fucker hadn't, and that made me want to find him and burn him down for daring to think of Jane as an object he could claim ownership over. I'd have to deal with him, too.

I managed to avoid running into another person until I was literally outside my bedroom door. That's when my luck ran out. Beadan turned the corner just as my hand landed on the knob. Normally, I would have called out a greeting, but I knew I still smelled like Jane. Like our coupling. And I knew Beadan would be able to detect it without much effort.

The two of us locked eyes for the briefest of moments. He raised his hand, looking as if he was going to say something. But his smile faltered as he sniffed, his brow furrowing. He sniffed a second time, and my stomach plummeted. Fucking wolves and their noses.

Beadan growled as if I'd fucked his sister or something. "Mick's gonna kill you."

I stood taller, not caring what Mick might do. "She's my mate."

"I thought you dragons didn't mate." His honest curiosity made me pause. Dragon lore was sparse and purposely seeded with untruths. But wolf lore was well-known. They had fated mates, their love was practically instant, and they defended those bonds to the death. Something I could understand. Something he and I probably had in common.

"Yeah, well, we do. We just get to choose our mates instead of dealing with what fate gives us." I stood taller, my chin up and my gaze hard. "And my dragon and I choose Jane."

He shrugged, huffing a sarcastic laugh. "Probably not going to matter much to Mick."

"She chooses us, too."

Beadan paused, staring into my eyes, not blinking. Weighing my words carefully. I held his gaze, reinforcing my truth.

A smile grew across his face, one filled with a happiness I had never seen from him. "Well, then, congrats, man. I'm happy you two found each other. She's always been kind to me."

"She is kind—and also tough as nails." I turned the knob, ready to escape, but I could never forget where I was or how this place worked. Especially not who was in charge. "Please don't say anything. We need to figure out what to do before we can really be together."

Beadan nodded, still smiling. "No worries, though you'd better hit the showers and quick. We've got a meeting in the arena in ten."

A trickle of fear weaved its way around my spine. "Meeting? For what?"

"New fighter." He shrugged, casual. Not knowing the full story yet. But he would. There was no way this meeting was about just another fighter.

"Who called the meeting?" I asked, squeezing the door handle until I felt the metal ball pop.

"Fuck if I know. I'm just the messenger."

He strolled down the hallway, his steps relaxed. A man without a care in the world, heading off to do what his bosses told him to. I envied him that.

"Spray yourself with the disinfectant shit they keep in the cleaning closet before you shower," he hollered over his shoulder. "It'll help hide the smell."

And then he was gone. I hurried into my room to grab fresh clothes and strip out of my current ones. No sense risking anyone smelling Doc on me after the shower. Within eight minutes, I was sprayed, showered, and basically free of all memories of my time with Jane. Something that made both my dragon and me unhappy. I wanted to bask in her scent, not wash it away.

"Humans are fickle," Mick called to the crowd of fighters and trainers spread out across the bleacher benches as I hurried into the arena. "They want rougher fights, more action, always needing the next great thing. Our own Tidal has brought in tremendous revenue due to his overwhelming fighting style, but even that seems to have slackened. We must invigorate the spectators. And I think I've figured out how."

Jane wasn't with him, a fact I found troubling. I searched the crowd for her to no avail. Only the other fighters and the training staff were present. Not even the two owners who partnered with Mick were there. This was his show, his decision. One I'd make sure he regretted.

Mick's eyes met mine for the briefest of moments, his smile making my blood run colder. "If I could get the good doctor to bring out our latest addition..."

I growled as Jane walked out from the back hallway with a man at her side. Her body looked stiff, her posture screaming how uncomfortable she felt. He, on the other hand, strolled in as if he owned the place. As if he weren't walking into a room filled with predators. And that told me all I needed to know. This was the other dragon shifter Mick had found. His dark jeans and black T-shirt outlined his muscled form, more bulky than lithe. He'd be a larger dragon than mine when he shifted, a different breed perhaps. There were many of us across the lands, some more dangerous than others. But really, that didn't matter. If he put a hand on my mate, he was dead. I'd make sure of it, no matter how big he was.

Jane tried to step away from the man, but he called her back. Wagging a finger in her face as if she were a naughty child. I rubbed my hand over my arm as my scales appeared, my dragon wanting to come out to defend our mate. But I couldn't—not yet. Jane needed our mating to be kept secret until we dealt with her father. Which meant I needed to stay calm.

"Meet our newest fighter, Midnight." Mick held one hand out in the direction of the man. The crowd clapped halfheartedly in response as Midnight slinked into the ring, the other fighters not impressed. "All you wolves can sit back and relax, though. Midnight will be paired with Tidal for his first fight."

Jane caught my stare, her eyes worried. Mick, meanwhile, was still smiling like a predator. Thinking he'd gotten one over on me. That he'd bested a dragon. A fact that almost made me laugh.

If I didn't get the chance, Midnight would certainly prove to him how wrong he was.

"I hope you've been training hard, Tidal." Mick moved to the side, giving the other dragon shifter a straight eyeline to me. "You've beaten all my wolves, but I'm not sure how you'll do against one of your own."

Midnight's eyes met mine, and my dragon roared. Motherfucker, Mick really was stupid enough to bring him into a warehouse full of wolf shifters. That was like bringing a wild animal into a preschool. None of these shifters had any idea how dangerous the man standing next to my mate was.

But I did, and I didn't like it.

I stood, ready to race down there, but the man called Midnight cocked his head. Watching me. Edging closer to Jane. Staring me down as he extended his arm. At first, I wasn't sure what he was doing, but then I saw Jane jump and I reacted on instinct. I was in the ring in a blink, the world a rainbow as my eyesight sharpened into my dragon sight.

"If you want to keep that hand, you'll take it off her ass."

Midnight smirked. "You think you can best me, tadpole? I'm not like these puppies you've been fighting."

I moved closer, boxing him in, dropping my voice so he'd hear the threat. "I know exactly what you're like."

"I doubt that," he hissed, leaning right into my space. He was a good thirty pounds heavier than I was but a few inches shorter. Not that height and weight would matter much if he shifted. And he would. Dragons—true dragons raised in the conclaves—were unable to stay human for long. They were too beastly, too beholden to their inner animals. Too out of control to go unnoticed in human society.

Keeping my eyes on his, refusing to let that particular challenge drop, I reached for Jane's hand. She gave it to me with ease, gripping my fingers with her own. My lips turned up at one corner as Midnight's arrogant mask cracked, a smirk fighting its way free. Midnight's eye twitched, and his jaw clamped tighter. Trying to control his instinctual reaction. This was a silent war for Jane, but where Midnight would probably just take her and demand she obey as his animal side wanted him to do, I was more human. I gave her the choice—come with me or not; it was up to her. And she came, so I pulled her gently behind me, using my body to shield hers. Protecting what I saw as mine. What I knew Midnight would want to take away from me.

"You'll regret that," he said with a growl.

"She chooses me."

He laughed, a growly rumble that sounded all wrong. "Silly child. You think I care what she chooses?"

"Oh, I know you don't care." I grinned as he smirked, letting him think he won. But then, "And that's why you'll never have her. Because you thought you could rule her. But Jane's her own person, and you can never truly enjoy her body without allowing her to decide when to give it to you."

I leaned forward, murmuring close to his ear. "And she's already given it to me. I've got the bite mark to prove it."

Midnight hissed, looking like a man about to lose control of his rage. I pushed Jane farther back, wanting her out of the way in case he shifted. In case he sparked up.

In case he tried to burn this place down.

"Now, now," Mick interrupted, stepping between us. Oblivious to the danger at his back. "Let's keep things civil. You can have your dick-measuring contest in the ring tomorrow night."

"Don't think so," I said, keeping my eyes on Midnight's. His smirk had kicked up, had turned into an almost mad grin. His eyes were dark, his pupils long and slitlike. No longer human eyes. He was losing control.

As scales appeared along Midnight's hairline, I pushed Jane back farther, wanting to tell her to run. But I couldn't look away from the other dragon. One second of distraction, and he'd be on me. Or worse, be on Jane.

Midnight must have noticed my move to protect Jane because his smile dimmed, his lip curling. "You'll really regret *that*."

Mick chuckled, though his bravado seemed quieter, less certain. "Gentlemen, I'm going to ask you to please separate and sit down."

"No," Midnight said, not even looking his way. "We are not your paltry wolves. We do not bow to your timing and rules. Do we, child?"

When I didn't answer him directly, Midnight leaned forward, hissing as he murmured to me just loud enough for Mick to hear. "I can smell you on her, tadpole. But it doesn't matter. She's my mate. My prize. I claimed her first—and she's delicious."

TEN

I stumbled back as Piers roared. Whatever Saern said had upset him to the point of losing control. Without a second's hesitation, Piers lunged for Saern, the two connecting in a flurry of fists and snarls. Six trainers rushed into the ring, all diving at the fighting pair. I watched in horror, wishing I could do something. Wishing I had been able to convince Piers to leave while we were still out by the river. I hadn't expected Mick to bring Saern tonight, but it didn't surprise me. Mick was looking to rile these two up so he could get a good fight out of them. Watching them wrestle on the mats, they certainly looked riled.

It took multiple tries and more than a few knocks to the wrong people, but the trainers were finally able to pull the two dragon shifters apart.

"Enough," Mick yelled once the trainers had done the dirty work. "You two should be saving that shit for fight night."

Saern smirked at Piers, his eyes positively black. "That's right. You young ones are too impulsive. Perhaps you need a little time-out to learn your place."

"I know my place, fucker. It's you who should worry."

Saern's arrogant look faltered, but only for a second. He quickly regained his attitude before turning to Mick and holding up a bloodied arm.

"I do believe I need medical attention."

Mick glanced at me, his eyes hard. "Take care of him, Jane. I need to speak with Tidal."

I jumped as Saern approached me, a move that had Piers yowling low and throaty. Two trainers grabbed his arms and another two jumped in front of him, holding him back. Restraining him as he tried to follow us. Something that broke my heart to see.

"You know, Tidal," Mick said, sounding too casual for my liking. "I've known Jane since she was a baby. In fact, I'm very involved with her family. Her father, particularly."

My stomach dropped with his threat. Piers must have heard it, too. He stopped fighting, his eyes locked on mine.

I nodded once, trying to calm my fired-up dragon even though we both had to know this was a bad idea. "I'll be back in five minutes."

"Three." Tidal gave Saern a glare. "Any longer, and I'm coming after you."

"I said go, Jane." Mick pointed toward the medical wing. My fear was a lead ball in my gut, but I had no choice. Mick had moved up his plan, so we were out of time. There would be no rescuing of my dad or running before the shit hit the fan. There was only this...doing what I was told to keep the people I cared about alive.

"You're an idiot to egg him on." I yanked my arm away when Saern reached for it, drawing a growl from him.

"Who, your little tadpole? The kid needs to learn his place."

I huffed. "I think it's you who needs a few lessons."

He didn't say another word as he followed me down the

hall. He didn't need to once we reached the exam room. His palm connecting with my face said more than words ever could.

I fell back, hitting my head on the exam table as I crumpled to the floor. The room spun, the ceiling refusing to stay in focus. I swallowed and tried to roll to a less vulnerable position, but my vision wobbled and left me unsure of which way was up.

"Jane, Jane, Jane." Saern stepped carefully around me, blocking the light, making me go blind in the shadows. "I thought I was clear when I told you that you were my mate."

He kicked my legs, forcing me to my side. My head spun again and my stomach revolted at the movement, but Piers' words kept running through my head. His advice on how to kill a dragon.

Put flame in the air, and we'll run.

If I could just get to the cabinets...

"Well?" Saern kicked me again, this time in the hip. "Was I or was I not clear?"

"Yes," I cried, closing my eyes against the pain. "You were clear."

"Then why would you spread your legs for that child when what's between them is rightfully mine?"

I huffed a pained laugh, inching my way back. Trying to look as if I was moving *away* from him, when truly, I was moving *toward* something else. Something I needed. Something that would make him run.

Saern growled and threw a metal tray across the room. "Answer me, human."

I managed to slide a few more inches. "No part of me is yours."

"Ja-ane," he said in a singsong way, the warning clear in his voice.

But I was done cowering for him. I was done thinking I had

no choice. I was simply done. "You can't claim someone who's chosen someone else."

Saern chuckled. "Of course I can."

My hand touched the bottom of the cabinet as he finished his sentence. I had one second of relief, one moment of thinking I might get out of this. But then Saern smiled, and my blood turned to ice.

"I'll show you."

His teeth in my neck made the blackness roll over me like a tide, and I fell to my side underneath the weight of him, convulsing and screaming as a burn unlike anything I'd ever experienced spread through my body.

ELEVEN

Piers

I fought against the hold the trainers had on me. I may have needed to wait for one hundred and fifty-six more seconds before I chased Jane down, but that didn't mean I had to put up with them touching me. Besides, my dragon was ready to explode out of me, and men clutching to keep me contained wasn't going to help that situation. I could feel the danger in the air, sense it almost like something physical and solid. Jane shouldn't have gone anywhere without me. I should have just killed Mick and gone for the throat of this Midnight-Saern dragon. Not being at her side was wrong—so very wrong—and every second I waited out my promise to her made my rage intensify.

"Relax, Tidal." Mick leaned against the side of the ring and watched me with disdain. "Doctor Jane's been visiting with Saern in his cave for weeks. She knows exactly how to handle him."

The innuendo laced through his voice stabbed a place deep

inside me, one that had my dragon thrashing to break free. To rescue his mate.

"One hundred and forty-six seconds left," I said, a definite growl to my voice.

Mick just smirked. "Perhaps she wants to be with Saern. Have you thought about that?"

"One hundred and thirty-nine." I brushed past the trainers and paced the edge of the ring, still counting. I knew Jane, and I'd seen her with Saern. She was afraid of him. He could claim her as his mate, but she wasn't a willing participant in that. I'd never let someone take her without her consent. Even if she were just Doc Jane and not *my* Jane, I'd have fought for her for no reason other than it was the right thing to do. Mick couldn't beat Saern; no wolf shifter could. Not without knowing our secrets. They were playing with fire —literally—and I wasn't about to let Jane be their collateral damage.

"Sit down, son," Mick barked. Laudon grabbed my arm and jumped in front of me, his eyes pleading. But there was no swaying me. Jane needed help, and I was done fucking around.

One hundred seconds too long.

"For your sake, let me go. I don't want to injure you," I hissed, showing him the modicum of respect he'd earned. Laudon watched me for a long moment, weighing his options, then let me go and took a step away. That was all the space I needed. I hopped past two trainers with ease, kicking a third in the knee when he tried to keep me from getting to the edge. One of Mick's goons raced toward me just as I reached the ropes, but Beadan rushed into the ring and caught him around the neck, tossing him to the floor with ease.

"Go get her," Beadan said, looking fierce and ready to back me up. I nodded once, worry becoming a heavy blanket around my shoulders. The need to blast through the crowd of wolf shifters between Jane and me growing with every passing second.

Eighty-five seconds too long.

And then there was Mick. "I said sit, reptile."

I jerked to a stop, my eyes locked on Mick's. The formation of scales along my hairline and my hands tickled, but I welcomed them. I welcomed my dragon this time.

"I'm not your son, and I'm not a reptile," I said, keeping my voice low and controlled. "My father was a dragon clan leader, a man of strength and honor. He left his world behind to be with my mother in an act of bravery I am only now truly understanding."

My wings unfurled, ripping my shirt in the process. Mick's eyes widened, his fear a bitter taste on the air. With a hiss, I jumped, landing directly in front of him, less than an inch between us.

"My father was too smart to fall for a dragon's manipulation. He was too caring to bring a human woman into a dragon's lair like some kind of sacrificial lamb. And he was too strong to have been corralled by the likes of you. You have no sway over dragons, dog." I pushed past him, heading for the ropes. "Saern isn't going to fight for you; he's going to kill everyone he sees as lesser. You brought a rabid beast into a children's story time, Mick. I suggest you let me do my thing to put him down."

Seventy-three seconds too long.

Once my feet hit concrete, I took off at a run for the medical wing, shoving past trainers and fighters in my way. Every inch of my body ached with the need to fully shift, to let my beast take over, but I held on to my human side. The halls were narrow, the ceiling low. If I fully shifted, I would do some damage to the building and that would slow me down. Would keep me from getting to Jane as quickly as possible.

Not acceptable.

A tug on my heartstrings and the soft sound of Jane screaming from too far away confirmed my worst fears. Jane was afraid. Even without a mating bite—with only the mark of her teeth in my skin—I could sense her deep emotions. Terror, anger, desperation. She needed me, and I'd wasted time dealing with those bastards in the arena.

Sixty-six seconds too long.

I ran faster.

TWELVE

Jane

His hands were everywhere at once, ripping my clothes, tearing at my flesh. I curled into a ball and pushed myself closer to the cabinet, kicked and tried to roll out from underneath him, but he was too big. Too strong. Too heavy on top of me. He was going to kill me right there in the exam room, and there was little I could do.

The sensation of my jeans being ripped from my hips sent my brain scattering. There was no way this was happening. I used my fingers as claws on his face, screaming with everything that I could as I punctured the skin. He yowled and tried to back away, but I dug my nails in deeper, pulled them harder, ignoring the dark liquid dripping down his chin and onto me. Let his blood run; his was the only kind that would. I would not bleed for him again.

Saern roared and swung, hitting me in the side of the head and giving himself the freedom to escape my hands. I'd never felt so much pain, never experienced such fear, but I had to keep my wits. I had to get out of this. Had to get to Piers.

Cupping a deep gouge my nails had caused along his jaw, Saern scrambled off me and backed away. His growling shook the room, but I refused to be scared into submission. I had one last chance to do something, and I was taking it. Mick had told me not to run, so I wouldn't. But that didn't mean I'd wait for more from the fucking animal.

Put flame in the air, and we'll run.

I just had to get into the cabinet at my back.

Saern spat blood onto the floor, his growl a deep, constant thing. "You shouldn't have done that, Jane."

I coughed a sarcastic laugh, rolling slightly to get into a better position. "Yeah, well, if you don't want scars, don't try to rape women."

He made a sound like a chuckle, one that sent icy fear straight down my spine. "Oh, Jane. You're my mate. Nothing I do to you could be considered rape."

I edged back, slipping to the side once my shoulder hit the cabinet I needed. Making sure I could get the door open without blocking it. Ready to fight back.

"I am not your mate, and I do not consent to you touching me."

"I claimed you, woman. My blood runs in yours, giving me ownership of everything about you. You *are* mine." He jumped into the air, hands out and mouth open, blood still dripping off his chin. Heading straight for me. I swung open the door and grabbed an acetylene torch, one of many in the cabinet. Something I'd used a million times before, just not for this purpose.

Put flame in the air, and we'll run.

I spun just as he landed, the torch in my hand, the tip already glowing red. "Back up."

Saern eyed the torch warily, but he didn't retreat. He didn't move forward, either, which I took as a win on my part. At least for a moment.

"What is this ridiculousness, Jane?"

I cocked one side of my mouth up in a sarcastic smile. "It's called payback."

I pressed the trigger, and the torch lit up, a spout of flame shooting toward Saern. He stumbled back, trying hard not to look afraid of the small thing... And failing.

"You are no match for me, mate," he said, but the shakiness of his voice and the panic in his eyes screamed his lie. I *was* a match for him as long as my torch kept throwing flames.

"Maybe not, but I won't go down without a fight." I turned up the gas flow, nearly sighing when the flames grew and the hiss of the torch increased. "And I'm *not your mate.*"

Saern roared but didn't come closer. He also never took his eyes off the tip of the torch. Piers had said they feared fire they couldn't control, and he'd been right. Maybe this little torch wouldn't be enough to kill him, but it seemed a good way to hold him off. For how long, I had no idea.

Saern began to pace, looking more and more like a caged animal trying to find a way past the bars. "That tadpole filling your head with lies about our species?"

"Nope." I edged toward the door, pushing myself to my feet and keeping the torch pointed at him. "I asked him how to kill a shifter, and he told me."

Saern laughed. "You can't kill me with that."

"Maybe not. But I bet I can cause some serious damage with it. Especially if I mixed this flame with that oxygen tank over there."

As Saern spun to look, I lunged for the door. Before I could make it out, Saern roared again. I could feel the wind as he came for me, could sense the predator at my heels. I spun again, falling backward, pointing the torch at his face just as the door opened inward.

Piers blasted into the room with a yowl that shook the walls. His red eyes took in the scene with a fighter's attention to detail. The torch in my hand, Saern growling and pursuing me, the blood on the floor, on Saern, on me. For a split second, those eyes landed on my face. I knew there had to be bruising from how Saern had struck me, had to be evidence of what he'd done. Between that and my torn clothing, I was pretty sure Piers would figure out what had happened in the moments since I walked out of the arena.

Piers didn't disappoint me.

Without question or pause, Piers roared and shifted, his dark red dragon breaking through the top of the doorway. Facing off with Saern.

THIRTEEN

Piers

Motherfucker.

My dragon took control before I could fully process the scene. All I knew was Jane was in trouble. She was hurt, and it was Saern's fault. My instincts were right. As soon as I could see through dragon eyes, I roared my fury. Jane had hot spots across her face and all over her body. Places where she'd bumped, where she'd bruise, where someone had hit her.

I was going to kill Saern.

The rumble of a wall crumbling behind me was nothing compared to the sound of Saern's tail taking down another as he shifted in response to me. Dust filled the air but it affected nothing. I could still see heat, still knew where Saern and Jane were. Still spotted almost every detail of Saern's black scales. And Saern could see me.

He attacked with a swipe from the right, a rookie mistake. I dodged left to stay out of his reach and swung my tail at him, making him retreat and keeping Jane in my sights. She was so small and fragile, so very *human*. I couldn't let Saern get anywhere near her. Not again.

As Saern edged closer, dropping to all fours, I grabbed Jane and shoved her into the hallway. The torch in her hand made me so proud. My brave mate had listened to me, had kept her wits about her. Had fought back. But it was time for me to do the fighting for her. She had to be safe, and only I could make sure of that.

"She's your weakness," Saern hissed in the language only dragons could understand. "You'll lose because you love."

He struck again, landing two blows before I could outpace him. But I wasn't some newbie off the street. Every fight I'd been in, every fighter I'd seen, had all led up to this. Saern was tough, older than me, with thicker scales and probably more experience, but he couldn't beat me. I'd been taught by the best, so I waited. I stayed back and made Saern come to me. Made him do all the work as I reserved my energy and analyzed his every move. As I looked for the chink in his armor.

The heat through his dark scales was minimal. They were too thick, too old for me to blast through. But every dragon had a weak point; I needed to find his. Then I would know how to take him down. How to use my inner fire to my advantage. I needed to wait him out.

Three more hits in quick succession, two connecting. I reeled slightly from the force but stayed alert. I could hear Jane in the hallway, so I kept myself close to that wall. Blocking the way to her with my body. Saern wouldn't touch her. Not again.

As he rose to his back feet to roar uselessly at the sky, I spotted it. A patch of orange among the dark. A spot where his scales didn't cover his more delicate flesh. I saw it, and I didn't hesitate.

The world went white as I called my fire forward. My chest and throat heated to an impossible level, the pain welcomed and expected. With a roar, I directed a stream of flames toward Saern, toward that spot of his body heat. Toward his weakness.

He hissed and fell back a step before taking to the sky, blowing right through the rest of the ceiling above. Running away and leaving behind piles of stone and twisted metal. But I couldn't let him go. Dragons had long memories and held even longer grudges. He would return again and again until he got what he wanted. Whether that was to possess Jane or to kill me was really up in the air and dependent upon his mood, but it would be one of those. I refused to let him be a threat to my mate's happiness ever again.

Saern would die by my hands tonight.

I followed Saern into the sky, my heavy wings cutting through the air with ease, roaring fire whenever I flew close enough. He circled and dove, trying to evade me. But bigger and older didn't mean better at flying, plus he seemed to be having trouble with one of his wings. That would eventually slow him down, and it was already making it hard for him to maneuver the way he wanted. I could tell. I could also tell that I would win up here for sure if I just kept up.

Saern circled around, spitting huge fire streams my way. The sight had me slowing, knocking myself off course. Okay then, I needed to avoid the flames. I curled slightly, dropping my arm, protecting my own weak spot as I flew above him.

Our roars and screams made the forests shake, made the mountains rumble to kneel at our feet. Our flames lit up the sky in oranges and yellows. Our dragons were older than those piles of rock below us, older than the oceans and many of the stars above us. We were the first of the shifter breeds brought to this land, and that night, we would take back our sky and battle the way we were meant to.

I dove for Saern as he arced into a turn that was too slow to keep altitude. My flames hit his back, setting his wings on fire.

Knowing his time was up, Saern screamed and doubled back. I followed, pushing myself as fast as I could. Zigging and zagging through the air in ways Saern no longer could. It wasn't until the building came into view that I figured out where Saern was going. Wasn't until I saw the crowd of people standing outside that I understood his plan.

Motherfucker.

I flew faster, working my wings harder, trying to push him off course with well-placed blasts of fire. Saern stayed just out of reach, but with every flap of his wings, he slowed. With every dodge, he lost a little more balance. It was going to be close.

On a cross directly over The Pack House building, his tail brushed my arm, and I reached for him. My claws scraped across his back leg, drawing blood. Saern roared and swooped lower, heading straight for the crowd outside the building. Heading for where my Jane probably was. Diving hard, I slammed into the side of him, trying to knock him off track. Succeeding in pushing him to the side by a few feet.

But it wasn't enough.

Saern rained fire down on the crowd, the screams from below enough to make my blood boil. I slammed into him again, this time rolling him, knocking him out of the sky with the weight of my body and plunging my claws deep into the spaces between his scales. The taste of burnt flesh flashed across my tongue as we swept over the crowd of people on the ground, but that only fueled me. Remove the threat, then go to Jane. Remove the threat, then help them. Remove the threat.

We hit the ground hard, plowing up dirt as we slid toward the tree line. I used my claws on Saern's belly, grabbing and pulling and working myself up the length of him until I could reach the orange area hidden almost beneath his wing. His weak spot. The flesh under the scales.

When I had him pinned, had him flat on his back and

completely exposed to me, I leaned over him so I could speak the language of my brethren.

"She is not my weakness. She makes me angrier, makes me faster, makes me hit harder. She gives me the will to never give up. Jane could never make me weak." I leaned closer, letting the smoke billow from my nostrils so he'd know his fate. Nearly salivating over the fear in his eyes.

"My mate is my true strength."

Saern cried out as I torched him, my flames finding that weak spot easily. Sinking through the delicate flesh. He burned from the inside out, leaving behind a husk of scales. Leaving behind nothing worth worrying about.

Remove the threat. Done.

When I was sure he was dead, I shifted human and crawled away from him, rolling in the dirt. My throat burned, my mouth tasted like ash, and my body felt as if I'd just gone thirty rounds with every fighter in The Pack House. But I'd done it. I'd gotten rid of the threat. I'd protected Jane.

Jane.

I was up and running for the building in a second, all thoughts on finding my mate. My heart raced as the scene came into view. Fire still burned in places, and smoke billowed high into the air above. But that was nothing compared to the bodies that lay crumpled on the ground. Some were burned to the point of no longer being recognizable, some barely burned but still lifeless. Most of the fighters and trainers at The Pack House were dead.

"Jane," I whispered, nearly frozen in fear. But I couldn't stop. I had to find her. I had to keep moving.

I searched through the melee, looking for anything that was hers. Shifting enough to taste the air for her scent. Finding nothing and growing more anxious with every second. I paused for one heartbreaking moment when I came across Laudon, but it was too late to help him. He lay in a charred heap, his body stiff, his heart silent. Dead because of Saern.

"Blessings, my friend."

I kept searching. Kept stumbling through the carnage. Kept hunting her down, but no Jane. Nothing of her around. No sign.

I wasn't sure whether to be thankful or terrified.

FOURTEEN

Jane

"Let me go." I fought against Mick's hold, but he only shoved me harder. Stumbling, I tried to look up, to look back, to see where Piers was, but the sky was too dark. I saw nothing but deeper shadows blocking stars and moving too fast to differentiate which dragon was which. Even when one spewed flames at the other, they were too far away to see scale colors. I could only hope Piers was winning.

"Quit fighting me, child," Mick growled, squeezing harder on the back of my neck. In his other hand, he held a flare gun, our only protection against a crazed dragon. For once, the man had actually listened to my advice. Though I didn't think it was enough.

"No." I swung around again, trying to reach him with my fists, but he squeezed and shoved, nearly knocking me to my knees. "Damn it, Mick. I need to check on Piers."

"What you need to do is move. We're not sticking around to watch this place be burned to the ground."

"Piers wouldn't do that."

Mick chuckled, a dark and dangerous sound. "You think I'm worried about him? Piers is a decent fighter, but he's tame compared to Saern. There's no way your precious Piers can survive with that thing after him."

My stomach dropped at the thought of Piers being in such danger, but a fire lit in my veins at the same time. A defensive streak that knew Mick was wrong.

"Piers is strong and a good fighter. He *can* win against Saern."

"He won't win, but it doesn't matter anyway. The Pack House will be destroyed or found out. It's time to move on to another venture."

If The Pack House closed, that meant...

"If we're done, then leave me here."

Mick pulled me closer, cocking his head, his words growled in a way that gave me no doubt he meant them. "Oh, I never said we were done, child. You still owe me. Besides, I'm sure you want to have the best care for your father. That care is with me."

The world tilted as my reality set in. Mick would never consider my debt paid. He would always hold my schooling or my father's life over my head. There was no escaping him.

But damn it, I had to try.

With Mick so close, I didn't have a lot of options. But I'd worked in the training facility for too long not to have picked up a few tricks. I lunged back, pulling Mick toward me where he hung on to my neck. Without pausing, I brought my leg up and kicked forward, hitting him square in the chest. He fell back, his eyes wide. Before he could regain his senses, I kicked again. Same spot. Aiming high. Hoping for a direct shot to his heart to interrupt the beating. Mick fell to his knees, the flare gun falling to the dirt at my feet. I lunged for it then danced backward, keeping Mick in my sights as I tried to figure out how the thing worked.

"You will regret that, child." Mick pushed himself to his feet. He looked ready to attack, though he wobbled a bit. I had limited time before he struck, judging by the growl rumbling from his chest. Killing him myself probably wouldn't work, but I knew someone stronger. Someone tougher. Someone who could do much more damage if he only knew I needed him. If he wasn't dying at the claws of another right at that moment.

I found the safety and clicked it into what I assumed was the off position, nearly laughing with relief. "No, agreeing to let you buy me is a mistake I regret. Giving you power over my father is something I regret. This is me having no more regrets."

I held my arm up and fired. A trail of sparks flew into the sky, lighting us up like a firework on Independence Day. At first, there was nothing but the sound of the wind and the quiet rumble of the fire burning behind us. But then the world shook as the night was torn in two by the scream of a great beast. What had to be a dragon.

And was hopefully *my* dragon, alive and well and answering my call.

Mick grew pale as he watched the flare burn bright and arc across the sky, though he tried to keep his growl rumbling. But as the sound of great wings flapping grew near, he lost all semblance of bravery and began to edge away.

"You'll pay for this," he spat. "Your father will pay for this."

"My father has paid for befriending a wolf shifter for the last fifteen years. I'm done living under that debt because of guilt." I closed my eyes for a moment as another dragon scream reverberated through the night, this time closer. "You'd better run, Mick. No matter which dragon comes, you're a dead man."

His eyes darted around the space behind me, his mouth falling open and his skin paling at whatever he saw there. I didn't turn, didn't bother looking for my fate. Either a dragon was coming to kill me or save me. No matter which, I was done with Mick.

Without another word, Mick turned and ran, leaving me behind in the night to wait for what was next. I hung my head and prayed, the flare gun gripped tightly in my shaky hands. Wishing for Piers. Begging for the strength to deal with the possibility that it may be Saern. Praying for guidance in a moment so beyond my control.

A boom sounded behind me, the definite sound of something large landing nearby. I closed my eyes and waited, too afraid to see if it was Piers. Too afraid not to as well. The moment dragged, time slowing to a crawl. Every heartbeat took an hour, every breath a year. And still I waited. Not moving. Barely daring to breathe.

"Jane?"

I sagged with relief, the flare gun falling to my feet. "You said to kill them with fire."

"I did. I said it, and you listened. You defended yourself and brought me to you with fire. And I killed Saern with fire." His voice grew closer, the tone warm but shaky. "Fuck, Jane, you'd better tell me if I have your consent because I'm about to—"

I spun and ran to him, jumping into his arms with a sob. Clinging to him as I thanked every god in heaven for sparing him.

"I've got you," Piers murmured, gripping me to him with strong arms. "I couldn't find you in the crowd, but I saw the flare. I knew it would be you. I found you."

I inhaled shakily, fighting back tears. "Mick tried to take me."

He tightened his hold. "I still would have found you."

"He said I'd pay. He said—"

"Shhhh." Piers grabbed my face, pressing his lips to mine in a kiss that stole my breath. I kissed him back, my tears finally falling. He'd survived. I'd survived. And we could be together.

When we finally broke apart, Piers placed his forehead against mine and whispered, "Are you ready?"

"For what?"

"To go." He leaned closer, kissing me again, moving to my ear to whisper, "To fly with me?"

There was no hesitation on my part. I nodded once and wrapped myself around him, tucking my face into his chest. Piers kissed my head, then shifted with me in his arms. His skin turned to scales, but I hung on. I always would. His dragon didn't scare me.

He roared into the night, and then we took off. The wind rushed past me, and everything below shrank as he seemed to fly straight up. With a dip and a turn, he roared again, circling. Flying high above the burning Pack House before heading down the mountain.

And I didn't look back.

Jane

Cold hands ran over my thighs, yanking me from sleep. Before I could move, a heavy weight crawled on top of me and held me in place. Pressing me into the mattress.

"Good morning, mate." Piers pulled my knees around his naked hips and rocked against me. Playful and teasing. The bastard. "It's moving day."

I smiled but kept my eyes closed. "Five more minutes."

"That depends." He hummed and lined his dick up with where I was already so wet for him. Where I was always wet for the man I'd chosen as my mate. I gasped as he nudged his way inside, as he stretched me open. As he took what I so freely gave him.

"On what?"

He grunted as he went deep, holding still to enjoy the sensation before rocking back and forth. "On what you want to do with those five minutes."

I finally opened my eyes, taking in his smile, his scruff, and his bright eyes. Irresistible. "You. Just you."

He grinned and thrust in earnest. "Thank fuck for that, Doc. Because if you didn't give me consent, I might have cried."

"Doubt it, but I could always tell you to stop, just to see."

He chuckled and kissed me, pulling away to whisper, "If you tell me to stop, you get no wake-up orgasms."

"Heaven forbid." I lost myself in his movements, in the way he knew my body. In the way he played me and drove me wild. Quiet moments like these were my favorite, when it was just him and me. When we could be together, alone and free to play and learn and be. So much better than I ever thought life with another person could be.

Piers nuzzled my neck, licking the spot where he'd given me my claiming bite. It overlapped the one Saern had forced on me, of course. Piers was nothing if not territorial when it came to me. He'd bitten that spot hard, wanting to erase the memory. Wanting to start new.

And we were.

Within a few hours, we would be loading my father in the old VW bus Piers had purchased and heading deeper into the mountains to join the wolf pack his cousin had mated into. The thought of being involved with wolf shifters again terrified me but not as much as the threat of Mick finding us without support. Piers swore he'd make sure everything was safe for me and my dad. He already had, breaking in to the nursing home with me to get my dad out before Mick could get to him. It had been a rough few days, and I was sure we'd lose him once or twice, but my dad was still strong. He made it through the changes with my help. He'd never get better, never regain his thoughts or personality, but that was okay. He was still my dad, and with my medical degree, I could take care of him better that any hired assistant. So I would—Piers had made sure of it.

The drive would be tough, the pack of wolves scary, but I

trusted Piers to take care of all of us. Trusted everything about him. He was my mate, the man I claimed. My heart.

We made love for far longer than five minutes, both of us whispering promises to each other. Falling into our bliss together, clinging to one another with no space between us. And even then, when we'd sated ourselves for the first time that day, we didn't separate or move. We stayed huddled under the blanket, sweat-slicked skin pressed together, lips finding lips for soft kisses. Perfect.

But even perfection had to end.

Piers groaned and rolled, keeping me tucked into his side. "We need to get up so we can get on the road."

I sighed, not wanting to let go but knowing it was time. A better life was ahead of us. A better world. He'd promised, and a dragon wouldn't break his promise.

"Okay," I said, stretching and pulling off the covers. "Let's get a move on, dragon."

Piers pulled me to my feet and kissed me again. "Your dragon."

And he was. Forever.

"My dragon."

———

At the request of my editor, I wrote a short story called A DRAGON'S PROMISE that is a little...naughty. This downloadable short is only available through my Facebook reader's group, Ellis' Elite. If it sounds like something you might want to complete your Fight Club Collection, check out the group!

Sometimes in the middle of an ordinary day, your dragon shifter decides to offer you oral sex using his forked tongue.

Join The Group - Get The Story

CLAIMING HIS GRACE

FERAL BREED FIGHT CLUB, BOOK THREE

One plus one equals two...or sometimes three

Wolf shifter Beadan fought at the now-defunct southern Pack House with solid results, so when the opportunity arises for him to continue his career in the ring at another location, he jumps at it. He's still on the hunt for his one true mate to take home with him, so easy money and being surrounded by people seems like a good plan.

Avory's a single mom with a dream—one that requires money. She comes to The Pack House to make that dream come true for her and her daughter Livia, not expecting anything other than a few fights, a few wins, and some cash in her pocket. What she definitely isn't expecting is to meet her fated mate the second she walks in the door.

. . .

Navigating those newly mated waters is tricky for everyone, but throw a six-year-old who loves unicorn marshmallow cereal into the mix, and all bets are off. The two adults in the relationship are going to have to make a few adjustments to accommodate their littlest priority. But adjustments aren't all that's needed when the other fighters figure out the two have a weakness no one else in the club does...and her name is Livia.

ONE

Beadan

You know what happens when a shitty situation goes up in flames...literally? You end up in an even shittier situation.

"Beadan, my boy. So good to see you." Mick—owner of The Pack House fight clubs and exploiter of shifters everywhere—reached for my hand. He looked a little pale, a little less the confident showman he'd always been. Considering the last time I'd seen him, we'd been fleeing a raging inferno as his other fighting arena went up in flames, I could understand why.

"Mick. Glad to see you made it here in one piece."

"Same to you, boy. Same to you." He darted a glance over my shoulder, obviously ready to move on to welcoming other, more important fighters. "If there's anything you need..."

Yeah. That statement would never be completed because if we needed anything, we went to our trainers. Mick was all talk, no action. I wasn't a big name or one of his top fighters, so he didn't waste a lot of time on me. That was fine. I wasn't here for notoriety—I was just looking for a paycheck.

I left Mick behind to play the host and headed inside the

training branch of the arena. The darkness of the hall caught me off guard, the length of time it took my eyes to adjust unusual. The thick and sticky air carried an odor that had me recoiling, humidity and whatever they put into the ventilation system to make us all go a little crazy slapping me in the face. I hadn't missed that smell or the way my body reacted to it.

"Bear."

I spun at my fighting name, catching the eye of one of the trainers. I recognized him from the last location but couldn't remember his name. Not that I needed to know it.

"Yes, sir?"

"You're in ring four—get your stuff put away and be ready in twenty."

I nodded and headed off down the hall to the living area of the place. A quick check-in at the training office, and I had a key and a room assignment. The closets we slept in weren't much— bed, dresser, TV, lamp—but they did the job. At least they were clean.

I tossed my stuff onto my new bed and changed into my workout shorts before making my way back to the training rings. Unlike most guys in the program, I wasn't there because I owed someone a debt. That's how most fighters ended up in the ring—they owed money, Mick bought that debt, then they owed Mick. Every time you competed—and won—the amount you owed him lessened. Big names and the guys who drew huge crowds didn't usually stay long, their fights depositing enough money into Mick's pockets for him to release them quickly. Me? I'd been fighting for almost six months with no debt to pay. I wasn't violent or a glutton for punishment—I just had nothing better to do.

"Right on time." The trainer—one I hadn't worked with before—set down his clipboard and hopped up into the ring.

"I'm Tony, and I'll be working with you for now. Let's start with some warm-up jabs."

I followed behind him, adjusting my stance to make sure my balance was solid. The workout started easily enough—jab, jab, swing, jab—but eventually, Tony began to move around more. To make me follow him. He danced all around the ring as I followed. I was a good fighter—strong and big and intimidating—but my endurance was shit. The trainers knew it. Tony wasn't letting me slide on it.

"Stay on your toes," he said as he danced across the ring again. I was beginning to get winded and was seriously thinking of letting a punch slip and knocking him in the chin to make a point when he finally stepped back and dropped his hands. "You need to work on your endurance."

No shit. "I'm not here for the long haul, man. So long as I can win, I think I'm fine."

"And when someone else gets you in that ring and wears you down until you're too tired to throw a punch? What then?"

I shrugged, still breathing harder than I'd like to. "Then I untape my hands and call it over."

"If you're still breathing at the end of it."

That was...well, harsh, but true. Shifters died in these fights. I didn't usually worry about such things because I was strong and had solid technique, but Tony wasn't talking out of his ass. If a smaller, faster guy decided to use his agility to keep away from me and forced me around the ring like the trainer had just done? I'd be in trouble. Can't win a fight if you can't breathe.

"I'll work on it, man."

Tony nodded, grabbing his clipboard and making a note. "I've got you with Rafe for the rest of the afternoon. Try not to drop dead of exhaustion, okay?"

Jackass. "Understood."

Rafe—tall, funny, decent fighter—hopped into the ring,

giving me a smile as he bumped fists. "You ready for me, big man?"

"When have I ever not been ready?"

We sparred for a good long while, both of us throwing easy punches and keeping the aggression at bay. The man had a good arm, but his best asset was his speed. He could be quick when he wanted to, knocking you on your ass before you even saw the swing coming. He was a fun one to fight.

"So," Rafe said, his feet still moving and his hands up close to his head more like a boxer than a cage fighter. "I have to admit, I was surprised to see you here. I figured you'd head home after the other place burned down."

I grunted, throwing a few jabs before bouncing back. "Nothing to go home to yet."

"No family?"

"Nah, I've got family. Got a good pack, too. But they're all mated."

He froze, his eyes going wide and his arms hanging still. "Your entire pack is made up of mated pairs?"

I shrugged, heading for my water bottle since we were obviously taking a break. "And a triad. Everyone blissfully mated, except me."

"That had to be..."

I could totally guess where his mind had gone and what word he was trying hard not to say. Others hadn't been so kind. "It wasn't awful, no. It was actually really nice. There has always been stability where I'm from. But when I got old enough to want some company of my own, there weren't any options. So, I left."

"For good?"

"Hell no." I tossed the water bottle and knocked my fists together, the international fighter signal for *get ready before I start destroying your facial structure.* "Once I find myself a mate, I'll head back. Got a house on a little farm and everything."

Rafe snorted a laugh, bringing his hands up to protect that facial structure and dancing on the balls of his feet again. "You do realize that the odds of you finding a mate in a warehouse full of men is sort of unlikely, don't you?"

Sort of unlikely. That was putting it mildly. "No shit. This is a job—when I'm ready to move on and have a pocketful of cash, I'll do so. For now, I don't have any idea where to go next, so I stay."

"And you followed Mick all the way here after the fire."

That was...yeah, more of a compulsion than anything else. I'd known the second word had spread through the rubble and the dead bodies that I'd be going with Mick to the next Pack House. Why, I couldn't have said. I had been besieged by an overwhelming need to follow him, though. So, I had, and here I was.

"More fights to win, more money to make," I said, knowing there was more to my move than that but not sure yet what that meant. Didn't matter. Everything would happen as the fates wanted it to anyway. "Speaking of fights and money, neither of us is going to get paid for gabbing."

Rafe laughed and shook his head, crouching slightly as he brought his hands up. We kept at it for a few more minutes, but eventually, something across the gym caught Rafe's eye. I saw him go stiff, noticed the way his pupils blew out and his hairline puffed up. The man was one step from shifting to his wolf. I spun, ready to fight off whatever threat might have walked in the door.

The threat turned out to be women.

Ten women, surrounded by about as many trainers.

Holy fuck, Mick was an idiot.

"That's not good," Rafe said, his voice low and husky.

Almost growling. I couldn't speak, could only nod. With the competitiveness of wolf shifters and their instincts to protect shewolves and keep them as their own, the presence of so much feminine energy in the space would be enough to throw off the balance. To knock the control out of some of my fellow fighters. Those women could start a war right there in the training gym.

"Gonna be a shitshow."

Rafe nodded, still staring. I couldn't take my eyes off the women either. Something inside me wouldn't allow it. My wolf —the beast I'd been blessed with and had shared a body with since birth—paced inside my head, uneasy. Anxious maybe. We couldn't take our eyes off—

"Gentlemen!" Mick yelled from across the gym, staring hard at each of us in turn. "The Pack House is now welcoming female fighters into our rings."

A collective groan sounded from around the gym, but I stayed silent. Kept watching. Why couldn't I look away?

Mick wasn't done yet, though. "These shewolves are here to fight and make me money, not to be entertainment for all of you. Mind your dicks and keep your hands off my merchandise, or I'll bury you myself. Understood?"

I nodded, unable not to. Still staring across the room toward where the women were being escorted to the far training rings. As they broke apart, I kept my eyes on one in particular. On a shewolf with reddish-brown hair tied up in a ball thing on top of her head. She wore a baggy sweatshirt, gray shorts, and an expression of total, uninterruptible focus. Aggressive was how I would have described her. The second her eyes danced past mine, though, that word reset to a more important one.

Mate.

My wolf practically stood up and howled, my entire body zeroing in on hers. I changed my stance, facing her fully, staring as her jaw clenched and her eyes narrowed. Looking flat-out mean. Was she going to make this difficult on me? Make me work to break that tough outer shell before giving in to me? Fuck, I hoped so. I loved a good challenge.

When she finally moved again, it was to bend down and talk to someone I couldn't see. Someone blocked by the trainers. Her body language shifted, her face softening as she said words I couldn't hear. When she was finished, she rose to her full height again and gave me a look that could have stripped paint off the walls. She spun around, moving toward the ring. Obviously about to do some sparring of her own. My eyes dropped to the person she'd been chatting with as the others around the ring moved. The one who had brought forth the kinder, softer shewolf. I was curious to know more about my new mate, about who could make her drop her guard. About who she cared for. So, I looked, and I waited to get a solid eyeful. And I...

Hold up.

Is that a...child?

TWO

Avory

I sought out Livia's little hand, needing to keep a solid hold on her for my own sanity. The Pack House was everything the man who'd sold me on the idea of fighting here had said it would be—dirty, smelly, and filled with men who could be dangerous for my daughter and me. Hopefully, the last thing he'd told me about the place would prove correct as well—that I could make enough money in just one or two fights to be set for the next few years.

Stability. Livia needed it. *I* needed it. And a wad of cash was the first step in acquiring it.

"Let's go, ladies," the trainer said as he continued down a dark, stinky hallway. The sounds of fighting rang through the space, huffs and grunts and thuds a soundtrack to our arrival. I wasn't the only shewolf looking a little nervous—most of the others did as well, though none of them had as much to lose as I did.

"Mommy?" Livia's quiet whisper had my head dropping, had me snapping my eyes to meet hers. "What is this place?"

At just six years old, there was no way she would understand what I'd gotten us into or the type of business we'd be staying in for a few weeks. I had to adjust my answer for those little ears.

"This is a club where fighters like Mommy train. We're going to stay here for a little bit."

She hugged Cornelius, her stuffed cow, a little closer. "And then we get to move to a farm?"

A farm. It was all she'd ever talked about—wanting to live on a big piece of land with lots of animals running around. Not usually the dream of wolf shifter pups, but her mind had been made up practically since birth. I had no intention of letting her down.

"That's the plan—a few weeks here, then we're off to our farm." We rounded a corner and came into full view of the training rings. Every male eye turned our way, and the energy around us took a hard jog sideways. The hair on the back of my neck stood on end, my inner wolf rising to her paws and growling inside my mind. Dangerous. Those men were dangerous, and we'd be sharing space with them for the foreseeable future.

I was going to need to get some sort of leash to keep Livia with me at all times.

Tugging my baby closer, I raised my chin and kept moving. Another shewolf—one who was a little younger than me and obviously a little more anxious about the men staring—caught my eye, looking absolutely terrified. That wouldn't do. I lifted my chin that much higher, holding her gaze as I let my expression go into full resting bitch face mode. She followed suit, hardening her eyes in a way that required no interpretation. We were nervous, but we weren't prey. If any of the men stepped out of line, they'd have a fight on their hands. And if a single one even looked at my Livia wrong, they wouldn't live to warn the others not to make the same mistake.

"Ladies!" the trainer yelled as he came to a stop. "I know you just arrived, but the trainers want to get started immediately so they can set up the first training pairs. Head over to the far rings where you'll be sparring."

He held up an arm indicating where we should go—which was right through the middle of the training area—and waited for us to follow his instructions. I kept Livia pulled tight against my hip, her little hand clenched in mine. This was definitely not the place for her, but I had no other choice. Her father was gone, my parents dead, and there was no family or pack that I could trust to keep her while I worked for our farm. This was the only option.

Just a couple of fights.

"You're here," a man said, catching my eye and pointing to a bench by one of the farther rings. He glanced at Livia but didn't say anything to her. "There's a bench on the far side."

I nodded, pulling Livia with me as I passed by the ring. I set her on the bench and made sure she had her stuffed cow—the one she'd been dragging along with her since she could crawl—before tugging off my oversized sweatshirt. The tank I wore underneath wasn't what I'd normally fight in, but I had no idea where our bags were, so it would have to do.

"Are you going to fight, Mommy?" Livia stared up at me, all wide eyes and pink lips. So beautiful, she made my heart hurt. So fragile, she made the wolf inside me want to come out and show these men what they'd be dealing with if they crossed a line.

I was almost glad for the time in the ring to work off some of the anxiety pulsing through my veins.

"I'm going to train for a little bit, baby."

She nodded, tugging on the cow's ear. "I'm tired."

Of course she was. We'd had a long day of traveling, and she'd been too excited watching the fields and barns fly past us to close her eyes even for a minute.

"We'll go to our room as soon as this training is done, okay? Then we can relax with Cornelius and read a story." I squatted before her, holding her gaze and keeping my face as serious as possible. "But right now, I need you to sit right here and stay quiet, okay? Let Mommy work for a little bit."

"Okay." Livia nodded, squeezing her stuffed toy close. "I won't move. I promise."

I dropped a kiss on the top of her head then crawled into the ring, ready to focus on fighter Avory instead of mommy Avory as much as possible.

"Okay," said the trainer, looking over a clipboard he held. "I want an easy match—light sparring, no need to dominate or win. Just throw a few punches, move around the ring, and let me get a feel for the way you move."

Easy enough. Once I had my mouthguard in place, I bumped fists with the younger girl from earlier, the one with the hard eyes. She had about three inches and twenty pounds on me, but that wouldn't matter much. I'd fought bigger over the years.

When the coach yelled go, I dropped into my stance and brought my fists toward my face, ready to defend. Just as I'd suspected, the woman came out swinging first, using her size to herd me back. That was fine—I always had been a patient fighter. I moved around the ring in reverse, ducking punches and throwing a few soft jabs her way. Nothing too crazy. She didn't go full out either, keeping her punches restrained and her feet moving. We were dancing around the ring and warming up our muscles, nothing more.

At least not until the coach yelled, "Now, show me who would win!"

The woman's stance changed, her head dropping and her fists clenching. Yeah, she thought she had me. That wasn't going to happen.

I didn't let her herd me this time. Instead, I was the one who went on the offensive. I charged toward her, swinging my right arm wide. My fist made contact with her jaw, which knocked her head back and to the side but didn't end the fight. She swiveled and rushed me, throwing rights and lefts as I dodged and bobbed. She connected with my ear on one punch, making the entire world go silent for a moment as the pain pulsed through my head. My wolf didn't like that at all. We attacked again, forcing her back. Jabbing with both hands until the opportunity we'd been waiting for presented itself. The woman moved as if to twist, but the action forced her left shoulder to drop. Target acquired. I jabbed with my left, knowing she'd dodge and open herself up even more, before putting every ounce of strength I had into my right and throwing the sort of punch that would knock a man to his knees. My fist made contact with her cheek, and I knew that was it. I saw the way her eyes rolled slightly and her mouth fell open.

Lights-out time.

The woman dropped to the mat, and I backed away, looking to the coach for what to do next. He nodded toward the bench where Livia sat.

"That's enough for today, Raven."

I spat out my mouthguard, frowning. "My name's not Raven."

"In here, it is—Avory like aviary like bird like raven. Everyone fights under an assumed name. Yours is Raven." He wrote something down on his clipboard before catching my eye once more. "You'll do fine here if you fight just like that. Dance a little, give the spectators time to bet, then take your opponent down. Understood?"

I nodded, flicking a glance toward my daughter. "Am I free to go, then?"

"Absolutely. Big Mike will show you to your room." He raised a chin toward the man who had brought us in. I let them have their chat, my eyes refocusing on Livia. She sat right where I'd left her, having what looked to be a deep and meaningful conversation with her cow. I couldn't help but smile at the image.

I hopped out of the ring and landed in front of her, ready to tell her it was time to leave, but something from behind Livia snagged my attention and wouldn't let me go. Something forced my eyes to lock on those of a man not ten feet away. He was tall and thick, built like a brick house and looking just as dangerous. And he was staring right back at me.

Some sort of force tugged at my belly, and the entire world twisted. It only took a moment—maybe three seconds—before reality rebounded and I knew. *I knew.*

"Fuck me," I whispered, unable not to. The fates loved to screw with me, and they'd just done it again.

The man was my mate.

THREE

Beadan

Big, wide eyes, a shocked expression, and plump pink lips that rounded into an "O" shape as she locked gazes with me. My woman. My mate. The end goal of all my traveling was *right there*. She'd been dropped into my lap, and I wasn't about to let her slip away. Which was why I'd crossed the gym—so I could be closer to her. So I could meet her.

"Fuck me," she whispered, still looking completely shocked by my presence. Understandable.

"That's sort of the plan...long term." I gave her my best smile, hoping to put her a little more at ease. My plan failed miserably. The woman took the hand of the little girl on the bench—the one who looked exactly like her but in miniature—and stormed away. Not that there was really any place for her to go—we were about to be spending a lot of time under the same roof. Something that gave me hope for a nice, slow wooing.

My mate stopped to talk to the guard at the edge of the training room, nodding as he looked over his clipboard and pointed down the hallway. She was heading to the barracks—

the small closets of space we were assigned to sleep in. Okay, so she *could* hide from me in there as I had a feeling men were not going to be allowed to be in the same living quarters as the women. I needed to act.

But she didn't turn to head down the hall. Instead, she sat on a bench near the guard and pulled the girl into her lap. The two created their own little world right there, both whispering and smiling and laughing. Looking like clones, just in two vastly different sizes. I wanted to sit on the bench beside them and know what they were talking about. Wanted to be invited into their pocket of happiness.

All things I was going to have to work for.

"Ladies!" Coach John yelled, catching the attention of not just the shewolves but the entire gym. "Thank you for your willingness to train so quickly after your arrival. Your evaluations are complete, so Trainer Tom will show you to your rooms, where we will bring you your dinners so you can have an evening off. Just follow him."

Tom—the guard—raised a hand over his head and took a few steps into the hallway off the side of the training room. The women began to follow after him, chatting softly with one another. I concentrated on my mate, who picked up the little girl and placed her on her hip. The two connected and headed away from me for the night. Something that made my chest hurt. I was about to retire back into the ring, figuring beating the hell out of someone or something might take my mind off planning for a future not yet earned, when something white caught my attention. I strode to the bench by the door where my mate had been sitting and bent down, reaching underneath it. My fingers found a soft and fuzzy...something. I pulled it to me and examined it, looking over the white-and-black fake fur. Turning it to find a small face looking back at me.

"Cow," I whispered, as if the damn thing could hear me. But

it wasn't just a cow—it was that little girl's stuffed cow. And she'd lost it.

Hang on, little one. I'm coming.

I took off at a jog after the women, cow in hand. It didn't take me long to catch up to them. The little girl was walking on her own, hand in that of my mate's, the two strolling slowly along the darkened hall. They stopped at a door, letting the other women pass. Being left behind by the crowd. I saw my chance, and I took it.

"Hey there, cutie." I dropped to one knee a good six feet away, giving them space so I didn't scare them but wanting to be close enough to make the vital handoff. "I was in the gym and heard something that sounded like a distress moo. This little guy seemed to be lost." I held out the cow. "Does he belong to you?"

The little girl's face lit up, those eyes nearly as round as the woman's had been when she first saw me. "Cornelius! Where did you run off to?"

The girl reached for her cow. The woman flexed, looking ready to attack if I made any sudden moves. I held still and handed off the cow, keeping my eyes on the girl. Keeping my body as relaxed as possible.

"Glad I could return Cornelius to his rightful owner."

Once the cow had been acquired, the little girl snuggled him close and stepped behind the woman, almost hiding. I rose to my feet and met the eyes of my mate, feeling that tug in my gut. Wanting so much to ask her a million questions and wrap her in my arms.

Not yet.

"I'm Beadan, cow wrangler of The Pack House. Let me know if you need my services again, little lady." I nodded toward my mate and pretended to tip the hat I wasn't wearing. "Ma'am."

The woman's lips twitched, a smile being fought for sure.

"Thank you for your services. I'm sure Livia is very appreciative and wants to say thank you."

The little girl—Livia—turned her face into the woman's hip and mumbled a quiet, "Thank you."

"It was no problem." I waited, hoping she'd tell me her name. Or invite me in. Or throw her arms around me and kiss me.

Alas, all pipe dreams.

"Well," she said, returning her focus to the key in her hand and the door before her. "It was nice meeting you."

Shot down. Hard. "You as well, ma'am. And you too, Miss Livia. I hope to see you at breakfast tomorrow."

Livia, still hiding behind the hip of the woman, suddenly seemed much more interested in me. "Cornelius and I like breakfast."

I grinned, unable not to. "They put on a good one here—lots of eggs and yogurt and about fifty different kinds of cereal."

Her little mouth fell open. "Cereal is my favorite."

"Mine too." I shot her a wink, grinning at her excitement. "You come find me tomorrow morning, and I'll take you around and show you all the cereal options." I leaned down, dropping my voice as if talking only to her. "There are even ones with unicorn marshmallows."

Those dark eyes practically twinkled as she jumped a little, sort of dancing in place. "Mommy, unicorn marshmallows."

I caught the woman's gaze, Livia having confirmed their relationship. Mom. My mate had a child. Something inside me roiled and reset itself in that moment, something dark and dangerous. A need to protect. The little girl was my mate's daughter, which meant she was mine now too. I'd make sure no one dared to even look at her the wrong way.

The woman leaned against the door, still holding on to that

key. Still looking far more anxious than I would like. "Thank you for your kindness. Little Livia does love her cereal."

"It's no problem..." I lengthened the word, waiting for her to jump in with a name. Hoping she took the bait.

She did. "Avory. I'm Avory."

Biting my bottom lip to keep from grinning like a fool, I nodded. "Nice to meet you, Miss Avory. I hope you both enjoy your room service tonight, and I'll see you in the morning for cereal."

"Unicorn marshmallow cereal," Livia said, a little sass in her tone. "It's my favorite."

I gave her a salute. "I will check in with the cooks at dinner tonight and make sure they'll have it out for you first thing."

Livia grinned, dancing in place again as if she couldn't control her excitement. Adorable. Avory smiled down at her daughter before shaking her head and reaching to unlock the door.

"Goodnight, Beadan."

Yup. That was a definite cue to get the hell out of their hair. "Goodnight. Welcome to The Pack House."

I waited until they'd walked into the room and shut the door behind them before turning on my heel and heading for the kitchens. Livia wanted unicorn marshmallow cereal, and I would not let the child down. I needed to make sure the kitchen had it in stock then lock it up so none of the asshole fighters ate it all.

I wasn't about to fail on my very first promise.

FOUR

Avory

The next morning, Beadan met Livia and me at the entrance to the cafeteria with a bright smile and two whole boxes of unicorn marshmallow cereal before leading us to one of the tables. I was pretty sure Livia fell in love with the man the second her eyes locked on those bright-pink containers of sugar. Me? Well...

Mate.

My inner wolf seemed interested enough—and by enough, I mean she wanted to jump his bones right there in the hallway—but the human side of me, the one who'd already had her heart broken a time or two, was far more cautious. I knew mating was far different from dating, but that didn't mean I was ready to dive in headfirst. Livia needed me to be smart about everything regarding us.

"Mr. Bay...this cereal is the best," Livia said, shooting me a sly look as she dove in for another spoonful. "Mommy never buys this for me."

Traitor.

"Let's get to eating instead of talking, Livia. I need to be on time for practice."

Beadan kept a smile on his face, kept his voice calm and nonjudgmental. "She's coming to the gym with you?"

"I don't really have another choice." I rose to throw away my garbage.

Beadan jumped to his feet and took the tray from me, whispering *I've got it* before heading for the nearest garbage can. I couldn't help but watch him—he was just so big and bulky, so very masculine. And handsome. He was definitely handsome.

Mate...mine.

I sighed and shook my head, trying my hardest to rein in the wolf pacing inside my head. She kept brushing her fur against my senses, knowing how much that bothered me. She wanted what she wanted, and that was Beadan. I wasn't ready to make that declaration yet.

The three of us walked to the gym together, Livia jumping and skipping and making a ton of noise. Unicorn marshmallows gave her a sugar high—hence why *Mommy* never bought them. Beadan kept her entertained, though. Me? I stayed quiet, my nerves kicking up. Today was a sparring day, and it wouldn't be an easy one like yesterday. We were going to fight, which meant I was about to find out how good some of the other women were.

"Right here," I said, my voice low and tight as I pointed to a spot on a bench. Livia sat right down, tugging her little bag of coloring books, crayons, toys, snacks, and juice boxes next to her. She knew the routine. "You good, baby?"

"Yup." She set Cornelius up so he could watch the ring too. "Mr. Bay, are you watching Mommy fight too?"

Beadan caught my eye, his lips pulled tight. Was he... nervous? "No, Miss Livia. I have to go fight in my own ring. But I'm sure your mommy is going to do real well."

Livia nodded, her feet dangling. "She's the best. I've never seen her lose."

"Way to hike up the pressure, kid." I shook out my hands and stretched my neck, wanting to get this over with already. Livia was right—I'd never lost. That didn't mean I was cocky, though. I still got nervous before even a practice match. At least, until I stepped in the ring.

"You good?" Beadan asked, still looking concerned. Dropping his gaze to Livia to make his question understood. Were *we* good—not just me. My heart pitter-pattered at the idea of him already looking out for both of us. One point for Beadan.

"We'll be fine."

He huffed, not sounding convinced. "Okay, well...I need to get to my trainer. Miss Livia, if you need anything, you holler for me, okay? I'll come running."

"Okay, Mr. Bay." She giggled, twisting so she could look up at him. "That rhymed."

"You got a nickname already," I said. "That's quite the compliment."

"At least I'm on the right path with one of you." He leaned in closer, dropping his voice. "Stay safe in there. You can holler for me, too—I'll come running for you, too."

I really hated how sweet he was. And handsome. And that he smelled good. "Thanks. We'll be okay."

He held my gaze for a long moment before finally nodding. "I'll see you after practice, then."

I watched as he walked off, trying hard to convince my heart to stop beating so hard and for my mind to stop thinking such dirty thoughts. I had other things to do. Such as—

"Raven."

I spun, catching the eye of the trainer—Big Mike—in the ring. "Yeah?"

"Time to fight."

There it was—the other stuff I had to do. I dropped a kiss onto Livia's head and climbed into the ring, holding out my hands so Mike could tape them while another trainer looked over a clipboard.

"You'll be sparring with Medusa."

A woman stepped into the ring, her thick, dark hair plaited into an art form on top of her head. The name was fitting. I took her in as we were both readied to fight. Tall, muscular, and with probably a solid fifty pounds on me. Seemed like they were playing for the whole underdog versus giant thing. That was fine. I knew my strengths, and I'd taken down opponents bigger than her.

I had this.

Sparring started as it always did—both of us dancing around a little, looking for a break or opportunity. Medusa swung first, a slow drive with her left that was easy enough to dodge. She then came with her right, still slow. Intentionally so. Medusa was smart—she was setting me up to assume her fighting style. I knew better than that, though.

So, I waited, and I kept my eyes on her shoulders, and I took advantage of one last slow jab by cutting up and under to connect with her ribs before dancing away. The whole slow, plodding tempo dropped right there, and Medusa came in hard and fast.

Now we had a fight.

Ten minutes of back-and-forth, of racing around the ring and taking more blows than I cared to count, ended with Medusa huffing and puffing as if she'd run a marathon, while I... well, I was breathing heavy, too. Just not as heavy as her.

I considered that a win.

"Good job, ladies!" the coach with the clipboard yelled, stepping into the center. "Take five, then we'll get each of you a new partner. Raven, you'll stay in this ring."

I nodded and headed to the corner for some water. My eyes immediately darted to Livia, who wasn't alone. Beadan sat beside her, the two playing a complicated game of what looked like patty-cake. Why he wasn't practicing in his own ring, I had no idea.

As if he sensed me looking, he glanced up, shooting me a wink and a smile.

Heart, behave yourself.

"Raven, let's go."

And so the day went—I sparred with what felt like every woman in that facility. During breaks, I caught Beadan either in his own ring, dancing around and throwing beautiful, arching punches, or sitting with Livia. The two seemed thick as thieves already, something that both thrilled and worried me. If he wasn't who he said he was, if this was all an act—

Mate. Good man.

Yeah, we'd thought that latter thing once before.

Livia and I spent lunch together but without Beadan, who was still fighting when we were released to eat. A quick meal, and then we were back in the gym, Livia playing and me fighting. For hours.

By the fates, was life at The Pack House exhausting.

When my training was done for the day—when I'd spent more hours sparring than ever before—I hopped out of the ring to find Livia by herself. She set down her crayons and coloring book as I approached, jumping up to give me a hug. One that hurt my sore muscles, not that I'd shirk away from her affection.

"Did you win, Mommy?"

I was still standing, so somewhere inside, I figured that counted as a win.

"Don't I always?" Her little giggle melted my heart, but I was tired. Tired and sweaty and starving. "How about we get some food?"

"We have to wait for Mr. Bay. I promised."

I looked up, spotting Beadan easily enough. He was still sparring in a ring across the gym, looking fierce and aggressive in his stance. The man was built like a linebacker but moved like a dancer, something that did not make sense to my brain. It was as if I were watching another reality, a dimension where gravity didn't affect people the same way it did in mine.

Either that, or I was really tired.

Livia packed up her bag and led the way to the ringside where Beadan was fighting, arriving just in time to watch Beadan knock his opponent to the ground. He practically growled, breathing hard and staring like a predator at fallen prey, but then he spotted us. His eyes softened, and a smile pulled at his lips around his mouthguard. He ripped the tape from his hands and spat out the guard, his long legs gobbling up the length of the ring in a handful of strides before hopping down to land directly in front of Livia.

"Did you win, Mr. Bay?" she asked, hugging Cornelius to her chest.

Beadan nodded. "I did. How'd your mommy do?"

"She won. She always wins."

Beadan tossed me a smile. "She's strong and quick. Good qualities in a fighter."

"Okay, you two." I grabbed Livia's hand, rolling my eyes at the brute grinning our way. "I think I've had about enough of fighting talk for one day."

"Understood." Beadan rose to his feet, suddenly looking a little more nervous than before. "Can I join you ladies for dinner?"

I was about to refuse—to go with the answer that popped into my tired mind and made my wolf a cranky canine—but Livia beat me to the punch.

"Of course. Mommy's tired and cranky, so I need someone

to talk to." She tucked Cornelius into her bag then grabbed Beadan's hand, dragging both of us toward the cafeteria. "Do you think they'll have unicorn marshmallow cereal for dessert?"

Beadan grinned, his eyes meeting mine. I rolled my own in response. His grin only widened, and he had the audacity to wink at me.

Jerk.

Handsome, sexy jerk.

I was in so much trouble.

FIVE

A simple meal had never been so much fun.

"Again, Mr. Bay."

I grinned at Livia's excited expression, placing my hands together in between us so we could play the most intricate game of patty-cake I'd ever seen.

"Ready." But I wasn't ready. Not in the least. I made it through about twelve of the 715 steps Livia had been trying to explain to me for over an hour before I screwed up. The girl laughed at my failure as always, tossing her head back and filling the room with the sound. She was perfect and funny and adorable—how could I not be entertained?

"Liv, baby," Avory said, fork still in hand. "You're being a little loud."

"Sorry, Mommy." Livia had a gleam in her eye, the one that told me she had the heart of a fighter. "Let's play again."

So that I could mess up and she could win. See? A fighter.

While I lost to Livia, Avory sat across from us, chatting with another female fighter occasionally and enjoying a leisurely dinner. I had a feeling she didn't get to relax and take her time very often. Livia was a great kid, but she was still a *kid*. Lots of energy, lots of desire to snag all the attention. Lots of needs to be fulfilled. Avory, as a single mom, likely didn't get a break from that very often. I was happy to offer her something as simple as time to enjoy her food and company, even if that company wasn't me.

I had patty-cake to play.

"Again, Mr. Bay. Again."

We played all through the meal service, not stopping until I asked if she wanted dessert. Those big eyes grew even rounder and wider than usual.

"Do you think they have ice cream?"

Fuck me, that face. If they didn't have ice cream, I was going to churn some myself.

"I'll check. What flavor?"

Livia gave that question some serious thought, even bringing her finger up to tap on her chin. "Vanilla."

Thank the fates she hadn't said anything crazy, at least. "Vanilla ice cream. And you, Avory? Want any dessert?"

My entire body clenched when she smiled my way, those dark eyes landing on mine and making the universe around us dissolve. One look, and I was hard as a rock and ready to take her to a dark corner to get my hands on her. That was...yeah. A lot to fight back.

Avory's head cocked a little as she watched me, her smile turning sly as if she knew what she was doing to me. That was fine—she needed to know how much power she held over me. Needed to revel in it so she could grow comfortable with me. Yes, I'd do anything for her. That was the shifter way. I'd never even look at another woman the same way, and I would beat down any man who dared to approach her. She was mine—once she said I could have her—and I would be hers. Wholly. Completely.

"Do you think they have any brownies?"

Such a simple request, and one I would fulfill. "I'll look. Be right back."

I was up and across the room in seconds, hunting for ice cream and brownies. Knowing if they didn't have them, I'd be spending some time in the kitchen to make them. My ladies deserved a little sweetness—I would not fail them. Thankfully, the kitchen had the ice cream machine working and a big platter of fresh brownies available. I filled a small bowl for Livia, tossing some rainbow sprinkles in a bowl just in case, and put a thick brownie on a plate for Avory. I made myself a brownie sundae, figuring it had to be the best of both worlds.

Avory took one look at my bowl when I sat back down, and her mouth fell open. "Oh, that looks—"

"It's yours." I pushed the sundae across the table, giving her a wink. "And I brought you some sprinkles, Miss Livia. In case you felt like decorating your ice cream."

She bounced in her seat. "Oh, yes please. I love sprinkles."

Jackpot on both counts.

We finished dessert in much the same way as we had dinner, but this time, Avory's attention seemed solely focused on Livia and me. A lot on me, to be honest.

"Where are you from?" she asked just before she licked a dollop of ice cream off the tip of her spoon. The pink in total contrast to the white. It took me a second for my shattered brain to understand those words because the sight had been so...distracting.

"Uh, New York. Upstate."

"What do you do there?"

Focus, Beadan. Focus. "Farming, mostly. We're a small pack, but we own enough acreage to be pretty self-sufficient."

Avory's face grew pale, her eyes widening in surprise, but Livia looked ready to jump out of her seat.

"Do you have goats?" the little girl asked, obviously highly interested in the topic.

I nodded, curious as to their reactions. "I don't personally, but my parents and brother do, along with lots of other packmates. My barn only houses a couple of horses and some chickens right now."

"Mommy!" Livia looked about to launch herself across the table. "He has chickens!"

"I heard." Avory shook her head, grinning. "This one is obsessed with farms. She wants lots of animals to take care of."

"You should come see my place sometime." I shot a look at Avory, my leg bouncing with nerves, knowing she could flat out shoot me down. "I've got a house and some acreage of good fields. There're even a few pastures for raising cows if that suits you. My pack is small and tight-knit, but we all work together to keep the farms running."

"How did you end up here...fighting?"

I shrugged, relieved that she hadn't completely refused my offer. "My entire pack is made up of mated sets. I left to help the fates bring me my match."

"They're all mated?"

I nodded, holding her gaze. Doing my best to impart as much feeling into my words as possible. "Every one of them, my brother being the most recent and having *two* mates. The rest are all happy and healthy and totally in love—exactly as they should be."

She shook her head, still looking a little surprised. "I've never heard of a pack of all mated pairs and even a triad. I wonder what that's like."

"Whenever you're ready, you can come with me to check it out." I let my voice drop, holding that gaze that was beginning to mean the world to me. I put every ounce of my truth into my words as I said, "My farm is ready for you."

As I should have expected, it was Livia who replied.

"Can I come too? I want to see the chickens."

Avory blinked, sitting back a little as I huffed a laugh.

"Can you? Of course you can. I wouldn't invite your mommy and not have you come along too." I leaned a little closer, grinning when she giggled. "You two are a matched set. There's no breaking you apart."

"Then we'll come," Livia said, returning all her focus to her sprinkle-covered ice cream. "I want to live on a farm."

I shot Avory a wink. "Whenever you and your mommy are ready, you can come home with me."

"I'm ready. Mommy, hurry up."

One down, one to go.

SIX

Avory

I let Beadan escort us back to our room, not yet ready to say goodnight. In another world, at another time, I likely would have invited him inside. He was my fated mate after all. But there was just one problem with that sort of thinking in my current reality. A problem just about three-feet tall.

"Goodnight, Mr. Bay," Livia said, reaching for the doorknob before I could. "See you at breakfast."

"You definitely will, Miss Livia." Beadan gave her a smile then looked at me, those dark eyes deep and filled with a heat I could feel. My inner wolf growled low, the sound eventually fading to a whimper. Making her wants known. Beadan breathed deep, a rumble forming in his own chest on the exhale. Both of us wordless, staring and...wanting.

"Mommy."

I jerked, my eyes darting to Livia of their own accord. "Yeah?"

"Are you coming?"

Not yet, but I want to be.

"Of course." I followed her to the door, shooting Beadan a weak sort of smile. "Thanks for today."

"It was my pleasure."

"Goodnight."

"Night." He looked each one of us over in turn, standing back to wait until we were safely inside our room. I shut the door and leaned against it, trying to catch my breath. To settle my mind. The sexual tension between us was growing, the need to mate deepening. I couldn't act on the instinct, though. I had a child to take care of and responsibilities to worry about. I couldn't make decisions all fast and loose like I had in the past. Livia deserved better.

"Can we go see Mr. Bay's farm when you're done fighting, Mommy?" The tiny person who ruled my entire world sat at the edge of our bed, kicking off her shoes and holding tight to Cornelius the cow. "He said we could."

"He did, and maybe we will. It's too soon to know for sure, baby."

She tugged off her clothes and pulled on her pajamas, our nighttime routine pretty well set. I followed suit, slipping into a pair of loose flannel pants and a tank top. Once we were dressed for bed, we headed into the bathroom, where we brushed and flossed our teeth and washed our faces. Totally normal. Nothing to be excited about, and yet my skin tingled in some sort of anticipation. I was completely on edge with no way to relieve the tension, but I didn't know why.

Livia crawled into bed when she was all clean and ready, snuggling Cornelius and handing me her favorite book. "Mr. Bay seems real nice."

The child was on a mission. "He does, but it's too soon to know anything about him for sure."

She frowned but laid her head on her pillow, closing her

eyes. "I know for sure. But that's okay, Mommy. You take your time—he'll be waiting for us."

I opened her book and rolled my eyes. "Thanks for the encouragement, kid."

And so, I read, and I let my mind wander a bit as I repeated the words I'd said a hundred times. And when Livia had obviously fallen asleep, I set her book on the nightstand and took a deep breath. Letting my wolf come to the surface. Letting her help clear my thoughts.

Mate. Mine.

So, maybe not clear. Maybe fill them with only one thought instead of hundreds. Beadan.

"I'm never going to fall asleep." I grabbed my own book— one that was definitely not child-appropriate—and slipped out of the room. I'd never leave Livia alone, but sometimes I needed a moment without the sound of her breathing to distract me. So, I closed the door to our room, I dropped to the floor with my back to the door, and I opened my book. Distractions. I needed distractions.

I was a good two chapters into the story of a small-town girl falling in love with her childhood best friend when someone suddenly sat beside me. No, not someone. *The* one.

Beadan.

"Can't sleep?" he asked, his voice quiet but husky. Deliciously deep. The sound sent shivers up my spine.

"I could ask you the same question."

"Oh, I definitely can't sleep. I keep worrying about these two people who have suddenly become quite important to me. Wondering if they're safe and comfortable. If they need anything." He turned and looked right at me, those dark eyes only increasing the trembling within me. "So, do you? Need anything, that is?"

Jerk. Caring, thoughtful, kind jerk.

"We're fine."

Beadan chuckled and shook his head slowly. "If there's one thing my momma and aunts have taught me, it's that nothing is ever just fine. What's on your mind, beautiful?"

I held up my book and shrugged a shoulder. "Everything. That's why I'm out here. I wanted a distraction, which is pretty hard to come by with Livia beside me in the bed."

He took a good look at the book in my hand. "So, you came out here to read and relax."

"Yeah."

"Cool. Don't let me stop you." He settled deeper against the wall and tugged, bringing me closer to him. Letting me use his arm and shoulder as a pillow. I didn't resist, instead falling against him and cuddling close. Taking advantage of how the contact soothed my inner wolf and warmed my body.

"What are you going to do?"

He gave me a smile. "I'm going to do the same as you—let the stress fall away and focus on my distraction."

Seemed reasonable.

So, we sat, and Beadan acted as a human pillow for me, and I read a book I'd been wanting to finish for weeks. There was no stress in that hallway, no tension, no need to fill the silence. There was only him and me and pretty words flowing across the paper and the warmth of our bodies touching. It was glorious.

At some point, Beadan began playing with my hair. There was nothing sexual about it—just a couple fingers running along the length of my waves—but the sensation was soothing. I sighed and snuggled closer, still reading. He continued with the motions, tugging slightly every few strokes, practically massaging my scalp. I could have fallen asleep right there, could have curled up in his lap and let him lull me into peaceful oblivion. But somewhere along the way, the characters in my book decided friendship wasn't enough for them. Longing glances and sweet arm touches turned more sensual, more erotic. My heart rate increased and my body warmed as I read their first kiss. As their love blossomed on the page into physical intimacy.

What had soothed my restless mind had become its own distraction.

Without thought, without allowing my mind to play through all the options of what could happen in the wake of my actions, I dropped my book and rose to my knees. I didn't give Beadan time to speak or question, simply hiked a knee over his legs and settled on his lap. Face-to-face. Eyes locked on each other. I raised a hand to run my fingers along his cheek, memorizing the feel of his skin. Wanting to learn more. Needing to.

Deciding to.

"Hold still," I whispered before leaning closer and pressing my lips to his. Not hard, not an attack, just a simple, slow kiss. Gentle, even. He did as he was told, not moving most of his body. His lips pursed against mine, though. Moved with them. He was kissing me back.

I wanted more.

Inching closer, I kissed him again. Deeper this time. Opening my mouth over his. He followed my motions, allowing our tongues to touch. Sneaking tastes of each other right there in the hallway. Anyone could have walked up on us, could have seen our intimate moment, but I couldn't worry about that. All I wanted—all I cared about—was memorizing the feel and taste of the man before me. Just this once.

"I'm done holding still," Beadan whispered when we broke apart, though that was all he had time to get out. He kissed *me* that time, raising an arm so he could grip the back of my head and holding me in place. Wrapping the other arm around my waist and tugging me closer. The feel of him, the press of our bodies together, awoke something inside me. I wanted. Needed. Craved more. More skin, more feeling, more touching, more contact. I shook with the power of it, jerked closer and rocked my hips to entice him into acting. I—

A door slammed somewhere nearby, and we broke apart. Beadan growling a thunderous sound as he yanked me closer and looked in the direction of where the sound had come from. Protecting me. Us. By the fates, the man was...impressive.

"It's probably nothing," I whispered, still clutching his face and trying to catch my breath.

He cut off the growl. "Probably, but you never know around here." He pushed my hair over my ear and dropped a kiss onto my brow bone. "It's late. You should get inside. I won't be able to sleep if I think you might be out in these halls all alone."

"Yeah, okay." I dropped my head onto his chest and took a deep breath. Not ready to let go just yet. He ran his hands up and down my back, not rushing to separate us. But when the sound of voices—male voices—met my ears from farther down the hall, I knew our time together had ended.

"Gotta go," I said, slowly untangling myself from his hold and rising to my feet. He followed, keeping my hand in his but his eyes on the far end of the hall. On guard.

"Lock the door when you get in there. I'll see you for breakfast."

"Okay." I rose onto the balls of my feet and gave him one last kiss—a quiet, closed-mouth one. "Goodnight, Beadan."

He smiled down at me, rubbing my cheek with his thumb. "Goodnight, Avory. Sleep well."

And with that, I headed inside to do as I was told—to sleep well while dreaming of another kiss. Of another cuddle. Of more. I really hoped the fates were right in pairing us, because Beadan certainly seemed like the kind of man I'd been looking for. Only time would tell, though.

Starting with another breakfast in just a few hours.

SEVEN

Beadan

One more fight. Just one more fight.

I spent the next morning—after a breakfast of unicorn marshmallow cereal, of course—sparring in the ring. Tomorrow, there would be actual fights with spectators and opponents, which meant I needed to show my stuff. Needed to make sure the trainers saw me. I needed to win one more fight.

"Good, Bear. Let's get a little more speed."

I hated the fight name they'd given me, but I nodded anyway and upped the beat in my head. Trouble was, Avory was sparring in her practice ring too. That woman was a distraction—a big one—and her daughter was the cherry on top of that focus-stealing sundae. I tossed easy punches and let my eyes wander to the two females who had overtaken my life, not a damn bit mad about it.

One more fight.

All I needed was the one win. That should give me enough money to take Avory and Livia home with me to the farm and live for a few seasons before I'd need to worry about turning any sort of profit. I couldn't wait for them to see my land. Couldn't wait for my family to meet them. They were going to love Avory, of course, but Livia was the one who was about to be spoiled rotten. They would *adore* her cheeky little personality. My mom would likely have a pasture filled with ponies by the time we got there if I told her my mate had a daughter. I wasn't telling them just yet, though—I wanted to give Avory a chance to get to know me first.

"Water break!" The trainer's voice was the only thing that could have stopped my thoughts or my punches. I had been in the zone—maybe being distracted by Avory was a good thing.

I hopped down from the ring and grabbed my water bottle, guzzling a little as I kept watching my mate. Damn, she was fast. Those punches looked wicked hard too. She was a scorpion hidden under a beautiful exterior. You wouldn't see the woman coming, but you'd know for sure when she struck.

"Check her out," one of the other fighters said from behind me, likely talking to another guy nearby. "Now that's what I call a MILF."

"You should make her call you Daddy."

The two jackasses laughed. I wasn't laughing. That was my mate they were talking about, but I couldn't clap back at them. Couldn't say a damned word because no one knew that fact. Hell, Avory hadn't specifically said she would accept my mating. Sure, the other fighters had likely seen me dining with the two ladies, but no way could they know the truth.

One more fight, and I was taking my girls out of this place. Period.

"Bear. Take on Ice."

I set down my bottle and turned, almost giddy to see that Ice was the fighter who'd been chatting behind me. Whether he was the MILF man or the Daddy one didn't matter—both needed to be put in their places, and I was the man to do it.

"You good?" Ice asked as I stepped into the ring. "You look a little flushed, Bear."

I shrugged, cracking my neck and getting ready to knock him on his ass. "Just looking forward to watching you fall to the mat, that's all."

"Never happening," he said. As if he had a choice.

I grinned as the trainer yelled for us to start, giving him a minute to step toward me. I had a solid six inches on him—an unfair advantage, really—but that didn't make me want to give him a break. He had to learn a lesson, and I was his teacher today.

Two punches and a lot of Ice dancing around doing absolutely nothing later, I was bored.

"That the best you got?"

Ice scowled, racing toward me and throwing a Hail Mary sort of punching spree. I took a few hits, blocking the majority, before I saw my opening. Ice moved as if to pivot, so I swung around and up, connecting with that fucking mouth of his. He went down like a tree in the forest—almost in slow motion and straight as could be. It was a glorious knockout.

When he was down, when I knew I'd won, I knelt beside him as if to help him to his feet, and I leaned in real close.

"Talk about women that way again, especially that one over there, and you won't be breathing when you leave the ring."

And with that, I stood, leaving him flat on his back, and I hopped out of the ring. The trainer met me at the side.

"Got beef with him I should know about?"

"Not anymore."

The trainer nodded, writing on his clipboard. "I've got a fight for you tomorrow. High-roller betters are coming in, and we need all the money we can make because of the fire."

The fire that had destroyed the other Pack House. Made sense. "What do you need me to do?"

"I need you to fight like you do—long and slow, drag that shit out so people have time to lay money down."

"Understood."

"You're a good man, Bear."

I nodded, leaving him behind in order to go check on Livia. I wasn't a good man—not yet—but my women would help make me one. I just had to win one more fight, and I'd have everything I needed.

One more win, and we were going home.

———

Avory

There were just some days when your entire body seemed to be on the same page and the fights came easy. This was one of those days.

"Faster, Raven. Make her work for it."

I did what the trainer wanted, throwing jabs and punches faster, keeping my opponent—a really nice woman from somewhere in Vermont—retreating. All the while, my mind stayed busy. Was Livia okay? Would watching her momma fight like this leave any sort of weird, emotional scars? Would she understand that I did what I needed to so we could survive? Take some hits or not feed my baby—the choice was really, really clear to me.

I threw more punches.

But while I fought and my mind spun with worry for my daughter, my eyes sought out Beadan. He was like a beacon for me, a lighthouse in a storm. The man stood out even among the other fighters, just bigger and thicker enough to seem menacing.

Not that he was—Beadan was about the sweetest, gentlest man I'd ever met. I felt safe with him.

A feeling I was not used to having.

My inner wolf growled and forced my attention back into the ring where my opponent was in midswing. I ducked and dodged, the punch glancing across my jaw instead of hitting me full on. *Stop thinking about Beadan and fight.*

I spent another few minutes dancing around the ring before the trainer called an end to the fight. He met me at the side of the ring.

"Feeling good?"

I nodded, ready for more. "Absolutely."

"We've got a fight for you tomorrow. You think you're ready for that?"

A fight. That was what I needed—a way to win some cash so Livia and I could buy that farm she so wanted. Like the one my mate already owned.

Focus, Avory.

"I'm ready. What do I need to know?"

He looked over his clipboard. "Your opponent fights a little dirty, so you'll need to pay attention to her tells if you want a chance to win. Otherwise, it should be a pretty even match." He looked up, giving me a wink that made me more than a little uncomfortable. "I know you can take her."

I nodded, moving away from him and throwing punches so my muscles didn't stiffen up. Maybe it was all the testosterone in the air—because you could practically smell that shit—but I felt more exposed today. More watched. I glanced over at Livia, making sure no one was bothering her, only to find Beadan sitting beside her, crayon in hand. The weight his presence took off my shoulders was immense. My girl was safe, which was all I wanted. I could focus on the fighting again.

I needed to win.

And then I needed to be alone time with my mate.

It was time to explore our connection. Sans little eyes and ears.

EIGHT

Beadan

Dinner with my girls was becoming one of my favorite times of day. Breakfast was nice too, but the evening meal tended to be quieter and more focused on the three of us. Avory no longer chatted with the other women fighters while eating—she sat across from me and kept her focus split between Livia and me. Kept a smile on her face and a sparkle in her eyes that I hoped meant she was enjoying herself. She kept me enthralled with her beauty.

Yeah, dinners were my favorite.

After dinner, the three of us took a stroll through the facility. Since we technically weren't allowed outside, this was a good way to let Livia burn off some energy. It also gave Avory and me a few minutes to talk. Alone.

"Help, Mr. Bay. I want to fight like Mommy." Livia reached up and grabbed the bottom rope for a ring, obviously trying to climb inside. I gave her little tush a shove and helped her the rest of the way, grinning as she started dancing around the ring.

When she became distracted playing with the ropes themselves, I sat down beside her mom. It was time for a talk.

"So..." I started, a little nervous. A little worried she might shoot me down. "I'm just going to come right out and say it."

Avory definitely tensed. "Say what?"

"I want to take you home with me. You and Livia. To my farm."

She sat perfectly still, her back straight and her eyes locked on Livia. I, meanwhile, felt as if I were melting into the floor. Readying myself for rejection.

Finally, Avory coughed. "That...could be nice."

Relief flooded me, and I moved a little closer, grabbing her hand so she would look at me. "Yeah? I'll take care of both of you—I promise. And my family will love you. I'll be honest, they'll love Livia more, but they'll love you too."

Her lips turned up a little, and her eyebrows lifted. "You sure about that?"

"Oh, positive. If I called my mom right now and told her I'd found my mate and I now had a daughter, she'd have ten ponies in the pasture waiting on Livia's arrival. Hell, she'd figure out a way to braid their manes into horns so there would be ten unicorns."

Avory sat and stared, quiet again. Eyes wide this time. "You called Livia your daughter."

"Of course," I said, frowning. "You're my mate and she's your child, so that means she's mine. Or..." I swallowed hard, fighting to hold back a jealous rage I had no real right to allow. "Is there a dad in the picture that I don't know about?"

Avory lurched forward, placing her hand on my arm. "No. Not at all. He's...long gone. He never even saw her and didn't want to. I just didn't expect you to claim her like that."

I placed my hand over hers, tugging her closer. Not wanting an inch of space between us. "I claim you both. You're a package deal, and I am so excited to have a jump-start on our future."

Her smile exploded on to her face, brilliantly bold and wide. "You mean it?"

I dropped a quick kiss on those lips, glancing up to make sure Livia—spinning, singing child of the ring—was still distracted. "I mean it. Now, what's your debt to The Pack House? How many fights are you in for?"

"I have no debt. I only came here to make money for Livia and me."

"How long were you planning on staying?"

"Two fights."

I grunted, my brain swirling. "I don't owe them either, but I'd like one last fight. That'll be a little extra money in the bank to pad the accounts so I can get us through a couple of growing seasons on the farm. I have one scheduled for tomorrow."

"Me too. So, one fight for you and two for me."

I grabbed her wrist, unable not to touch her. "Then we leave. Together."

She sighed and leaned into me, resting her head against my shoulder. "It'll be good to get Livia out of here."

"It will," I said, watching the little girl in question. "The farm is quiet, though. We're a small pack—family bonded and close, but small."

"I think I might like that. I've never had a pack."

My heart broke a little for her, my childhood memories of love and attention flying through my mind. She hadn't experienced any of that. It was my job to show her how good a tight pack could be.

"You will love it. Every person is kind and loving. They will all spoil the two of you rotten." I glanced up as Livia danced closer, grinning when she smiled my way. "Speaking of rotten."

"I'm not rotten," Livia said, putting those little hands on her hips. "Mommy, am I rotten?"

Avory laughed and rose to her feet, reaching for her—*our*—girl. "You are the rottenest, but I love you anyway."

I stood and reached for Livia, laughing when she dove into my arms from between two of the ropes. I grabbed her airborne body and flipped her, settling her hips on my shoulders. "Ready to head back, ladies?"

Livia laughed and pointed. "Giddyup, Mr. Bay."

And with that, I giddied. Or rather, I walked a bouncy step to jostle her around and hear her giggle. Avory walked beside me, grabbing my hand and hanging on. The three of us... connected. Like any family should be.

Man, my heart could not have gotten any lighter than in that moment. But all good things must come to an end.

"Bear!" Trainer Tony yelled from farther down the hall, giving the three of us a hard once-over. "Mick wants to see you."

I stared him down, making sure he had his eyes on the floor before I set Livia on her feet. "You two get back to your room, you hear me?"

Avory looked worried. "Are you going to be okay?"

"Of course. I'll be fine." I kissed her forehead then gave Livia a big hug. "I have to go talk to the trainers. Just head on back and stay safe."

Avory grabbed Livia's hand, still looking nervous. "I might be reading later."

"I'll bring my book." I gave her one last forehead kiss then headed for Tony, making sure to keep a scowl on my face. "Is there a problem?"

Tony shook his head. "Nah, but Mick said he wanted to see you." The man was quiet for a ways, leading me deeper into the facility. But then he murmured, "You know you're not supposed to—"

I didn't let him finish. "Mind your own. You don't want to piss me off."

He nodded, still walking. I, meanwhile, felt completely torn. I knew I needed to see Mick if he was asking for me—without his approval, I'd never get in the ring again, and I needed one last win for my plan. But I hated leaving Avory and Livia alone. Hated knowing they were exposed to whatever the other fighters might want to do. Avory could definitely hold her own in a fight, but little Livia... I would kill for either of them, but that little one was special. I needed to get this over with so I could check on my girls.

Tony led me to a room at the far end of the facility, one that looked like a storage area. One containing a very unkempt and obviously rattled Mick.

"You wanted to speak to me?"

The man jumped, his eyes wild as they found mine. "Bear. I need to know what you know about the fire. Have you heard from any of the other fighters?"

I shook my head, staying a good distance away from the man. "All I know is there was a fire—" *a bad one that caused a lot of deaths and total destruction of the facility, but I certainly wasn't bringing all that up* "—and I haven't heard from anyone else. I came straight here when I heard about the second facility."

"Fine. That's fine." Mick began to pace, mumbling to himself. Putting me even more on edge.

"Sir, are you—"

"I expect a good fight from you tomorrow, Bear. A good, long one. We need all the bets we can get, so don't let me down."

I nodded slowly. "Of course, sir. I'll do my best."

"Good. Good. And no fraternizing with the females. Someone said they saw you eating with Raven. I'll kick her out of she's—"

The growl I issued was instinctual and unstoppable. "You don't get to threaten her."

He jerked to a stop, staring at me. "You know the rules, Bear."

"I do, and I know I haven't broken them. So, don't worry about Raven and me."

Mick didn't look happy. In fact, for just a moment, I saw the old Mick. The put-together, powerful man behind The Pack House industry. That moment faded, though, and he returned to the disheveled, mumbling man he'd become.

"In my day, there wouldn't be so much strife. You told fighters what to do, and they did it." He wandered through the room, mumbling to himself for several minutes. Meanwhile, I waited. Wishing he'd shut up so I could get back to Avory and Livia. Worrying far more about my girls than this old man.

Finally, after way too long, he wandered away from me, heading toward a door at the back of the room. I didn't follow him or wait for an official comment that it was okay for me to leave. Instead, I slipped into the hall and jogged toward the housing units. I needed to make sure Avory and Livia were okay. Needed to know they were safe.

I needed them to calm the beast within me that was ready to burst free and protect them.

Something was definitely wrong with Mick, and I didn't want that man anywhere near my girls.

NINE

Avory

Once Livia was in bed, I took my book and headed into the hallway to wait for Beadan. He'd told me he'd show up, so I had no doubt that he'd follow through. Okay, maybe a little doubt. Not because of him but because other people in my life would have failed to deliver on their promise.

I should have known not to let even the memory of doubt shadow the man in question.

"You good?" Beadan asked as he jogged around the corner. "Livia okay?"

I nodded, holding up my book. "She's asleep, and I'm reading. Are you okay?"

Because he definitely didn't look okay. In fact, he looked nearly panicked. He recovered well, though.

"I'm fine. I was just worried about you two." He slid down the wall to sit beside me, tugging me closer as he did. "How's the book?"

"I'd rather hear about how the meeting went with Mick."

"And I'd rather talk about the book." Beadan stared down at

me, his face softening as he apparently realized I wasn't kidding. "It was fine. He wanted to know if I'd heard from anyone at the southern Pack House."

"There are other Pack Houses?"

He shrugged. "There were. The southern one burned down —that's how I ended up here. I've heard about two more, but I can't say for sure where they are or if they even exist. Mick wanted to know about the southern one. I didn't have whatever info he needed, so it was a short conversation that lasted way too long."

That seemed...contradictory, but I wasn't going to question him. Instead, I gave him a kiss on the cheek. "Well, I'm really glad you're here now."

"Me too." He sighed, resting his forehead on mine. "Read, beautiful. I need to know you're calm and relaxed."

Such a sweet man. I cuddled into his side and held up my book, falling back into the imaginary world within. Beadan sat quietly, running his fingers over my hair. Seemingly just fine with me giving most of my attention to the book in my hand instead of him.

But I was still reading my romance novel. I had just reached a scene of physical intimacy, had begun devouring the words and reading faster as I gleefully read about a hero settling himself in between a heroine's legs for what he described as a feast, when the picture I'd developed in my head of the two characters changed. No longer was the hero a tall, muscular man with more of a swimmer's body and light, unruly hair. He became a behemoth of a man with dark hair and eyes who looked as if he could move mountains. He became Beadan. Which meant the heroine looked exactly like—

"Avory?" Beadan frowned down at me, his fingers still running through my hair. "Are you okay?"

Was I? Suddenly, all the moments leading up to the chapter

I was on shifted in my mind from hero and heroine to Beadan and me. What would it feel like to have those huge hands on my body? To be thrown around by him? I had never felt small or soft growing up, had always been the strong one, but Beadan's physical strength made mine pale in comparison. And I sort of wanted to find out what all he would do to me if he had me alone.

I coughed, trying really hard to focus on the moment. "I'm fine."

He chuckled and shook his head slowly. "As I've said—my momma and aunts taught me long ago that *fine* does not mean fine. What's happening in your head, beautiful?"

Tell him, my wolf intoned, pacing and huffing in my mind. And I could have told him—could have admitted why I'd gotten a bit excited and squirmy. But telling Beadan wasn't what I wanted to do. I wanted to show him.

So, I set my book down.

And I sat up, swinging a leg over his lap as soon as I could.

And I kissed that man with everything I had, grabbing hold of his face and holding him to me as his lips and tongue tangled with mine. He didn't hold back, didn't question me and my impulsiveness. He simply went along for the ride, letting me lead. At least until we finally broke apart.

Then, he chuckled. "Something in that book of yours got you a little worked up, mate?"

By the fates, the way the word mate sent tingles up my spine would be the death of me. "It may have gotten a little steamy."

His eyes darkened, his hands gripping me tighter and sliding lower to grab hold of my ass. "How steamy?"

I liked that deep, growly voice. I liked it a lot. So, I leaned in and bit his bottom lip, letting out my own growl. Telling his wolf how much his obvious strength made me feel.

"The hero was about to go down on the heroine when I started picturing you in his place and—"

Beadan didn't let me finish. He gripped my ass and tugged me closer, shoving me back in the next movement. I adjusted my position a little, and then there it was. The pressure. The feel of his cock right where I wanted it to be. Well, almost. As close as we could get to *that,* considering we were in a hallway. The thought of possibly getting caught almost made the moment more delicious, not less. I leaned in close and bit his neck. His earlobe. His jaw.

"Someone could see."

He growled deep, thrusting up against me as I writhed and panted. "I'll blind any motherfucker who tries to get a look at you right now. This face, those unfocused eyes and dark lips... those are only for me." He kissed me deeply, groaning and growling and pulling apart way too soon. "No one gets to see you come but me."

I nodded, my head falling against his shoulder as I realized he really was going to make me come right there in the hallway. He had his cock firmly placed against my pussy, had the motion just right and the pressure slowly increasing. Had his growl sustained and just low enough for me to hear it. A moment of privacy in a very public space.

And then he started talking.

"You're so beautiful, Avory. So strong and amazing. Give me a chance to show you, and I'll be the best mate. I'll kill anyone who threatens our family, and I'll work every day to provide you with everything you deserve." He groaned and adjusted his grip, his fingers spreading my ass cheeks wider. "Fuck, beautiful. Give me a chance, and I'll work all day, every day to provide for us, then come home and murder this pussy every night. You want me to play a pirate so you can be a damsel in distress? Done. I'll wear the hat and crawl under your skirts without hesitation. I'll fuck you for hours, show you how a real man takes care of his woman. I'll have you screaming my name every single day."

I cried out, not doubting him a bit, but far too gone to make sense of anything else he said. The intention was there, though. If I gave him a chance, he'd be my personal hero. He'd take care of me. He'd make sure I was satisfied *in all ways*.

And wasn't *that* an intriguing idea?

"I'm gonna come," I whispered, opening my mouth to bite his neck again. Rocking my body over his hips as every ounce of my world funneled down to that one moment, that one place, that one feeling of pleasure and anticipation. Until I crashed against him, rocking and writhing and biting him hard. Collapsing onto his chest and feeling the growl he released through my entire body.

Until he jerked and groaned and whispered my name as a chant against the top of my head.

Until we were still once more.

And then I laughed. "Well, that was unexpected."

Beadan ran a hand along the length of my back, patting my ass when he reached there once more. "Good unexpected, I hope."

I leaned back so I could give him a kiss, tugging him closer. "Definitely good unexpected."

He stared at me with a look that was pure want, pure openness. Pure loving mate. My wolf practically purred, content for the first time in our life. This was right. This man had been delivered to me practically on a silver platter, and I wanted to accept the gift. To be sure the fates knew how appreciative I was.

I wanted to surrender to him.

"One fight," I said, leaning in and kissing those plump lips again. "One fight for me, and I'll leave with you. That way, we're done sooner."

He grinned, watching me. "That means tomorrow."

I nodded, unable not to return the smile. "Tomorrow."

He yanked me in for a hug, wrapping his arms around me and growling low and soft. A sound I could more feel than hear. "You'll be safe with me, Avory. You and Livia both. I'm going to give you two the best life possible."

And somehow, I believed him.

TEN

Beadan

I spent the next morning wishing I could have more time with my girls instead of handling all the last-minute details of a fight day. There was training, carbing up, massages, and basically a lot of hours of being distracted because I didn't get to have unicorn marshmallow cereal with my little girl. And Avory—fuck, that woman had me tangled up in knots. I just needed this one fight, just one more win, and I was taking her home with me.

But if there was one thing I was having trouble with, it was superstitions. I hadn't called my family to tell them about my mating because I was too worried speaking about Avory out loud would make her disappear. I was looking forward to doing that tonight after the two of us were done fighting—I had a feeling my mother was going to cry. In a good way, of course.

That was what got me through the day—thoughts of leaving The Pack House, of my mom crying when I told her I was coming home with a mate *and* a daughter, and overall good feelings about my future. A future with one obstacle in the way.

"Bear," Trainer Tony hollered as I was getting my hands taped. "You've got Ice in the ring. Warm up."

I caught the eye of the guy taping my hands. "Didn't I spar with him the other day?"

"Yup." He kept his eyes on what he was doing, not speaking again until he tore off the last piece of tape. "And he's been talking shit about you ever since, so keep your eyes open."

Good to know.

I took a few moments to bounce around the changing room, letting my muscles loosen up and my mind switch to fight mode. All thoughts of sexy Avory and sweet Livia had to be tucked away, all plans for my future shoved into a vault for safekeeping. Tonight was about one thing—winning the fight.

Once I got the call to come to the ring, I hyperfocused on the moment. There was no crowd, no screaming, no betting. There was just me and Ice, whom I could see coming toward me from the opposite side of the facility. We met in the center of the ring as was ritual, neither giving the other a moment of respect. There were no fist bumps in The Pack House tonight— there was only fighting or not fighting. It was time to start fighting.

The match started the same way most did—a little dancing, a few easy punches thrown, maybe a kick or two, depending on positioning. I kept my feet moving and my body gliding, kept watching him for an opportunity to attack. He didn't give me one. In fact, he went full floor fighting, something I wasn't the biggest fan of.

The Pack House had no rules about what style of fighting was approved. Most of us boxed—hence the ring instead of the octagon more commonly found in MMA clubs—but it wasn't a requirement. Ice had apparently learned some sort of wrestling-style fighting. Maybe jiujitsu or some shit. I couldn't tell; all I knew was one second the guy was standing and in my face, and the next he was crouching and swinging an extended leg in my direction. I fell like a ton of bricks, actually bouncing on the mat.

"Motherfucker," I spat, rolling and jumping back up as soon as I was able. Ice kept coming at me, though. Kept staying low. Kept throwing off my center of gravity and taking me to the mat. The bastard definitely had the upper hand in the match.

Until he didn't.

See, I might not have known those wrestling-style fighting moves, but I was actually really fucking fast for a man my size. I let Ice take command, let him think he had skills that beat out mine. I let him work and strike and roll until I started to see his tells, and then I made my move.

On a drop and leg swing that he'd performed at least three times, I timed a hit just right to land a downward punch to the center of his thigh. The resulting charley horse must have been super painful because he screamed as if I'd cut off a limb, and he hobbled away from me. He also glared. Probably didn't like me grinning at him. Pity that.

Didn't take him long to rise again, though. Next time, I might have to attempt to break the bone.

"You trying that same move again, Ice?" I crouched low, arms spread. Ready for anything. "I won't go easy on you this time."

"You're awfully arrogant for someone about to lose."

I snorted. "I ain't losing shit."

And I didn't. I fought hard, swinging every chance I had and making contact with the majority of those moves. Using brute force and a little speed to keep him off balance. He didn't try that leg swing again, but he did go low a few more times. I stomped him hard, though, in those moments. Probably breaking a few rules as I fractured a bone or two along the way.

"Fuck," he said after a particularly vicious attack that resulted in my stomping on his leg. "You broke my foot."

I shrugged, hands still up even though he had crumpled to the mat. "It'll heal. You still fighting, or are we through here?"

Ice growled low and deep, his pupils growing. He was close to shifting for sure, something we were definitely not allowed to do. I took a step back, giving him room to pull himself together. Time the refs forced on him instead.

"Fight called," the announcer said as the entire crowd hollered and cheered. "We have a man down with broken bones. Winner by default is Bear!"

I accepted the cheers but kept my eyes on Ice. That man was not happy—in fact, he looked positively murderous. I waited until they had him on a stretcher and were carrying him out of the ring before giving him a finger wave and a wink.

"Better luck next time."

Ice looked ready to jump off the stretcher, not that he did. Instead, he was moved out of the arena and into the locker room. Disappearing without much fanfare. I, meanwhile, held my arms up and took in the cheers, letting the crowd's energy revitalize me. I really did like winning these fights, but my last one was over. I unlocked the vault with the thoughts of taking my girls home with me and refocused on them. Avory would be fighting soon, which meant I had some time to see her before she climbed into the ring. That was all I wanted, all I cared about.

Just one more fight, and we were out of there.

ELEVEN

Avory

The Pack House training rooms where we were to get ready for our fights looked like hospital rooms. Dirty, understaffed, unequipped hospital rooms. That didn't exactly fill me with a sense of calm.

I bounced around the room, trying to ignore the grime and the dark spots on the walls that were most certainly old bloodstains. I had about forty minutes until my fight if my calculations were right. I was ready to go, though. Energized, pumped, prepared...and absolutely certain I would climb out of the ring victorious. There was just one thing missing.

Okay, two—Livia and Beadan. We were a trio now.

As if summoned by my thoughts, a very sweaty and somewhat bloody Beadan slipped in through the door. He stood for a moment in the room, just staring at me. Looking as if he was trying to decide whether to kiss or kill me. I really hoped for the former.

"Are you okay?" I asked, inching forward. My voice must have broken whatever spell he was under because he suddenly moved, twisting to lock the door, then rushing at me. Those big arms lifted me right off the ground and held me close, Beadan's entire body seeming to surround me. He even dipped his head into my neck and breathed me in as if he wanted to consume every inch of me. I was surrounded, owned.

Claimed.

"I won," he finally said, still holding me close. Every inch of him absorbing me and waking up my basest instincts. "You're up soon... Just one more fight, and this is over."

I nodded against him, running my hands over his neck. Unable not to touch more of him. "Are you okay? Did you get hurt at all?"

"I'm fine." He set me back on my feet and inched away, looking me in the eye. "You got this?"

As in the fight. As in winning. As in stepping into the ring. I knew I technically didn't have to—I could have walked away without fighting. But I'd made a promise to Livia and myself. I'd made plans for our future. Sure, Beadan coming into my life made those plans a lot easier to succeed at, but that didn't mean I was giving up on my own goals. One fight was all I needed. One win.

"I've got this," I said, nodding and trying really hard to focus. "I can totally do this."

"Good. Where's Livia?"

"Back in our room. I don't mind her watching me practice, but I don't want her seeing me in a real fight."

"Makes sense. Should I go check on her?"

I shook my head. "She won't answer the door, even for you."

"Shit." He tugged me closer, practically rubbing himself against me. Seeming needy and handsy and craving the feel of me. "But she's safe?"

"Absolutely." My wolf growled low and quiet, sniffing and practically purring in my head as she became enveloped in everything Beadan once again. Focus, gone. Fight? What fight? I had my mate in my arms, and he was making me want to do all sorts of physical things that did not involve fists. "By the fates, you smell good."

He chuckled low, reaching to grab my ass and tug me closer. "I smell like sweat."

"You smell like man." I rose onto the balls of my feet and licked up the length of his neck, biting the cord of muscle there when he groaned. "You smell like *my* man."

He had me off the floor again and wrapped in his arms in an instant, had his lips crashing into mine almost at the same moment. A quick stumble, a deep kiss that had my toes curling, and suddenly there was something hard at my back. Beadan lifted me a little higher and then set me down—a counter. He'd put me on the counter.

Oh, things were about to get interesting.

"I have a fight soon."

"Hush," he said, biting his way up my neck on his way back to my mouth. "We've got time."

And we did. He rocked and rolled against me, worked his way between my legs and kept that delightful pressure exactly where I wanted it. He had me teetering on my way to an orgasm in seconds as I held on for dear life. Legs around his hips, arms around his neck, teeth unable to be kept to myself and instead biting into the flesh of his shoulder. Yes, we had time, all right. We'd *make* time for this.

On a particularly hard thrust, one that nearly sent me falling over backward, I squeaked. Beadan must have taken that noise to mean something specific because he groaned and picked me back up, transferring me to the gurney that looked to be used as a hospital bed when needed. He tossed me to the head of it then crawled onto his knees at the end. Spreading my legs. Stalking his way between them.

"Beadan—"

"Let me make you feel good, beautiful. I promise it'll be worth it."

Was I really supposed to say no?

I nodded my consent, and Beadan immediately got to work. First order of business, yank my fighting shorts down and off one leg. Second, grab me by the hips and flip me over until I was on my knees and elbows with my ass in the air. That one wasn't something I was used to.

"I don't know if you want—"

But the feel of his mouth on my pussy cut off all rational thought. My entire body jerked at the first contact, a moan loud enough to be heard over the sounds of the crowds out in the arena escaping my mouth. I'd never been in this position before, never had someone use their mouth to make me come while I knelt before them. And he would make me come—I had no doubt about that. The man had a magical mouth with thick lips and a tongue that flicked and laved and drove me absolutely wild. And his hands—I'd been right, his big hands gripping my body were a thing of pleasure. He held me tight, almost massaging my thighs. Kneading the flesh and bringing me to the brink.

I gripped the edge of the table as the anticipation grew, as my legs began to shake and I started chanting Beadan's name. Head all the way down on the table, knees spread wide to give the man room, I rocked and gyrated and basically rode his face until I couldn't hold out any longer. I came with a growl that shook the table, reaching back to hang on to Beadan's hand. Shaking and slipping and finally falling flat on my stomach on the table as pure pleasure roiled through me.

Beadan took the opportunity to smack me on the ass and laugh. "You okay there, beautiful?"

I slapped at him, not really wanting him to move. The man

had settled sort of half on/half off the table, leaning his body into mine without crushing me under his weight. Warming me with his presence.

"I think I just died a little."

Beadan laughed again, tugging me up and adjusting us until he had me settled on his lap. "Sorry—couldn't help myself."

"Don't ever apologize for that." I ran a finger over his lips, still feeling a bit shaky. "Though, the timing is interesting. My muscles feel like Jell-O."

He gave me a kiss to my chin. "Trainers always say to stay loose."

I laughed as we cuddled more, neither of us seeming to be ready to let go. At least not until there was a knock on the door and a call of "Five minutes!" hollered through it.

I sighed and edged my way to my own feet. "Guess it's about that time."

Beadan rose to his feet as well, his face growing serious. He flipped both of my hands, checking the tape. Making sure the edges were tucked just so.

"You sure you're ready?"

I nodded, my mind focusing in on the task at hand. "Yeah, I am. Are you ready?"

"For this to be over and to take you and Livia home for good?" He leaned in, giving me one final kiss. "Abso-fucking-lutely."

My heart jumped at his words, my soul settling. This was it. One last fight and we would be together. We would be a family.

A family without secrets. "Livia's safe word is Austen. If you need to go check on her, say that through the door, and she'll at least talk to you."

Beadan grunted. "Thank you for trusting me with that."

There was nothing left to say. Not really. I had a fight to win, which meant I needed to get my head in the right place. I needed to focus on the upcoming physical strain and the strategies I'd learned over the years. I needed to win.

Just one more fight.

"You'd better go," I whispered, tugging him in for one last hug before stepping away. "I need to get my head in the game."

"Understood." He headed for the door, pausing with his hand on the handle. "I'll check on Livia as soon as your fight is over. Let her know her momma kicked ass."

I grinned, biting my lip to hold it back. "And then we leave."

"First thing tomorrow."

I could hardly contain my excitement. "I'll win for you."

But the man shook his head, looking completely sexy as he leaned against the doorframe. "For us, beautiful. You're winning for all three of us."

And with that, he was gone. Disappearing into the hallway with all the crowds and the people and the noise. I was left alone to fight my instincts that screamed at me to follow him and instead get ready to fight my opponent in front of hundreds of humans who could not care less about us. About our future. About the things that made us special.

One more fight. One win. And then forever with my mate.

TWELVE

I couldn't get my leg to stop bouncing. I was pretty sure the humans in the seats around me were getting pissed about it, but my size and general *don't fuck with me* expression likely convinced them to hold their tongues. Good, because I was not in the mood.

Avory was about to start her fight, and as much as winning seemed important, the end goal was for her to be able to walk out of the ring.

What a thought. A fucked-up, depressing thought. Avory needed to fight and wanted to win, but our future only required her to stay alive. Something that could be made impossible depending on how hard her opponent fought her. And I was supposed to just sit there in the audience and not rush to her aid at the first sign of trouble.

Tonight was going to be a shitshow.

"Get it, Raven!" I yelled when Avory bounced into the ring. My sweet, soft woman—Livia's loving mother—was gone. All that was left in her place was hardness and aggression. Avory looked ready to decapitate someone with her bare hands, an energy of brutality floating around her. I kind of liked it. I was also kind of afraid of it. But on a particularly quick spin as she punched at air and moved into her fighting stance from all angles, she caught my eye. That little vixen winked at me, too. She knew what she was doing.

The fight started as they all did—both women moving toward the center of the ring and on the defensive. It was Avory's opponent—a woman with a fighting name of Serpent— who went on the offensive first. She rushed forward, using her size to overpower Avory. The move was fast and hard, ugly to watch, and if the way Avory hit the mat and grabbed for her ankle any indication, likely as close to illegal as we got at The Pack House.

"Fair fight, ref!" I sat back down, not even realizing I'd risen to my feet until I had already taken a step toward the ring. I needed to control myself and my inner wolf, who was definitely not happy watching his mate in danger. This entire scenario went against my nature—I should be protecting Avory. Should be in there fighting the battle at her side. I wouldn't, of course, but that's what I wanted to do.

But so help me—if Serpent tried to make a death move against my mate, all bets were off.

Avory recovered well, looking even madder and meaner than before. She limped for a few strides but regained her footing just fine. And then she went on the attack, fighting fair but going all in. Swinging, punching, kicking, and just overall beating Serpent down. It was a solid minute of Avory attacking before she backed off from a fallen Serpent.

"That's my girl," I mumbled, clapping and staring and totally missing it when someone sat down beside me.

A trainer. The one who'd been working with me in the ring. Tony.

"Your girl looks good out there," he said, watching Avory. Not looking toward me at all. "I was wondering if you two were together."

Fuck, this wasn't how things were supposed to go, but Avory was already in the ring. She was fighting, and we would be leaving in the morning. There was no point in keeping secrets anymore.

"She's my mate."

His head whipped in my direction, his eyes a little wider than usual. "Doesn't she have a child from someone else?"

The question irked me, so I voluntarily looked away from my girl to stare the man down. "She has a child, yes. One I now see as my daughter, so you'd better watch your mouth."

He put up his hands, refocusing on the fight. "No offense intended, Bear. I'm only just learning your...*culture*."

I snorted a laugh, watching my woman go back into an aggressive mode in that ring and swing hard on Serpent. "Is that what you call it? Culture?"

"I wasn't around people like the fighters here before I came to The Pack House." He dropped his voice, leaning forward so his elbows rested on his knees in a forced casual sort of position. "Your very existence took me a little bit to come to terms with."

I could see that. "Understandable."

We watched Avory fight for a few minutes, watched her definitely winning her match even as Serpent tried again and again to go after the injured ankle. Avory was quick and smart, though. She saw that shit coming. I was so proud of my girl. She'd make bank if we stayed—would likely become one of Mick's darlings.

We weren't staying, though.

"So, the reason I came by," Tony said, reminding me of his presence. "Ice had a few things to say about you and your girl after the fight."

Of course he did. "The man is all talk and no action."

"I hope so, but I thought you should know. I ignore most of the shit-talking you guys do because it's just that—shit. This was a little different, though."

I frowned, my mind spinning. "Different how?"

"He seemed pretty confident that he was going to be able to do something to get back at you for the loss."

I shook my head, still watching Avory. "This is our last fight. We leave tomorrow to go home, so he has no leg to stand on."

Tony nodded before patting me on the back. "Good. Good. I felt inclined to tell you in case he really was coming after you somehow, but it seems like you've got yourself covered. Best of luck to you, Bear. I've enjoyed watching you fight."

I took my eyes off Avory to look at him squarely and reach out a hand for a shake. "You were a good trainer, and thank you for coming to me with Ice's threat. That's upstanding shit right there."

He nodded, shaking my hand before turning to leave. "Stay safe, Bear. You and Raven both."

I turned back to the fight, trying hard to focus, but that final statement nagged at me. Me and Raven both...plus Livia. I could take care of myself against someone like Ice. I had no worries there. Avory likely also could handle herself, plus I'd make sure to stick close to her tonight and tomorrow until we left. The only vulnerability in my plan, the only way Ice could hurt me at that moment, was the little girl with the big eyes and the love of sugary cereals who sat alone in her mother's room.

My wolf rose to all fours, growling. The sound becoming a howl as if to mentally call to his pack. Avory and I hadn't truly completed our mating yet; we hadn't had sex or bitten each other. That sort of internal call would go unheard by her wolf. And whether or not Livia would ever hear it as she technically wasn't my own would be determined at a later date. I was alone in my fear.

But Livia was the one truly alone.

I was up and running from the arena in a flash, wanting so badly to keep an eye on Avory but knowing Livia was the weak link at that moment. I'd never forgive myself if something happened to that little girl, and Avory likely wouldn't forgive me either. So, I ran through the arena halls and into the living area of the facility, not even pausing in my quest. I was halfway to the room where Livia should be when my wolf barged forward, shifting us in midair and landing heavy on four paws before continuing the race toward Livia. We growled the entire way, ready to fight. Ready to go all in against any threat to my family.

Because Livia was my family. More than that, she was my sweet baby girl. If that motherfucker put even a single finger on her...

I ran faster.

———

Avory

The bitch broke my ankle. Not that it would stay broken or that the fact that my bones were likely knitting together wrong would end the fight, but still. That was dirty pool.

I kept my hands up and my mind focused, limping for a few seconds before my wolf side took care of the pain. As soon as that irritation was over, I went full attack. Serpent had caught me a little off guard with a move that would have been illegal anywhere else, but the ref hadn't called it. Lesson learned—all bets were off in terms of what I could and could not do.

Swinging hard, making contact, and throwing more punches —that was my plan. Harder, faster, and unstoppable. The crowd cheered around me, but I didn't care. I had one intention, one focus for the moment—teach this bitch that breaking my ankle was a bad plan. I went hard on her for longer than my usual style, beating on her with my fists, throwing in a kick or two to prove to her that the illegal ankle-break meant nothing, and refusing to let up for a second. At least not until she fell to the mat.

I bounced away, keeping my eyes on hers. Serpent—snake. She *was* a snake, all right. One who needed to be beheaded and tossed into the forest to rot.

"You good yet?" I yelled above all the noise from the crowds. "I've got more payback for you."

Serpent glared at me as she slowly rose to her feet. I might have laughed at the wobble in her first step. Might have grinned like a lunatic, too.

"That hurt?" I nodded toward her left side, where I'd landed a number of solid blows to her cheek. "Anything broken yet?"

"Fuck you." Serpent broke away from the ref and moved toward me, her gait unsteady for about three strides. I knew better than to assume she'd continue being weak in any way, though. Our wolves healed fast—example, my ankle that didn't even twinge anymore—which meant she was likely back at 100% in seconds. I still had my work cut out for me.

I waited for her to advance, for her to shift her weight forward and rush in my direction, before I dropped low and swung upward. I didn't aim for her head this time—I aimed for her gut. The woman doubled over, a loud grunt leaving her body when I made contact. Once I had her in such a position, I rose up and slammed an elbow into her back. Once, twice, three times, before she fell again. I was in the middle of a windup to kick her in the head when something caught my eye outside of the ring. I wasn't one to be distracted during a fight, but this was impossible to miss. Beadan—huge and fierce and totally intimidating from a size perspective—ran through the arena. Away from me. Why he wouldn't watch me fight, I had no idea. That didn't seem right to me. And why he'd need to leave so fast, I had no idea. There was nothing to be afraid of unless—

Livia.

My wolf howled, ready to claw herself from my skin. In that split second as realization slammed into me, I wanted to rush from the ring and head for my baby. But at that moment, Serpent caught me off guard with a slam to the face. My eyes stung, watering heavily as I crouched slightly and backed away. I couldn't leave yet, couldn't jump from the ring and go running after my mate. I needed to finish this woman and—

My eyes were still watering. That definitely wasn't normal. The bitch just couldn't fight fair.

"You can't win without cheating, can you?" I bounced around the ring, avoiding her. Blinking as I waited for whatever chemical Serpent had on her taped hands to dissipate so I could see again. "You're truly not a worthwhile opponent."

"Yeah, well, I thought beating the ass of a single mom would be more fun. You're a total bore."

As if that were somehow an insult. "Stop fighting and read a book—that comeback sucked."

She growled and rushed at me, giving me my opportunity. I caught her with an elbow to the throat, following up with three quick and hard punches to the back of her neck. Serpent collapsed into a pile of unconscious goo at my feet, the ref stepping in between us and ending the fight right there.

"Your winner is...Raven!"

I let him do his thing, let him hold up my arm and show me off to the crowd, but the second he released my wrist, I was in motion. Running out of the ring and straight toward my room. Fuck the trainers and the medical staff who would want to see me—if Beadan was running, there was a reason for it. And that reason was quite likely my little girl.

Please be safe. Please.

My wolf took over the second we were out of human eyesight, bursting out of me with a growl. She took off at full steam, paws clicking on the concrete floor and low growl rolling through us.

If anyone dared to touch my Livia, they'd be met with teeth and claw. There would be no surviving their grave error.

If anyone touched my daughter, they were dead.

THIRTEEN

Beadan

When my wolf reached the door to Avory and Livia's room, there was no door. The whole damn thing had been kicked in, leaving the room wide open. I rushed inside without slowing down, paws scrabbling on cement to gain traction into the turn. Not that my speed mattered—Livia was gone.

A giant rock sank into my gut, but that didn't stop me. Instead, it set a fire under the rage already burning inside me. This night was not going to end well for whoever took my baby.

I spared a few seconds to inspect the room. Nothing appeared out of place other than Cornelius the cow, who sat on the bed all alone. Livia *always* had that toy with her. If she left the stuffed animal behind, it wasn't voluntarily. Someone had snatched her, and fast.

I made a quick pass around the room, sniffing deep in every corner. Looking for any sign or hint of who had come so I could track them. I found nothing, so I gave Cornelius a solid sniff instead. Livia's scent filled my head, making my wolf whimper. That sound turned into a growl, though. Ice was a dead man for touching my child. Whether that death was quick or slow would depend on what he did to her before I found them. And I would find them...no matter what.

Once I had Livia's scent locked down, I headed out of the room, my pace slower than before. The halls were filled with scents of various shifters and humans; even Livia's light smell led me in different directions. It was really hard to get a lock on tracking anyone in multi-unit housing. Not without them touching things along the way. There were too many scents, too many trails overlapping and running back on themselves. It would be far easier outside, which was likely where the fucker had taken her.

I headed outdoors.

If I had wanted to do anything to someone from inside The Pack House, I'd drag their asses outside first. It was too busy in that building, too filled with other shifters who had amazing hearing and humans who could be just plain nosy. No, I'd head for the outdoors to get a little privacy. I doubted Ice was any sort of criminal mastermind, but he was a shifter. He'd do the same. Unfortunately, I was betting—with Livia's life. We didn't have time to be wrong.

Thankfully, the second I made it outside, tracking little Livia became much easier. Her scent lingered in the air, the acrid smell of Ice right there with it. I followed the trail away from the facility and into the woods, slowing my pace once I entered the tree line. Not by much, just enough so as not to be taken by surprise. I doubted the man had had time to booby-trap the path, but I couldn't be sure. I was Livia's only hope—I couldn't let some stupid trip wire get in my way.

As I raced deeper into the woods, Livia's scent increased, and the normal energy of the forest dissipated. Eventually, even the sounds around me changed—night animals going quiet and staying hidden. Prey avoiding the predators in their midst.

When the entire world seemed to fall into complete stillness and silence, I knew I was close. And I was right, because I made one last turn along the path and spotted a flash of light ahead of me. It had to be them.

With a deepening growl, I ran faster, no longer concerned about trip wires or booby traps. She was *right there*, and I needed to get to her. To make sure she was safe. To bring her home. I needed her away from Ice.

And then I needed him dead.

The second I was close enough to feel comfortable shifting, I switched to my human form. Some things needed a voice.

"Ice. Stop."

The man did as I demanded, breathing hard as he spun to face me. There was a nasty gleam in his eye and an evil sort of smile on his face. I was far more worried about the little girl in his arms, though. Livia clung to Ice's neck, her face red and streaked with tears. The look in her eyes broke my heart, but I had to deal with him first. It was the only way.

"Ice, give her to me."

Ice laughed wildly, taking a single step as if to continue up the trail. "You're so weak, you have to chase after someone else's progeny? She's not yours, Bear. Why the fuck do you care what I do with her?"

My wolf growled, the sound rolling out of me. The man was about to learn just how much I cared.

"Livia, baby, close your eyes. Okay?" I took a step closer, knowing my nakedness would likely take her by surprise. The fact that we shifted without clothes meant nudity was not a big deal within wolf packs and shifter scenarios, but Avory had said she'd never been in a pack, which meant Livia likely had no idea. I didn't want her to see me like this or to know what I was about to do. "Close them, angel."

Livia did as I asked, releasing Ice's neck and sitting calm and patient though practically shivering in his arms. Once I knew she wouldn't be watching me, I gave my wolf a little more rein. Let him begin to shift out of me. Hair sprouted over my body, and my fingers turned to claws as the beast within hung out just past the surface of my mind.

I focused my canine eyes on my prey and let my growl permeate my voice as I said, "You are going to give that little girl back to me. Just set her down so she's safe."

"Safe from what?"

"From me, when I beat your ass to the forest floor."

Ice's grin widened. "You're not wolf enough to take me on in the wild."

"Prove it." I shifted first, knowing he'd follow. Praying to the fates that he was at least careful with Livia.

He wasn't as careful as I'd have liked, though. In a single move, he tossed Livia to the side and shifted, hitting his paws at a run. I had a split second to watch, to see that Livia had landed softly and rolled, so would likely be unharmed, before all my focus was forced to the attacking wolf. I had one moment of hearing Avory yelling for me before Ice grabbed at my shoulder with his teeth. I feinted and dodged, rearing up to dig my claws into his flesh. Both of us growling and yipping into the night as we clashed.

I fought Ice hard, forcing him to pivot so I was between him and Livia as much as possible. Ice battled in wolf form like he did in human—slightly messy and fast, but without true skill. Still, he managed to get his teeth in me a time or two. Slipped past me once to claw at my haunches, too. Nothing that would end the fight or leave lasting damage, though. No, all of that came from me. First with my claws—slicing, digging deep, tearing muscles and drawing blood. The last, though, came from my teeth.

I took my shot as Ice reared up, popped from underneath

him and aimed right for his throat. He caught my shoulder with his claws, digging deeper than ever and causing a massive explosion of pain, but I didn't falter. The warm, metallic taste of blood flooded my mouth the second I made contact, so I doubled my efforts. I dragged him to the ground by his throat and flipped him onto his back. I held him down, growling the entire time, until he stopped fighting me. Until he lay still and losing heat. Until I had killed him right there in the woods.

When I was certain his fight had ended, I stumbled back, my growl softening. Motherfucker, my shoulder hurt, but I wasn't done yet. I stumbled my way across the path to a very scared and shaky Livia. She hadn't kept her eyes closed, the little troublemaker. Not that I could blame her. I walked right up to her then lay down, my head resting on my front paws. Trying my hardest to look kind and not scary. I even wagged my damn tail. Then I did my best to growl the word Avory had told me.

"Austen." Wolves couldn't talk, though, so what came out of my mouth sounded very little like I needed it to.

Livia smiled, though. "Are you trying to say Austen?"

I raised and lowered my head, frustrated at being in wolf form but needing a few moments to heal before I shifted. So maybe Ice had hurt me a little more than I'd been willing to admit. Just...maybe. Wouldn't stop me from getting the little girl back to her momma, though.

I inched forward, whimpering and moaning. Booping the girl with my nose. Doing my best to get her to move. She finally laughed and did as I had wanted, rising to her feet. Once she was up, I bit the back of her nightgown and tugged her to my side, flipping my head up when I released her and staying on the ground. She took the hint like a champ, throwing one leg over my back and straddling me.

"Mr. Bay?"

I jerked my head around, not able to really see her but giving her a signal that she had my full attention, especially since I definitely heard the little wobble in her voice.

"I want my mommy," she whispered, once again breaking my heart. I nodded and rose to my paws, wincing silently as my shoulder burned. Pain didn't matter—I had a job to do, a little girl to protect. I could live through the pain just fine.

We left Ice's body behind, me padding softly and slowly through the woods as Livia rode on my back. Both of us silent. Her little hands wove through my fur in her effort to hang on, tugging on the flesh of my torn shoulder. I couldn't stop to rest, though—couldn't relax. Not until I had Avory with me, too. Not until we were reunited as a family. Then I could deal with the pain. Maybe.

Thank the fates I didn't have to wait too long to find my woman.

"Livia." Avory raced around a tree, her eyes wild. She beelined straight for Livia, grabbing her off my back and holding the little girl against her. "I was so worried about you."

Livia wrapped her body around her mother, clinging to her. "The bad man grabbed me, but Mr. Bay came to my rescue like a prince in one of those stories."

Avory caught my eye, looking completely teary-eyed and still terrified. As she should have been—someone had threatened her daughter. That couldn't stand. She needed to know the threat had been taken care of.

I dropped to the ground, growling deep as I shifted to my human form. The shift took longer than usual, the still-damaged muscles and tendons tearing and reforming in ways that were far more painful than usual. I gritted my teeth as much as I could, accepting the pain as part of what I needed to deal with. Still, once I was fully human, it took me more than a few seconds to be able to speak through my panting breaths.

"Livia, baby," I said, trying my hardest to sound normal. "Close your eyes, okay? Just for a few minutes."

Livia nodded and closed her eyes, tucking her head into Avory's neck. Once I knew she wasn't watching, I sat up. Slowly. Really, really slowly.

Avory frowned, but the second her eyes darted away from my face to my shoulder and side, her frown turned to an expression of surprise. The damage must have been worse than I'd thought.

"It's fine," I murmured, holding still and forcing calm on myself. "Everything is fine."

"You keep telling me fine doesn't mean fine."

Okay, so...she had me there. I chuckled, wincing when the shaking of my body caused a stab of fire through my shoulder. "Okay, yeah. It's messed up, but *it will be* fine. My opponent from earlier took Livia, thinking he would get back at me for beating him, but I caught them. I took care of it."

Avory looked ready to cry as she cuddled her daughter close. "Will he come after us?"

I shook my head, holding her gaze as I repeated what I'd said but in a deeper, more significant tone. "I took care of it."

Eventually, Avory nodded, looking a little calmer. As if she understood my meaning.

"Now what?" she asked, still clinging to Livia. "Do we run?"

"No," I said, shaking my head. "We go back to The Pack House. We get my shoulder looked at, we collect our winnings and our stuff, and *then* we leave."

"Okay." She came to my side, leaning down to run her fingers over my shoulder. "Is it painful?"

I tried to shrug, cringing a little. Fuck, it was so much easier to deal with pain in my wolf form. "It'll heal, but I'd like to make sure it's set correctly before we go. Just in case."

I didn't need to specify what the *just in case* was.

She nodded again, glancing down the rest of my body. "You're naked."

"I'm aware." And I was going to need her to stop looking at me naked because parts of my body that weren't in pain were responding to those looks in ways that weren't appropriate around Livia. "We'll cut in through the back. There are spare shorts and stuff in the training center. Once we're inside, I'll throw some on, and then we'll get started."

"See the doctor and collect our money."

"Exactly."

"Grab our stuff and...leave."

I rose to my feet, tugging her closer. Making sure to rest a hand on Livia's back as well. "And leave. You ready to head to my farm, ladies?"

Livia practically jumped out of her mother's arms, her head popping up and those bright eyes meeting mine. "Definitely. Can I get a pony?"

Avory laughed, cuddling closer as I took Livia from her arms —carefully, so fucking carefully—and began the trek back to The Pack House.

"Let's worry about getting there first." I met Livia's pouty gaze, grinning at her. "Your mother's right. We need to worry about getting out of here first. But I'll call my family and tell them we're coming—what they do with the stalls and paddocks around my barn are up to them."

Avory smacked my arm—the good one—but laughed, the three of us happy in the moment. Sure, I was still in pain and we still had a few hurdles to jump over, but we were leaving. No one would be able to stop us. I wouldn't allow it. I wanted my mate and my daughter safe, which meant heading home to the farm.

Immediately.

EPILOGUE

Avory

Being a single mom had always been hard. Being a single mom without a support system had been even harder. There had never been any time alone, never any breaks or chances to rest. I'd envied all those who had mates or spouses and packs or families for years when it had been just Livia and me.

There was nothing to envy anymore.

I stepped into the shower, sighing as the hot water ran over my shoulders. Beadan had the *best* shower—huge and open to the bathroom with multiple shower heads to bring water at you from almost all sides. I could spend hours in there—in fact, I had. The first time his family had taken Livia for the day, I'd spent far too much time under the water. Relaxing. Remembering how to be Avory instead of Mommy. Hours of alone time I hadn't even realized I'd needed.

This time, I wasn't alone, though.

"Where's the princess?" Beadan asked as he stepped under the water. His hands found their way to my hips as they always did, his body pressing against mine immediately. The man was so handsy and totally affectionate. He was even a snuggler in his sleep, and I loved it.

I turned to face him, kissing his neck and sighing when he grabbed my ass. "She's spending the night at your parents' house."

He paused, his body freezing into place. "The whole night?"

My grin was unstoppable. "The *whole* night. It's just us tonight. What should we do?"

Beadan wasted no time whatsoever. He immediately pushed me against the wall and dropped to his knees, grabbing my thighs and lifting until he had me resting on his shoulders. Then he dove in—laving my pussy in a way that had me screaming and fisting his hair. The man was a machine at this, could spend hours lavishing my pussy with attention from his mouth. That wasn't what I wanted, though. Not what I needed. So, I tugged on him, purposely moving my legs off his shoulders until I could place my feet on the ground. Beadan let me go, looking up at me with those adorable, dark eyes.

"What do you need, beautiful?"

"You," I said, reaching for his hand. "I need you."

He followed me to the bed, collapsing on the mattress with me. It didn't matter that we were dripping wet, didn't concern me that the sheets would be soaked. All I cared about was feeling this man inside me. The need was immediate and overpowering. And Beadan met it.

He nudged his way inside, sighing and groaning as his cock slid deep. I clung to his shoulders and closed my eyes, enjoying the feel of him stretching me. Of us coming together. This was what my life had been missing—a connection to a mate who felt safe and solid, a community surrounding me with love and support, and the joy only stability could bring. Beadan made sure I knew Livia and I were always safe, that we were cared for, that we had an entire pack ready to stand beside us at all times. The change was very freeing—as was the ability to send Livia off for a night so I could be alone with my mate.

Packs were amazing.

"Fuck, beautiful." Beadan pushed my leg up over his shoulder, opening me wide for him. Sliding deeper as he adjusted his angle. "I'm not letting you out of this bed tonight. I'm going to stay here and make you come all damn night."

I reached for him, tugging him down to deliver a sloppy, wet kiss to his lips. Both of us breathing the same air and grunting as we coupled. This was heaven—no fighting, no stress, no fear. Just me, Beadan, Livia, and our pack.

Plus the two ponies and six goats that had magically appeared the day after we arrived.

Home and safe.

Forever.

ABOUT THE AUTHOR

A storyteller from the time she could talk, Ellis grew up among family legends of hauntings, psychics, and love spanning decades. Those stories didn't always have the happiest of endings, so they inspired her to write about real life, real love, and the difficulties therein. From farmers to werewolves, store clerks to witches—if there's love to be found, she'll write about it. Ellis lives in the Chicago area with her two daughters and a German Shepherd that never leaves her side.

When she's not writing paranormal romance, Ellis Leigh can be found writing romantic suspense as Kristin Harte and erotic shorts as London Hale.

Sign up for Ellis Leigh's newsletter for release information, promotions, swag opportunities, and early access to free reads!

www.ellisleigh.com/newsletter.